C000077498

Roman Co

Book 13
in the Sword of Cartimandua Series
By
Griff Hosker

Roman Courage

Published by Sword Books 2017
Copyright © Griff Hosker First Edition

A CIP catalogue record for this title is available from the British Library.

Contents

Prologue

When Decurion Marcus Gaius Aurelius finally reached his home in the Dunum Valley, he realised the dying curse of Caronwyn, had come to fruition. The frontier was a volatile place. He would not be granted leave for a further three months. Sent north with the rest of his ala he had spent the time hunting raiders who had descended from the north and raided the land south of the wall. His service had been in the land of the Selgovae, in the west. The chase had been expensive. Many settlements had been destroyed. Slaves had been taken and animals stolen. For Marcus what was even worse was that he had lost men from his turma. When the Selgovae were finally routed or driven into their holes he was granted a brief leave.

The farm where his brother and family lived, the place he had grown up, was not far from Morbium. He had been looking forward to seeing his wife and his family. His brother farmed the family estate and his wife and children lived there with them. He expected to be greeted by smiling faces and hugs. What he was not expecting was the lack of smoke spiralling from the farm. He expected to see animals in the fields and to hear dogs barking. What he found was an empty and deserted home. The last time he had been home the bad news which had greeted him was that his mother had died. As he dismounted from Raven's back he wondered what could have happened in the three months he had been away.

His first thought was that the farm had been raided. The Brigante and the other northern tribes were unhappy with Roman rule. His family supported the Romans. The door to the family home was closed. When he opened it, he was struck by a smell he did not recognise. Nothing had been disturbed. The cooking pots and the Samian ware his brother's wife had so prized were still there. The small pots with the spices, worth a small fortune, still remained. The farm had not been raided. It begged the question, where were his family?

A familiar and reassuring voice behind made him turn. It was Drugi. "I wondered when you would return."

Drugi stood in the doorway. He had been a bear of a man. He had once been a slave but now he lived in the woods of the Dunum. When Marcus saw him, he was shocked. His friend looked thin and emaciated. He could see his cheekbones.

Marcus was perplexed and held his arms out in confusion, "Drugi! What happened?" He started towards his friend.

"Stay! Do not come closer." He took a step back. "It was the plague or the pestilence. It started just four days after you left. It struck the children first and then the old ones. Your brother sent for healers from the fort. As soon as they saw the pustules, they knew what it was. They forbade any to leave."

"The plague?"

"That is what the healers said. I had never seen such a disease. Within a month all were dead but for your brother, Decius. He hung on for another month. He was a tough man. He could not eat and I fed him soups and broths. We spoke of you at great length." Drugi coughed. Marcus saw blood. Drugi took a step backwards as Marcus moved towards him. "No, I beg of you. Stay away. I have it too. It began when I was caring for your brother. I do not have long to live." He gave a rueful smile. "I know the signs."

"I am sorry."

"It is the will of the Allfather."

"Or the curse of the witch!" Marcus looked back into the home he had shared with his family. "My wife?"

"She is safe. She was away with the children. They had travelled to the market at Morbium. She is with the wife of Rufius Atrebeus, Mavourna, they are safe at their farm to the west of Morbium.".

Marcus dropped to his knees. He thanked the gods for saving his family. The raiders had come to his home many times and had always been beaten away. Now an even more dangerous enemy had crept inside and killed all within.

"I burned the bodies. When I die then burn me too. I have made the pyre already." He looked up at the sky. His voice was so calm that

Marcus could not believe it. "Perhaps I will come back as a hawk. I should like that."

Marcus was an officer in a Roman Ala, Marcus' Horse was not named for him but he was proud to serve in the Ala named after his father. He knew how to make decisions. On a battlefield he was never uncertain. Now, in his own home he felt helpless. What could he do? His hand went to the Sword of Cartimandua which hung from his waist. As he did so it felt hot to the touch.

Drugi noticed it, "The magic weapon speaks to you."

"How did you know?"

"I could feel it. You were saved for a purpose Marcus. You brought Frann and me to this land and we were both happy here. I am happy to go to the Otherworld. The life I had here was unexpected and the memory of your children and of you and your wife will stay with me when I am a spirit. The sword has more that it needs you to do."

"No, this is not the sword. This is the curse of the witch! I thought, when I buried her in that cave that it was done, it was over. When I heard that my mother had died, I wondered if that had lifted the curse! I was wrong."

"Do not give up. When you were captured, and taken far to the east, you never gave up. You can defeat this witch." He shrugged, "I know not how but you will find a way. Marcus, I know you are greater than I could ever have been. You are the son I never had. Live long and care for your children." He turned.

"Drugi!"

"No, my friend. I have to go and find somewhere quiet to die. It will not be long. I have lived from the drink I make for the last ten days. Each time I go to sleep I sleep on my pyre. You need not touch my body. Just burn me and know that when the black smoke rises then the spirit of Drugi rises with it."

He nodded and in that nod, he disappeared. He never saw his friend in this world again. Marcus Gaius Aurelius' world was shrinking. He had a wife, a son and a daughter. Other than that all that he had left were the men of the ala. Rufius, Metellus and Felix, Drugi's acolyte, were all that he had left. His blood was gone. He and his two children were the last of his blood. Now he would have to make Marcus' Horse replace his family. He sat on the chair on which his mother had sat and he wept.

Decurion Marcus Gaius Aurelius spent a week at the farm. Drugi died two days after his arrival. He did not get to speak to him again. He

knew his friend was dead when he saw birds pecking at his eyes. He lit
the pyre and burned the former slave. He was going to do the same to the
farm but he could not bring himself to do so. His family had carved a
rich farm from the land and fought to protect it. He could not just let it
go. He rode to Stanwyck and spoke with the head man there. All knew
Marcus' family. He was greeted with sympathy. They were Brigante but
they were Brigante who liked Rome and the Roman way of life. He told
him of the disaster. The head man clutched his amulet.

"What will you do now, Decurion?"

"I will return to my ala but I need someone to work the farm. It is
still a rich farm. Have you any suggestions?"

He nodded, "My son Arthfael has just taken a wife. He needs a home.
He could run the farm for you."

"And the profits?"

"If you split them, equally, with him Decurion you would guarantee
yourself as much money as it was possible to get from the farm. And,
when you leave the army, my son would have enough money to buy his
own farm. This seems to me to be a solution which serves you both."

"Aye it does. Where is he?"

"He went to trade at Cataractonivm. He will be back tomorrow."

That single day enabled Marcus to bury the most precious items
belonging to his family and to collect the weapons his father had kept
after he had left the army. The meeting went well and Marcus was happy
that the farm would be run as his brother would have wished. As he rode
north to Coriosopitum he knew that his life had changed forever. He
would have to throw himself into the ala. Perhaps he would try to
become Decurion Princeps. He would speak with the Legate. Julius
Demetrius was wise. He would know what to do. Marcus needed an
advisor now. He felt like a stick in a spring river. He was going where
the river took him. The only constant was now the sword which hung
from his waist.

His horse neighed. Patting his neck Marcus said, "And you Raven.
When I see Felix and Wolf I will be happier and on the return of Rufius
and Metellus I may even smile but right now my spirits are below the
soles of my boots."

He rode hard for the fort at Morbium. Guarding the Dunum it was as
vital to the defence of the land as Coriosopitum, further north. He barely
acknowledged the sentry on the bridge. He galloped at full speed for the
farm. Rufius had a good farm. It lay northeast of the fort. Scealis ran it

for him. Scealis was a good man. He would protect Marcus' family. Even as the thought came into his head he realised that he had thought Drugi more than capable of protecting his family. When he saw Frann playing in the yard with Marco and Ailis he felt such relief as he had not felt for a long time. He leapt from his saddle. The noise of his arrival brought Mavourna from inside the villa.

Frann looked around in delight, "You are back!" Then she saw his face. "Drugi?"

"He is dead. All are dead. You three are the only ones that the Allfather has saved."

He threw his arms around the three of them. They were now his world. He heard Mavourna for his eyes were closed. He did not trust himself to open them. "I will have food prepared. It is good to see you Marcus and I am sorry for your loss."

Later he sat and talked around the table with Scealis, Mavourna and Frann. He told them all and what he had done. "I knew not what to do. I hired a man, Arthfael, to run the farm for me."

Scealis nodded, "I think I have met him. He is a good man. I think you have made the right decision Decurion. Your brother would want a farmer to run the farm. You are a warrior."

"And you will be safer here." The short ride from Morbium had shown Marcus that. Aware that they would be imposing on Mavourna he turned to Rufius' wife. "If that is a satisfactory arrangement, domina?"

She laughed, "Of course. My husband is away more than you!"

"I would stay longer but I am almost out of leave as it is. I will need to ride in the morning."

Just then there was the sound of hooves in the yard. They had been talking for some time and now it was dark. Scealis frowned. "This is late for visitors. Decurion, we may need your sword."

Drawing his weapon Marcus joined Scealis as they went out to see who had arrived. To Marcus surprise it was Rufius. "A happy meeting, sir! Were you seeking me?"

Rufius laughed and picked up his wife, "No, it was for my wife that I came. The ala has been ordered south. There is trouble on the border close by Deva. We go with the mixed cohort."

Marcus nodded, "Then I will leave with you in the morning."

"No, my friend, there are orders. The new ala at Coria is the Ala Petriana. They have come from Gaul. At the moment they are down at Lindum. You are attached to them as liaison officer. You will be returned to Marcus' Horse when this trouble is over." Rufius saw Marcus' troubled face. "Is something amiss?"

"I will speak with you before you leave."

Rufius was up in the small hours before false dawn. The noise of his movements woke Marcus and he too rose rose. "What is wrong, old friend?" Marcus told him. "My wife told me the news last night but your face suggests something more is troubling you."

"I had thought to throw myself into the ala. Become Decurion Princeps. I want to achieve something."

"You would have Metellus' position?"

Marcus laughed, "I am not ready yet but if you are in Deva then who knows, I may be stuck with the Ala Petriana."

"You will achieve that position. You are highly thought of. It was I recommended you for this task. It keeps you close to home." He pointed to the sword. "And it keeps the sword in its homeland. This is all good."

Marcus felt better as he saddled Raven and left in the early morning.

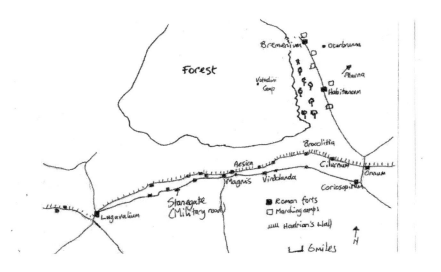

Chapter 1

Province of Britannia 130 A.D.
North of the Wall

Randel watched the column of legionaries as they marched up the Roman Road. He and his men were lying in the bracken. They knew how to hide in plain sight. The Romans built such long straight roads that it was possible to see down them from a long way off. Here, north of the wall, the Romans had built to cut his homeland in two. They rarely went abroad with less than forty men. This was a larger number for in this column there were sixty of them. Randel had fought them since he had been a boy. He had learned to respect them. He hated them but that respect was tinged with admiration. They knew how to fight and they knew how to die. Today Randel, now a chief of the wolf clan, planned for them to die. He and his clan lived high in the valley north of the town the Romans called Coriosopitum. His clan had no name for it. The place had been little more than a couple of crude, rude huts before the Romans came. If it had been named it would have had a name like Ardh's home by the river. Randel had been told of a clan who had lived there many generations ago. Their chief was Ardh and he had died. The Romans did that. They came to a place and disregarded the people who lived there and the rituals they had. So far they had not built a fort in Randel's valley. Perhaps that was because they lived north of the wall. The White Wall offended the land but Randel and the other tribes had long ago realised the futility of trying to destroy it. The Roman soldiers barred the gates and waited for their horsemen to appear and slaughter the tribes. Randel's tribe had lost

Randel might have left the Romans alone. He and his clan might have carried on, in their remote valley, much as they had for generations. They would have raised their cattle and sheep. They would have raided their neighbours and, in the good times, they would have traded their surplus. That had all stopped with the wall. The White Wall meant that they could no longer either raid or trade with the Brigante. For the last six summers they had traded and raided north, in equal measure. The pickings from the raids were lean and the barters for their animals were poor. Randel's clan were becoming poorer. The young warriors and their families were leaving. He had decided to make a raid on the Romans themselves. A mark in the land had to be made and Randel would make it. Part of it had been his wife. She was a priestess and had had a vision which showed Randel wearing a golden torc. Roman forts had been seen burning. It was too clear a dream to ignore.

They had built a number of forts to guard their road. The people who had lived there had been moved away. Randel remembered that the chief of the fort closest to Coriosopitum was called Abitus. He had never met him but his father had told him about the clan and how they had been moved. They had farmed the valley of the Rede. The fort they called Bremenium was the closest to his valley. Habitancvm, however, barred the old road which his people had used for generations. He and the warriors of his clan had decided to punish the Romans and make themselves richer. Every warrior knew that the Romans paid their men in gold, salt and food. They men who guarded the forts wore mail. Randel realised that the mail they wore might make his own men as hard to defeat as the Romans. He had to strike soon. Each year more of the young men in the clan left and the clan became weaker.

The sixty men were marching to the fort. He knew the Romans called it Habitancvm. They looked to be replacements for they were encumbered with gear. They had a couple of carts being pulled by their soldiers. His men were waiting. Fifty of them were a thousand paces up the road with his brother, Baradh. Randel had sixty. Baradh was on the sunrise side of the road and Randel was on the sunset side. The attack would begin when the Roman with the red horsehair helmet reached his brother. The Romans would outnumber his brother and they would react as Romans always did. They would form three lines and present a forest of spears. They would advance to flick away the barbarians. When that happened then Randel would lead the rest from behind. He knew that many of his clan would die. When you fought the Romans that was inevitable but the victory would draw more warriors to the clan. They would see the strength that lay in Randel and his clan.

These were not the dreaded legionaries. He knew that by their shields. They carried the oval shield of the weaker warriors. They still wore mail but they wore mail made from rings and it could be pierced. They carried a long spear and two throwing spears. They showed that they were not as tough as the legions for they wore trousers which went to their feet. Randel's people wore trousers but they respected the legionaries who did not. Theirs came to the knees. The men they would be attacking were heading to the fort to reinforce the garrison. One of the other clans had raided the fort a moon since. Tadgh had led a clan who eked out a living closer to the sea. He and his warriors had fought bravely but they had been beaten. Tadgh's head was displayed on a spike on the gatehouse. Although they had lost the battle their attack had depleted the fort's garrison. The survivors had come to Randel and were eager for vengeance. It was they who followed Baradh.

Randel could smell them as they passed him. They smelled foreign! Some smelled like women. Their skin was not white like the clan. Randel did not know whence they came but it was not from this land. He heard them talking. Their words meant nothing to him. It was just sounds but the noise showed that they were not expecting trouble. The fort was just four Roman miles away and they thought that they would soon be there. Randel had learned about Roman miles from the stones they laid next to the road. He could not read but he could count. Baradh was waiting at the next marker. The men were marching in fours. The leader had a helmet with red horsehair and next to him was a warrior with a wolf skin over his helmet and a pole with a bird of some description. The men carried their belongings hung from their spears.

The Romans passed Randel and his men. Randel did not need to look at his men. They would attack as soon as he stood and raced towards the Romans. He carried no shield and he wore no helmet. None of his tribe did. He had a sword in one hand and a long dagger in the other. They would be more than enough. Randel had a chest like an oak tree and his arms were so strong that he could lift any of his warriors above his head. He was also fast. He could outrun most men.

Looking up the road Randel saw that the Romans were almost level with the stone marker. Randel knew where Baradh and the men lay hidden but he could not see them. Suddenly there was a shout and Baradh led his warriors from hiding. Randel was already on his feet and running towards the road. The leather shoes he wore were not like the ones worn by the Romans. They were not studded with iron. He was silent. He felt, rather than heard his eager warriors rise behind him. Their movement was like a sigh. Ahead he saw the Romans moving into a defensive formation. A scream told him that one of the men his brother was leading had died. It was one of the Romans pulling the carts who alerted them to their danger. He saw Randel and the sixty men behind him and, even as he shouted a warning, it was too late.

Randel was fast and his long dagger tore into the Roman's throat. Without waiting for the others Randel hacked his sword across the neck of another Roman. He did not have the best blade nor the sharpest edge. It did not matter for the blow was so powerful that it broke the Roman's neck. His men were amongst the Romans. The Roman auxiliaries had spears and they had shields but they were facing Baradh and his men. It was not a battle, it was butchery. Even when some turned to face the new threat and presented shields, it was to no avail. The barbarians were inside the shield wall and they outnumbered the Romans. Randel dropped to one knee and used his sword and dagger to hamstring two Romans. As they fell other warriors slit their throats. It was all over faster than Randel could believe. There had been sixty Romans and now there were sixty corpses.

Randel looked up and saw his brother. He raised his sword, "Aieee! Victory!"

His brother, bloody but unwounded, raised his own sword and shouted, "Aieee! Victory!"

The men from Tadgh's clan had paid the largest price. Twenty of them lay dead but the survivors were exultant. They took the heads and the manhoods from the dead Romans.

Randel turned to his men, "Strip the bodies. We have mail and we have weapons. Now we can take the fort!"

He had a plan. It was basic and it was simple. They would take the mail, weapons and helmets from the dead. Sixty of his men would don the Roman war gear. They would wait until it was almost dark and then run towards the gate pursued by the rest. They would now be a much smaller number. Baradh knew a few of the Roman words and he would wear the uniform of the leader. He would shout for them to open the gate. Even if the garrison was suspicious and kept the gates closed, they would not use their deadly weapons which threw the long man-sized bolts. They would wait to speak with their comrades. It was those long bolts which had slaughtered many of Tadgh's people.

Randel donned the clothes of the man carrying the bird. The wolf's skin would hide Randel's long hair. That was another reason for the timing of the assault. His clan favoured long hair. The Romans cropped theirs. The leather vest felt tight against his skin and the mail he donned did not feel right. It smelled of blood. He had no time to clean it. The metal which hung down between his legs also felt strange. The helmet was a tight fit. He was loath to discard his sword and so he jammed it in the belt behind his back. The Roman's sword might have been sharper but his own sword had been handed down from father to son since before the time of the Romans. The sun was fading when all were ready.

He turned to the ones dressed in Roman war gear, "Remember we run as the Romans run. We run in lines of fours. Keep together. Those who are supposed to be attacking us do not risk yourselves. Make sure you are far enough behind us that you cannot be hit by their bolts and their javelins. Keep screaming insults at the Romans. The more noise you make the more of you they will think there are."

He turned and Baradh raised his spear and they began to move. Randel glanced around. His men were not marching in time, as the Romans had done. How did they do that? It would not matter for when they neared the fort they would be running. They spied the burning torches in the dark before they saw the fort. They glowed in the sky to the sword side. They marked the position of the fort.

Randel said, "Run!"

They began to run. The slapping of their feet on the stones sounded loud. Some of his men had taken the hobnailed sandals worn by the Romans. They made an even louder noise as they ran. As the fort came into sight they heard the sound of a Roman horn. That was to be expected. Each time visitors were seen the Romans sounded it. Randel admired the Roman forts. They were solid. He and his brother had visited a few. They were identical. With towers over the gates and at the corners they were a formidable bastion. As they ran he saw the deadly bolt throwers and their crew at the towers. He had seen a body transfixed by one of those. The hole through the dead man had been as big as Randel's fist! Behind the fake Romans, those chasing were screaming loudly and lewdly!

A Roman voice shouted something. Even Baradh could not make out the words but his brother shouted in reply, "Open the gates!"

The voice shouted something else. They were less than a hundred paces from the walls. There was no sign of the gates swinging open. He saw now why the Romans ran in the formation they did. The bridge over the ditch would accommodate four men. As they turned from the road Randel braced himself for the javelin or the bolt which would end his life. It was young Ragdh ap Tadgh who saved them. He ran ahead of the mob of warriors and screamed a challenge to the fort. He hurled the javelin he had taken from the dead Roman. It was a good throw. It landed on the bridge just before Baradh. There was a mighty crack as the bolt thrower hurled its deadly missile. Glancing over his shoulder Randel saw the chief's son impaled by the bolt. He had a smile on his face.

The javelin, however, had convinced the commander that the men running towards him were genuine. The gates opened as arrows and bolts flew from the walls. Behind him, Randel heard the shouts as men were struck. His orders had been disobeyed. His men had been too close. Had they been Roman they would have obeyed. He needed to make his men Roman! The smiling Roman auxiliaries who greeted them were taken in by the mail and the helmets but as soon as they saw the tattooed arms of the warriors behind they knew they had been tricked. The knowledge came too late and did them no good. Baradh gutted one with his sword while Randel brought the bird standard down and smashed it upon the head of the Roman. He drew the Roman sword and his own. He was no fool. He held the sharper and better Roman sword in his sword hand. His father's sword was a good luck token. Every warrior needed one.

"Now is the time for vengeance!"

All need for pretence was gone. Those who had been in Tadgh's clan hurtled up the steps to the bolt throwers. The son of their chief had died to one of the bolts and they would make sure that the crew paid with their lives. They were reckless as only barbarians can be. The first warrior up the ladders was struck in the shoulder by a javelin. The Roman thought it would stop him. It did not. I pulled it from his shoulder and ran at the man who threw it. He hurled him over the side of the wall to land in the stake seeded ditch. The optio rammed his sword into the warrior's middle. Even though he was mortally wounded the warrior wrapped his arms around the officer and took them both over the side. Erre's comrades ran down the fighting platform. All were eager to emulate their brother. He would be with the Allfather. He had died well. Without their officer and, facing overwhelming numbers, the auxiliaries on the fighting platform and in the tower were butchered. Using the captured Roman swords, the tribesmen hacked the bolt thrower to pieces.

The clerk of the cohort had been hiding in the Principia. He was not a fighting man. The centurion had led the last of his men towards the barbarians who had sneaked into the fort. The foolish Optio who had ignored standing orders and opened the gates had just been hurled over the walls. Gaius Mateus knew that if he stayed he would die. He ran to the east gate. All the sentries from that wall had run to join the centurion. Opening the gate Gaius slipped out. He ran east. It was away from the road. Once he was out of sight he would head back south and make his way to Coriosopitum. It was only fifteen or so miles but he would have to escape the natives first. They were barbarians. He had had enough of life north of the wall. He would ask for an easier posting, closer to Eboracum.

The centurion who led the cohort of Dalmatians could not believe that he would die because of Optio Metellus Caster. The lad had seemed to have so much potential and yet he had cost the centurion and the rest of his comrades their lives. Brutus Cassidius knew that he was going to die. No one surrendered to barbarians. All that he could hope was that they took enough of them with them so that one or two of his men might survive.

"Right lads. Today we fight like legionaries. Lock your shields and protect each other."

He had twenty men left with him. In a double line of ten they held their shields before them. The spears from the second rank poked over their shoulders. The barbarians would throw themselves at the wall of spears. It was their way. Even as the barbarians ran at them Brutus wondered where they had acquired the mail and helmets. Wearing mail they would take some killing. The first ten barbarians were easily despatched. The Roman spears found faces for the barbarians did not know how to use the shields properly. That first attack broke some of the spears. Brutus drew his sword. The next attack was more organised. The leader of the barbarians was wearing the uniform of the imagnifer. That made Brutus more determined than ever to kill him. The man shouted something and the barbarians formed ranks. The barbarians stood and hurled javelins. The centurion took two on his shield. Four of his men fell. A second volley followed and Brutus felt his shield becoming heavier. Three more men died.

Randel saw that the javelins had worked. He shouted to his brother. "Attack from the sides. We will keep them occupied."

He now saw the benefit of the Roman javelins. Even when they did not strike flesh they impeded the one defending against them. He saw one Roman attempt to pull one of the javelins from his shield. One of his men pinned the arm to the shield and another of Baradh's men dashed in and slew him. The last to die was the centurion. Randel lost four men unnecessarily. All wanted the honour of slaying the Roman chief who fought on with mortal wounds. When it was over his men despoiled every single body that they found. He and Baradh did not waste their time on such things. They hurried to the building the Romans prized so much. He knew that within it lay the gold they paid their soldiers and there would be other treasures. Tadgh had discovered their hiding place when they had captured four horse soldiers. They had made them tell all that they knew before they had killed them. They took two days to die.

While arms, mail, grain and food were collected by the clan the two brothers descended the stairs to the tiny space where the chest containing the pay resided. They took every box and chest that they could find. By the time they emerged dawn had broken. Randel knew that they could not carry back all of the treasures they had collected and the bodies of their dead. Barely thirty-three of the men who had attacked were without wounds. They took four carts. There were no horses but they would be able to pull the carts and their treasures home.

"Pile the bodies together by the gate. We will burn them. Our brothers will understand. Save me the head of the mighty warrior and two others who fought with him until the end. They will be trophies for our families."

None of the clan objected. Randel had done what none had done in their lifetime; he had led a raid which destroyed a Roman fort. His star was rising. As they headed east, laden with mail, weapons, food and chests the sky behind them was filled with smoke from the fire. The wooden walls would burn. All that would remain would be the ditch and a pile of burned bones.

Far to the north, unaware of the sudden success of Randel and his clan, the chiefs of the Votadini were gathered at the hill fort they called Din Guardi. The council of chiefs met regularly. it prevented blood feuds. It also served to keep those who ruled in remote parts of the land apprised of what was happening in the rest of the land of the Votadini. The King of the Votadini, Clutha, was in his palace, further north. He spent all of his time there. He feared assassination. Childless he was protected by devoted bodyguards. The chiefs who met were less than happy with their king. The Romans had advanced and taken large tracts of Votadini land. Worse, they had cut it in two with their road and their forts. The proud Votadini had to ask permission to walk about in their own land. It was unacceptable. They knew that the Romans paid money to King Clutha. He did not share his bounty.

Agnathus was the most vociferous and belligerent of the chiefs. When his daughter's husband Tadgh had been killed it had been the last straw. His lands had not been threatened. He lived by the coast south of Din Guardi but he had watched as increasing numbers of Roman warships had sailed up the coast. He was no fool. They would soon seek a port in his land.

Góra spoke first, he was the youngest chief there and he was attempting to assert himself. "I have heard that the Selgovae and our brothers the Brigante almost succeeded in defeating the Romans last year. Perhaps we should do as they did and use the power of the witches."

Agnathus shook his head, "I have nothing but admiration for witches and the cult of the Mother but I fear too many warriors put all of their faith in witches and in magic. They will not defeat the Romans. Victory will take a warrior and his sword."

"We have tried the sword and the Romans line their roads with the heads of the warriors who have tried."

"You are right Góra. Perhaps it is time we joined forces. The Romans have defeated us because we fought with them one by one. We should gather our armies into one and attack them."

Vinicius was a rival of Agnathus. He did not trust the ambitious chief and he feared his son even more, "With whom as our leader? You?"

Agnathus shrugged. "I care not so long as we fight together."

Another chief, Witan shook his head, "None of us will agree to follow anyone else in this room. It must be someone who has proved himself in battle against the Romans."

"Is there such a man?"

Agnathus nodded, "There was, Tadgh, my daughter's husband attacked a fort in the south. He and his tribe killed forty Romans."

Even Vinicius was impressed, "He sounds like the warrior to lead us."

Agnathus held up his hand, "He died in the attack but there are others in the tribe, including his son, Ragdh ap Tadgh. He has only seen twenty summers but he is a brave warrior."

Old Baglos had not said a word. This was his hillfort and he was respected by all. He spoke only to make decisions. He would not fight for he was too old. Indeed, he had no need to fight for his home was impregnable. "Then summon him here. If he cannot lead us he may know of some other who can. At the very least he can tell us how his father achieved his victory. If we meet here again in one moon we still have time to raid before the summer is gone." He looked at the faces of the chiefs. Each one, seated around the table, took out their dagger and pointed the hilt towards the centre. Baglos nodded, "Then it is agreed. I have high hopes for this confederation. We have reached a decision quicker than at any other time. The Allfather must smile on this venture."

Agnathus chose his own son, Creagh, as the messenger. Already groomed to take over from his father Creagh was both cunning and fierce. He had slain many in single combat but he was not afraid to take a knife into the night and slay his enemies with the cloak of night to hide him. He rode south on the hill ponies with his six oathsworn. They were all dedicated to keeping him alive. In their company, he felt safe. Creagh did not use a sword. He had had a war hammer made for him. It was a crude weapon but it suited the big man. With a wicked spike on one side and a hammer on the other even Roman armour could be pierced. He also affected limed and spiked hair. With his tattooed body Creagh was well aware of the effect he had on his enemies. It was one of the reasons he had won so many single combats. They had fifty miles to travel. It would take more than a day. As the son of a high ranking chief Creagh and his men would be made welcome wherever they stayed. He travelled down the coast. That way he ensured servitude. He and his father hoped that one day they would be the rulers of the tribe. Agnathus would be King and Creagh would be Prince and heir.

The first night they stayed at the mouth of the small twisting river which led up to Tadgh's heartland. Ammabile was a fishing village of a dozen huts. It was at the southernmost part of Creagh's father's land. The headman gave his own hut for Creagh and his warriors. Creagh was known to have a short temper.

As they sat around the fire eating the shellfish stew the villagers had made and drinking the strong ale, Kerryn, one of the oathsworn, asked, "Why does your father wish to speak with Tadgh's son? He is but a boy!"

"If truth be told the boy is not important. He will be the next chief and it is a courtesy only. It is the older warriors with whom we will speak. My father is wise. He wants to know the secret of defeating the Romans who wear mail, hide in wooden forts and use the deadly bolt throwers. Whoever has that knowledge will lead the tribe against the Romans."

Kerryn nodded, "And that leader would be you."

"I can think of none better. It is why my father sent me. The other chiefs do not want my father to lead but Tadgh's son might be acceptable. When we reach his village, I will flatter him and he will bring his men to follow me and then it will be easy to tell the old men how to defeat the Romans. King Clutha is old. It is time for a new king." He smiled, "A younger king who knows how to fight and to win." Although his father hoped to be king Creagh dreamed that he would persuade his father to let him become the ruler.

They left early the next day. As they headed for the village which lay just to the east of the Roman Road they noticed birds swarming to the west and to the south of them. Creagh was curious. He waved his arm and led his men south.

"What of the Roman fort which lies there?"

Creagh laughed, "We ride ponies. Do you think we cannot outrun Roman soldiers wearing hob nailed sandals?"

As they neared the road, however, Creagh kept a better watch. He was not a fool. His men were equally vigilant. Kerryn pointed south, "Look yonder, lord. The fort! It is burned!"

Creagh did not believe Kerryn. He had heard that Tadgh had killed Romans. How could he have destroyed it? The closer they came the more they saw. Kerryn was correct. His sharp eyes had seen what Creagh had not. The birds were further south. "Kerryn take Aedh and investigate the birds. We will see what magic has destroyed the fort."

The ash had cooled and there were charged timbers showing where buildings and walls had stood. They dismounted and scrambled over the remains of the bridge. There they saw pieces of bones. Bodies had been burned here. His men clutched their magic amulets around their necks. They had never seen a burned Roman fort. What disaster could have overtaken the vaunted Romans? They saw dark patches between the burned-out buildings. It was blood. There had been a battle here.

Kerryn galloped up, "It you think this is a mystery then down the road is an even greater one. There are sixty dead Romans. Our people have killed them. They have taken their heads, manhoods and despoiled the bodies. Perhaps Tadgh's son is a greater leader than we thought."

Creagh whirled around, "Fool! A boy could not have done this! There is another war chief and it is he with whom we need to speak.

Come we waste time. We ride to Tadgh's settlement. I will speak with the boy myself."

The village was almost deserted. There were children, there were the old, but they were mainly women. Creagh made for Tadgh's hut and his sister. She was older than he was. The daughter of his father and his first wife, Creagh and he had never been close. He dismounted. "Where are all the men? Where is my nephew?"

"The men are up the valley of Otarbrunna in the Ceμed. They have joined his clan. My son is dead. Randel and his brother attacked the Roman fort. My son died. I have lost my husband and now my son. My life is over."

Creagh nodded. He had the information he needed. It was unimportant to him what happened to his half-sister. "Come we ride."

He knew of Randel. He was an ambitious chief. His valley had two hill forts. Neither was as strong as Din Guardi but if the Romans wished to take them then they would bleed. Now it made more sense to him. It had been Randel who had destroyed the fort and not his nephew. Creagh would have to tread carefully. Randel could be a powerful ally if he was treated right. Creagh could still take over the tribe. The difference would be that all would be watching Randel to see what he did. Creagh began to smile. This might prove to be an even better plan than the one he had had originally. Randel and his brother Baradh were not related to Creagh. No one would suspect that Creagh was using him.

Chapter 2

As he approached Coriosopitum Decurion Marcus Aurelius knew something was amiss. He saw frantic activity at the Roman fort. It was as close to panic as he had ever seen. The sentry at the gate was a Batavian. He recognised Marcus and saluted, "What is going on?"

"Search me, sir. Three days ago, they sent your lot, Marcus' Horse and the Mixed Batavian cohort, south. Trouble in Wales sir. Nice and quiet it was and then this morning a clerk ran into the fort shouting about an uprising. I reckon you will be needed sir. The last three riders were sent south and west just an hour since. You are the only horseman left here now!"

What was going on? The decurion spurred Raven. He rode directly to the stables. When he saw Felix, his scout, he was relieved beyond words and almost hugged him. The thought had been in his head that he had gone south with the ala. Dismounting he said, "What is happening here Felix?"

The young scout shrugged, "From what I have learned the fort at Habitancvm was destroyed and the garrison massacred. First Spear asked me to go and have a look. I was about to leave I am glad you are here. I felt lonely amongst all of these Romans!" He smiled. "Decurion Rufius was sorry to have missed you. He and the ala were sent south. He was given command of Marcus' Horse. He hoped you would be following him."

"I know about Rufius. I spoke with him this morning." He nodded. He wondered if it meant he was leaving the land of his tribe? When he had returned from captivity, across the Eastern sea he had kissed the land of the Brigante. The sword he bore was meant to stay in this land and defend it from enemies. Marcus ruffled the fur behind Wolf's ear.

Felix finished fitting the halter to the pony. "How are your family? Is Drugi still well?"

21

Marcus' face told the young scout all that he needed to know. Felix realised that the officer had terrible news to impart. His ashen face warned him. The Decurion told him all and of Drugi's last instructions.

Felix smiled a sad smile, "That sounds like Drugi. He thought all things through." He looked out of the stable doors. "He will come back as a bird. That was his belief. I will listen for him." The youth put his hand on the Decurion's shoulder, "It is right to grieve but your family are together now in the Otherworld. At night when it is dark listen for their spirits. They will talk to you."

"I do not think so."

"You are more Brigante than you know, Decurion. Let go of the civilised side. The sword will help you to talk to them."

Just then Julius Longinus hurried in. Marcus was still standing in the shadows and the clerk did not see him. "Felix! They want you on the road now!"

"I am going."

As Felix kicked his pony in the flanks the decurion stepped from the shadows, "Hello Julius."

The clerk almost jumped. "Decurion! I am glad that you are here!" Felix galloped out followed by his dog, Wolf. "I thank the gods that I will be leaving here this afternoon and even that may be too late."

"You are leaving?"

He nodded, "The Legate is going back to Rome. He left two days ago. He was riding with Marcus' Horse as far as Eboracum and then making arrangements for our passage home. I should have left this morning but for the news from the north. The wagons are almost ready and I shall leave as soon as I can." He put his two hands around Marcus' shoulders. "I am glad I got to say goodbye to you. You will have to tell your family that I am sorry I could not speak with them."

Marcus shook his head, "Drugi, my brother and his family; they are dead, Julius."

He told him everything and the clerk wept. He sadly hung his head and began to wring his hands. "It seems that war is not the only killer in this land, Decurion." He looked over his shoulder, "And I should warn you, Decurion, that you are not to be sent with Marcus' Horse. There is a new ala of auxiliary cavalry coming here in the next few days and you are to be attached to them."

"I knew that news for I spoke with Rufius. It does not make me any happier."

"Come, you need to put sad thoughts from your head. First Spear will need all of your skill and knowledge to help us in the next few days."

First Spear was Quintus Licinius Brocchus on detachment with a cohort of the VIth Legion. He was a grizzled veteran. More importantly he liked Marcus. That had not always been true of some of the other senior officers Marcus had met. Julius, as the legate's clerk, did not have to knock and he just entered the inner sanctum. Quintus Licinius Brocchus looked up. He was surrounded by the senior centurions of the auxiliary cohort. When First Spear saw Marcus he smiled, "Well, we have one horseman at any rate. Come, Decurion, you need to hear our news. Thank you, Longinus. The wagons with the Legate's baggage should be ready to leave whenever you are."

"Thank you, First Spear." He turned to Marcus, "Watch out for yourself. Dangerous times are coming. I daresay the Legate will write to you. He was fond of you. I fear he may not return to this land again." He nodded and closed the door as he left. It was the last time Marcus saw him.

The centurions were eager to get back to the business at hand. "Sorry, First Spear. I understand we have lost a fort."

"Aye, and it is worse than that, Decurion. The reinforcements for the fort were also slaughtered. With the departure of your ala and the mixed cohort we have no men left to seek the barbarians out."

Marcus nodded. He had patrolled up the road many times. "That means that Alavna and Bremenium are also cut off. When the Votadini realise that they will attack those as well."

Decius Brutus Maximus laughed, "There is some hope that they will not find those two as easy. The Commander at Habitancvm made a mistake; he trusted a half-witted optio. The other two are made of sterner stuff."

Marcus was the only one who had a native mother and had lived among the Brigante. Only he knew how their minds worked. He knew he was the youngest in the room but he had to make a point. "Sir, this is more dangerous than you realise. In the last twenty years no fort has been attacked and destroyed. To have the garrison massacred means that the flood gates will open. Every Votadini, Selgovae and Brigante will join whoever did this."

"But the Brigante are south of the wall!" There was the hint of fear in the voice of the First Spear. It was bad enough having so many enemies to the north without the south rising too.

23

Marcus said, "And they are just as keen as the Votadini to rid this land of Rome. Just because the wall is there does not mean that their spirit is cowed."

First Spear nodded. He trusted the Decurion. "I have sent riders to Luguvalium and Eboracum. We have just one cohort of legionaries here now. It is the First Cohort but if I sent that out then Coriosopitum would be in danger. There would just be a cohort of auxiliaries to defend it."

Marcus had worked a long time with First Spear. The man was a rock and he was certainly no coward but he had always had plenty of men to deploy. Now he did not. "You sent Felix north; I assume it was to scout out the fort?"

"We need to know what they have done with it. Have they occupied it? Is the road still open?"

"Felix is a good scout, sir, he can track and follow signs which are invisible but he is no soldier. You need a soldier to interpret what he discovers. I ask permission to follow him. He can tell me what he sees and I can inform you of what we discover."

"Are you certain you wish to go there alone? There will be no troopers alongside you this time."

Marcus realised that the First Spear did not know of his tragedy. Outside of a wife and two children Marcus had little to live for. Rome had been good to his family. It was not Rome's fault that they had died. He smiled, "I will have my horse, Felix and Wolf. I will not be alone. We may be away for a few days. I intend to ride to Alavna and Bremenium. I take it their commanders know nothing of the disaster?"

First Spear said, "A sound suggestion. Tell them that the barbarians have auxiliary uniforms and weapons." He shook his head. "We can hold here. My legionaries will ensure that but we need more men to take back what the barbarians have destroyed."

As Marcus rose he saw that the situation was getting worse by the minute. The departure of the Legate and so many men at one time was a sign that the Parcae were in a mischievous mood. Heading back to the stables he quickly ran through what he would need. A good blanket, grain for his horse, a wineskin and a water skin and some cereal. Hanging his clipeus from one of the four saddle horns and his bag with three javelins from the other, he was ready. He left by the north gate. The sentries looked at him apprehensively. As the gates slammed behind him it felt ominous.

Heading along Via Trajan, he did not hurry. Felix would have been stopped at the wall. He was a native riding a pony. They would question him. They would closely examine the pass given to him by First Spear. Onnum was just down from Cilurnum. It had been the barracks used by the mixed cohort. With a depleted garrison to guard that fort they too would be vulnerable. It was lucky that the river there could not be forded and the bolt throwers would guard the bridge.

When he reached Onnum he was recognised. The optio waved his hand and smiled, "Your barbarian friend just left." He pointed to a pile of horse droppings, "That is still warm if you want to catch him."

He dug his heels into Raven. He might as well have company. He found Felix, just half a mile up the road. He was waiting. He was sombre, "I heard the hooves and wondered who else had a horse. Are my orders changed?"

"No Felix. I will come with you. First Spear needs to see what the barbarians are doing and I need to see how they managed to attack and destroy sixty auxiliaries."

"Good, Decurion, I will enjoy the company."

The birds were still feasting when the two came upon the bodies. Both Felix and Marcus were used to death. Felix dismounted. Wolf drank some water and lay next to Felix's horse. There was no danger. Felix did not examine the bodies, he went to look at the ground by the side of the road. He had been trained as a tracker by Drugi. He owed it to him to do the best job he could. Marcus just needed confirmation that it had been the Votadini who had done this and not Selgovae or Brigante. He found the proof he needed when he discovered the broken dagger in the auxiliary's back. It had broken through the mail but then broken on the man's spine. When the mail was removed the head had fallen one way leaving the blade embedded. He saw the carved wolf in the bone handle. They were the wolf clan of the Votadini. He frowned. They were a small clan. They must have had help.

For the first time since he had left Coriosopitum Marcus felt hopeful. This could be just an unlucky accident. If the Legate in Eboracum could send an ala up here quickly then the trouble might be quelled quickly.

Felix approached him. Marcus stood and asked, "Well?"

"They were clever, Decurion. Half hid there in the bracken and then the other half stepped out to draw their attention. The Romans did not watch their backs."

"Let us go to the fort although it looks to be burned out."

25

There was little to be learned from the fort save the level of ferocity the attackers had used to reduce it to a pile of ash. As they headed up the road Marcus peered left. "We need a tribesman to question."

Felix nodded, "Aye Decurion, but that will not be so easy."

"Does anyone watch us?"

Felix half closed his eyes and sniffed the air. Then he looked down at his dog. "I sense nothing, nor does Wolf."

Marcus rubbed the stubble on his face, "I am just thinking out loud, Felix, bear with me." Felix nodded. "If a tribe had a success like this then they would do one of two things: they would raid another fort or they would celebrate. We will try to reach Bremenium before dark."

That, in itself was easier said than done. The road was almost perfectly straight but lay within bow range of the forests. Marcus was truly grateful that they had Wolf with them. He would alert them to danger. Felix and Drugi had trained him to growl at enemies. The Votadini used the forest only for hunting. Their homes lay up the valleys which crossed it. Marcus knew that they were hard men to live in this land. The farm on the Dunum valley had yielded more crops than some of the settlements in the valleys they would cross. The Decurion was relieved when he saw the lonely fort rise above the road.

They waited at the ditch while a centurion was summoned. It was dark and Marcus expected close scrutiny. He had heard the command to 'Stand to!' as they had approached and the clicking of the bolt throwers as they were cocked.

The centurion leaned over, "State your business!"

Had Felix been on his own then he would not have been admitted. In fact, he might already have been struck by a bolt. He was not in uniform. All that afforded Marcus the courtesy of a conversation was his helmet and saddle. Marcus had donned his plumed helmet for the last mile or so. The horsehair plume marked him as an officer.

"I am Decurion Marcus Gaius Aurelius of Marcus' Horse and this is my scout Felix. We have been sent for Coriosopitum with urgent news for your First Spear." He saw the centurion nod and an auxiliary disappeared.

Felix was used to waiting. He was chewing on a piece of dried animal meat. Marcus knew that it could be anything. Felix was a good hunter. When he rode the land, he was never short of dried meat. He threw half of it to Wolf. The dog was also waiting patiently. Both knew the Romans and their systems. The gate opened and Marcus saw a reception committee.

The centurion stepped forward, "I am First Spear Julius Sextus Sejanus of the First Cohort of Lingones. I have been expecting someone this last three days. I did not expect one of Marcus' Horse. I recognise you, Decurion."

"I have dire news." Marcus looked around at the others. Did the First Spear want this news to spread like wild fire around the fort?

First Spear caught the look, "Come we will speak in the Principia. Your scout and his dog will have to sleep in the stable."

Felix grinned as he slid off the back of his horse. He held his hands out to Marcus for the reins. "Do not worry about us, Decurion, a stable is more comfortable than many places we have slept."

Marcus nodded, "I will send you hot food. There is grain on the saddle for our horses. Make sure they are fed well."

As we headed towards the Principia First Spear laughed, "That young barbarian had my men worried, Decurion."

"And with good reason. He is a deadly and silent killer. I am just glad that he is on our side."

Marcus took off his helmet as he entered the Principia. First Spear did the same. The centurion poured a beaker of ale and handed it to Marcus. "We have had no supplies for six days. There must be problem at the supply depot. We ran out of wine. You will have to make do with ale."

"I do not mind ale. My mother was Brigante."

"I know and that must be the sword they speak of; the magic one." His voice displayed his scepticism.

"You do not believe such things?"

"It may be a good sword. Of that, I had no doubt but magic? There is no such thing."

It was an argument Marcus could not win. "I fear you will not be receiving supplies for some time, my friend. The fort at Habitancvm has been destroyed. The garrison and their reinforcements were slaughtered."

First Spear did not seem surprised at the news. He drank heavily from the beaker. "We saw smoke to the south and wondered. How did it happen?" Marcus told him. "So they have mail, helmets, shields and weapons. It will avail them nothing. You can dress a pig in armour but it is still a pig. I hear more behind your words, though, Decurion." He poured some more ale. "Come, honesty between soldiers."

"Marcus' Horse has been sent south to support the Second Legion along with the Mixed Cohort. There is no ala in the east. You are looking at the only horseman for fifty miles. Legate Julius Demetrius has been summoned back to Rome. I do not think that this was planned but the barbarians have managed to strike at an almost perfect time."

The centurion raised his beaker, "Here is to Brutus Cassidius. He was a good man but, from what you have told me, one of his eager young officers has done for him and all the others. That is a valuable lesson. I will have to go around and ginger up my officers." He emptied the beaker and placed it on the table. "So, it was the Votadini. You know that Brutus Cassidius and his men repelled an attack and killed a local chief?" Marcus nodded. "Then I think I know who is behind this."

He took a map and unfurled it. The road was clearly marked, as were the forts. They had been drawn professionally. The lettering and the ink work were perfect. Also on the map were the charcoal marks made by another. Marcus guessed it was First Spear. He jabbed a squat finger at a blue line. "This valley here is where the most dangerous local chief lives. Randel is his name. He has a hill fort at Otarbrunna. Actually, he has two but it is only the one at the lower end of the valley which is manned and occupied."

Marcus peered at the valley on the map. It was not far from the road. It lay to the south east. He knew that the land on that side was heavily forested. It was country for auxiliaries and they did not have enough of them. "I will take Felix tomorrow and investigate it. If they are celebrating then others will gather there with them."

First Spear Julius Sextus Sejanus laughed, "You know your barbarians. A little dangerous isn't it?"

Marcus shrugged, "I served under an Explorate and Frumentari and I have Felix. I will be careful. Have you the means to get a message to Alavna? They too will be exposed."

"Alavna? Yes. It will be difficult but I can send a couple of men." He shook his head. "I have not got enough men to risk. Do not worry, Decurion. Our standing orders mean that the commander will have guessed there is something wrong. They will be rationing their food and they will be suspicious. Barbarians wearing our uniforms will not fool them. However, until the horsemen return north we will have to hunker down in our forts and weather the storm. One man made a mistake at Habitancvm. I will make sure it does not happen here."

Felix and the decurion left after dawn and headed towards the hill fort at Otarbrunna. First Spear had told them that it was also the name of the stream which wound its way down to join the bigger rivers. The decurion led Felix's horse, Flame, while the young scout ran ahead with Wolf. Both adopted the same position. Felix sniffed the ground as did his dog. He picked up leaves and stones. When he was satisfied he led the decurion off the trail and up the side of the narrow valley. They were looking for a way to the hill fort which would keep them hidden. Felix had found the trail of the single barbarian close by the road. There had been blood on the trail suggesting that the barbarian was wounded. Perhaps he had been left behind. Whatever the reason he was their best chance of finding a quiet way to approach the hillfort.

Marcus realised that they were following a small stream. It was so small that it hardly made a cut in the land. It wound its way through scrubby trees and stunted bushes. Felix made the sign for the decurion to dismount and tie the horses up. Marcus was not precious about being ordered around by a youth. The youth could save his life. With his cloak over his mail and no helmet, Marcus could blend in with the undergrowth. He dropped on all fours and joined Felix. Along with the dog they crawled through the wild blackberry bushes and tangled, overgrown, elder. At first, Marcus could not see where they were headed. All he knew was the ground was rising but Felix's movements exuded confidence. When the sky became lighter Felix slowed and he bellied along the ground. Wolf just stayed on the ground.

When Marcus finally reached Felix he saw that they were on a piece of ground which was level with the top of the hill fort. It was just half a Roman mile away. The ground descended from their vantage point. They had walked a straight line to get to this point. The wounded warrior they had followed had obviously chosen the quickest route. Marcus realised that the stream had stopped some time ago. Fortuitously it afforded a view into the heart of the hillfort. He saw a great number of warriors. The ramparts of the hill fort prevented an accurate count but there had to be more than two hundred warriors. It was tempting to ask Felix what he saw but he would remain silent until they were back with their horses. As he scanned the hillfort he also saw that the gates had the heads of two Romans adorning them. He had the proof he needed. These barbarians were the ones who had destroyed the fort. He tapped Felix on the shoulder and they backed away through the trees.

When they reached their horses he said, "What did you see that I did not?"

"I saw that some of the barbarians sported Roman war gear. They must have taken it from the ones they butchered. I counted more than two hundred and fifty warriors. There were the signs that it was at least six clans who were gathered but I saw warriors from a seventh clan there. They had horses and limed their hair. The majority of the clansmen did not have limed hair."

Marcus had realised that there were a number of different clans gathered for they had their standards. The seventh clan, the ones with the limed hair, did not have a standard. "Well spotted. We will head back down to the bottom of the stream head north and make camp."

"You wish a prisoner."

"If we can get one. I think any movement will be from east to west or south to north. We need to place ourselves where we can see any tribesmen travelling alone."

Felix nodded, "There was that small rise to the west of the road just before the forest on the road to Bremenium."

Marcus remembered it. It would be a good place to hide and, hopefully, ambush a barbarian. "Good, then let us ride there."

Chapter 3

In the days before Marcus and Felix had scouted to view the fort Randel had entered his hill fort and his people had rushed to acclaim him. A runner had preceded them for it took some time to travel up the road. The wounded messenger had travelled up the trail to the Holy Spring of Olwen and bathed his wounded leg in the goddess' magical water. The Allfather smiled on them for every person, young and old lined the walls as the victorious warriors, with their trophies, entered. His wife, Olwen, named after the spring where she was born, greeted him. She garlanded his shoulders with wild flowers and the mystical mistletoe.

When Randel reached his hall in the centre of the fort he turned, "Today we have begun to claw back our land from the hobnailed boots of the Romans. I wish runners to go to those clans who live nearby and to tell them of our victory. We have swords, spears, helmets and shields. We can be armed as the Romans are. We have tried to fight them as our fathers did and it availed us nothing. Perhaps Math Mathonwy felt like playing a trick on our people or maybe the Allfather thought to set us a challenge. Whatever the reason we now have the means to destroy every fort within our tribes' lands. Tonight, I will lie with my wife and eat of the magic mushrooms and I will dream. When I awake I will tell all of you that which I dreamed."

Olwen held his hand tightly. Her fingernails made marks where she dug them in. She whispered in his ear, "Lord let us lie together now! I am ready for you. My body hungers for your touch."

He smiled, "Be patient. We must feast with my men. They did well today but men were lost. They need to mourn. We need to praise those who are dead. Trust me, this is just the beginning. We could not have dreamed that our attack would be so successful. We need to build on that!"

Randel, too, wished to lie with his wife. He felt such power in his body as he had rarely felt. It felt as though a god had taken over his body. The cries of acclamation had been as a draught of heady beer. He craved more and he saw a way to achieve his desires.

When Randel and Olwen had retired to their sleeping chamber it had been to a hush from those watching. The next morning the clan were waiting from before dawn. When they emerged it was almost as though they briefly stopped breathing. Olwen clung on to Randel's arm as he spoke. He did not shout and he did not rant. His tones were almost hushed and people pressed closer to him so that they could hear every syllable that he uttered.

"I dreamt that I was a dragon. I was a dragon without fire. I searched the earth until Morrigan took pity upon me and she gave me fire. She told me to use that fire and burn the Romans from this land. Fire can destroy their stones and can cleanse this land. As a reward she promised that we would unite the Votadini, Selgovae and Brigante! All would follow my banner. I know what we must do. From this day forth we gather an army and we fight the Romans wherever they are. There are two more of the forts within a day's ride of us. We will attack them first."

The sound of the ululations, shouts, and screams seemed to echo through the valley. Olwen whispered in his ear, "You will be the king of a land which is greater than that ruled by the Brigante! Our children will be kings and queens!"

He turned and smiled, "I know."

Men began to flock to the hillfort within a day. Creagh and his oathsworn were taken aback as they rode up the greenway to the hillfort. Kerryn said, "I have rarely seen so many warriors save at the coronation of a king. Is this all for Ragdh ap Tadgh?"

For once Creagh was without words, "I know not." He pointed at the skull topped spears. "They are the ones who killed the Romans but I do not see Ragdh."

He knew Randel but only slightly. As a minor chief this far south in the land of the Votadini he had not been seen to be important. His hillfort was not the best in the land and he could have been quashed by his father at any time. Yet he had not shown any desire to be a leader. The numbers of warriors who Creagh saw milling about suggested otherwise.

He reached the entrance and a young warrior, standing on the rampart shouted, "I am Baradh, brother of the mighty Randel, destroyer of Romans, do you come here to serve under him?"

Kerryn's hand went to his sword, "Impudent young…

Creagh snapped, "Peace! We have to discover all that we can." He dismounted. He could tell that riding horses into Randel's home could be seen as an insult. "I am Creagh son of the chief of our tribe, Agnathus. My father sent me to discover how one of his clans managed to destroy a Roman fort and all its garrison."

Baradh jumped down, "We used courage and cunning! The Romans were brave but we outwitted them."

"And what of Ragdh ap Tadgh. How did he die?"

"He bravely drew a bolt from a bolt thrower and enabled us to get close. He will be remembered. The men who followed his father now follow my brother." Baradh smiled, "See all the other clans who have chosen to join us. This is just the beginning. Soon we will have many more. Perhaps you and your men would like to follow us?"

Creagh was becoming irritated by the young warrior's arrogance. "Perhaps we should speak with your brother, the chief!"

"Come then but leave your horses outside. We have too many warriors within our walls as it is. More flock here as the day progresses. We thought, at first, that you were volunteers too."

They had made a raised platform for Randel and he was addressing some chiefs and their warriors. Randel saw Creagh. He had met him but he had not liked him. He had dismissed both Creagh and Tadgh as being beneath him. However, he was acutely aware that he dared not offend the chief of his tribe and his son. "Welcome Creagh son of Agnathus. You are here to celebrate our victory?"

"My father heard of the burned fort and wished me to come and speak with the warriors who achieved that miracle."

Randel was a clever warrior. He could read men's thoughts, "You mean you thought to come and see if it was true? You have seen the fort and, I daresay, you have viewed the bodies. You could tell your father that the tribe now has a warrior who can beat the Romans!"

The other chiefs all cheered.

Creagh did not like the way that Randel was being accorded the status of a god-like hero! He had done well but he seemed to have ideas which were too grand for a hill chief. "My father would like you to join us."

"Join you? Has your father burned a fort? Has he slain over a hundred Romans? Has he captured a chest of Roman gold, not to mention the arms and armour?"

33

Creagh remained silent.

"I respect your father. He was a great warrior." A sudden thought came into Randel's head, "Does he wish me to lead his armies? That would be acceptable."

Once again all the chiefs and their oathsworn cheered and roared as though this was the finest idea they had ever heard. Creagh needed to get Randel away from these men. Isolated he could use the weight of the older chiefs, the ones who really mattered, to put him in his place and to use his skills to their advantage.

"You would have to speak to my father about that. Return with me to Din Guardi and we can speak to all the elders of the tribe."

Baradh laughed, "Brother, why should we waste our time with old men? That is more than two days riding from here! We can use the time to raid another fort. Our trick worked once. It can work again."

Creagh's ears picked up the word '*trick*'. "How did you trick the Romans?"

Baradh was as clever as his brother. Some said that he was cleverer for he could speak Roman words and he was able to decipher some of their writing. "When my brother leads you to war, Creagh son of Agnathus, then you will find out."

Randel nodded, "My brother is right. That is too long a journey. More men are arriving each day. We will raid the fort they call Bremenium in four days' time. I have not got time to ride to Din Guardi!"

For the first time ever Creagh was outwitted. What he wanted to do was to tell the young chief that he could not attack without his father's permission but he knew that was not going to happen.

"You may join us Creagh. I would relish the thought of fighting alongside someone who has slain so many men in single combat. Think how many more Romans you could kill."

Creagh was not certain if he was being insulted or mocked. "I cannot fight alongside you without permission from my father. I will ride to Ammabile. It is just a short ride away. Perhaps he has already reached there."

Randel nodded but Baradh could not resist one more jibe, "And when he does visit us perhaps, we will control more of the tribe's land than he does for we will have taken two Roman forts!"

Even Randel realised that his brother had gone too far, "My brother is just excited about the prospect of driving the Romans from our home.

When we destroy the second fort then the nearest Romans will be south of the wall. That is all. I will send one of my men to King Agriragus to explain my actions."

As Creagh and his men rode east Agnathus' son was troubled. The King of the Votadini had no sons. When he died the tribes would choose a new king. If Randel captured two forts then he might be chosen to succeed him. That would ruin all of his father's plans. Drastic action needed to be taken.

Baradh asked, "You really mean to send a messenger to King Clutha? He is even less warlike than Agnathus and the other old men."

"This is a game Creagh plays. He plays it for his father. They wish to use us to defeat the Romans and then, when the King dies, they will seize power. I know what is in their hearts. Remember my dream brother, I am to be king of a land greater than King Clutha. I will send someone to persuade him that he should support me and I will support him. We need a warrior we can trust and one who is not as young as we are. I have noticed that old men resent the young."

Baradh nodded. He had a warrior in mind, "Caractus would be the best choice. He has a wound and his beard is flecked with grey. I doubt that we will use him to help us fight. This might suit him. He is very loyal to you."

"Good, send him to me."

Caractus was a lonely man. His wife had died in childbirth. His two daughters had married men from other clans and his two sons had been killed when raiding the Romans. He had nothing left in his life and so he had tried to become the best warrior that he could. His farm was largely neglected but he didn't care. He was not, however, a very good warrior. His leg wound had come because his hands were just too slow with his sword. The Roman who had wounded him had died but he had had nothing to do with the blow. When Randel asked him to take a message to King Clutha it was the crowning glory in his life. Baradh even let him ride his pony. He spent the night before his journey making sure that he knew where he was going and that he had memorized the message he was to give to his king.

Creagh reached Ammabile even when Caractus was still preparing for his ride. He sent Kerryn on a fast pony to ride to his father's stronghold further up the coast. He gathered the warriors from the settlement. He noticed that there were not as many of them as he had expected. "Where are the other four?"

"They left this morning to join Randel at Otarbrunna. We thought you might have passed them."

Creagh bit back the angry retort. "I want every other warrior who is within half a day's ride from here. Tomorrow we march to Bremenium." On the ride to Ammabile Creagh had decided to pretend to throw his lot in with Randel. He would join in the attack on Bremenium. That way he might see how the young chief had succeeded where others had failed. He would be part of the success. Of course, he would make sure that he was nowhere near any real danger. That was always the trick. When he had fought single combats against other champions, he had studied them before he fought them and always had some trick to use: a poisoned edge to his blade, a secreted blade in his boot, a stone in his mouth to spit into an opponent's eye. He had used all of them and many others. He would use his guile to survive.

When the other chiefs had returned to their home the word of the destruction of the fort had spread. Góra wondered if this was the work of the Mother and she was spreading the news on the air. His wife served as a priestess of the cult and she was eager for him to wreak vengeance on the Romans for the deaths of Caronwyn and her priestess. "Husband, this is your opportunity. The others are old men. This Randel is young. Join him and it will be the two of you who hold the power in this land and not that popinjay, Creagh."

"But what could I do? Do you want me to simply turn up at his camp with my warriors?"

She laughed, "Of course! Word has been sent that he seeks warriors to destroy another Roman fort. With your men that victory should be assured."

Góra trusted his wife and the next day he led his forty warriors south. His tribe lived far west of the road towards the higher ground. They could reach Randel in just two days. They would not be travelling on Roman roads. His men rode hill ponies. Broad backed and hardy, they were perfect for moving through the high ground in which they lived. They rarely fought on the backs of them but they knew how to. The problem they had found was using weapons effectively. Góra admired the Roman cavalry. They had saddles which seemed to hold them in place and allow them to throw javelins, fight with a sword and even use a bow. If they could capture one then he would see if his craftsmen could make one.

Even Baradh was impressed at the number of warriors joining them. Some came alone or in pairs. Their chiefs had forbidden any to support an attack not sanctioned by the council of chiefs. Even so many minor chiefs and chieftains gathered the fighting men from their farms and hills and made their way to the hill fort. Randel and Baradh stood on the gate and watched another twenty head towards them. They were not the same clan, they just shared the same journey.

Randel swept a hand before him, "What the Romans fail to realise, brother, is that they have pushed us too far. Their forts and their roads are bad enough but the wall stops movement. We cannot go south. For years our father and his father raided the land of the Brigante. It showed them that we were better warriors and they came back richer. These men have nothing to lose. They may be poorly armed but they are willing to fight to rid the land of the Romans."

"But brother, I still do not see how we destroy their wall. Their forts which lie north of it will soon be a memory but the wall? How do we remove it?"

Randel shrugged, "I know not but I knew not how to take a fort until a few days ago. We are learning as we go."

Baradh pointed, "It is Creagh. He has returned and he has with him forty men."

Randel's eyes narrowed. Talking to himself as much as his brother he said, "That is not the whole of his father's clan. They would be as a flock of crows if it were. They would fill the ground. What is he doing here?"

"Whatever it is I do not trust him."

"Nor do I but I confess that having him and forty men gives me even more hope. And, if he follows my standard then he cannot undo the action. He will have taken orders from me. I wonder if his father knows? Come we will welcome him. Put distrust from your face and let him think he has duped us." He took his brother to one side. "Listen, I have a task for you. I want you to choose the best forty men we have left and issue them the spears and swords we captured. Use some of the helmets and mail shirts. I want you to go ahead of the main warband but do not go close to Bremenium. Instead I want you to wait close by their other fort at Alavna. If we succeed then those who escape are more likely to

37

flee east to that fort. If they do then your men could join them as they entered and we might be able to take a second fort on the same day."

Baradh looked less than thrilled at the prospect of sitting out a battle while others bled. "Give that task to another brother. I would be at your side."

Randel put his arm around his younger brother, "It has to be you for I can trust you and Creagh will wonder where you are and what you do. If we get the chance then I intend to take Alavna. You are the only one I can trust to achieve that without losing too many men."

Baradh bowed, "I know I am in the shadow of greatness when I am with you brother. You will be the dragon which devours the Romans and I will serve you in any way that I can."

When Agnathus heard the news from Kerryn he was, at first angry. His son had acted without commands and then, as he let his head take over from his temper, he saw the wisdom on his son's action. "A whole fort and its garrison were killed?"

"Yes lord. It was burned to the ground and there are many warriors flocking to the side of this Chief Randel. He has a chance. There are more men at the fort he intends to attack but he has so many men and Roman weapons that your son thinks he will succeed."

Agnathus lowered his voice and leaned in a little. "And this Randel, he is a reckless warrior? He leads from the front?"

Kerryn understood what Agnathus was implying, "He sees himself as a dragon. He will lead the attack."

"Then my son has made the right decision. We will leave in the morning. I have a hundred warriors close to my home. We will take those." He spread his hands and adopted an innocent look. "First we will camp outside the Roman fort at the river. I will order the Romans to leave. When they do not we will continue to join the rest of the tribe. It we do not arrive in time then that will not be our fault, will it? It will be the will of the gods!"

Olwen did not just rely on her husband's skill and his weapons. She took the Roman sword he had adopted and the mail shirt he had chosen to wear. She used her powers to make a spell and a potion. The potion was spread on the mail and the blade. She also made a draught for her husband to drink on the night before he left. He trusted his wife completely and drank without fear. The drink made him sleep but also made him powerful. His whole body felt stiffer and harder. It was as though she had made a potion to give him flesh, armour. They coupled in the hours before dawn and Randel took that as a good sign. The Mother would approve of such actions and Morrigan, the Goddess of war, would certainly approve. When Randel stepped from his hall and looked up at the rising sun he saw a single raven flying lazy circles. It was Morrigan. The goddess would be at their side and victory was assured.

Chapter 4

Caractus' leg was hurting him. He had not wanted to say to the chief that he was not recovered. It began to bleed not long after he left the hillfort. The chafing from the pony did not help. Caractus was determined to continue, no matter what. It would be worth the pain and the blood for he would be speaking with King Clutha. That in itself would be the pinnacle of Caractus' life. As he headed along the trail which ran parallel to the Roman Road, he began to visualise himself as an adviser to Chief Randel. Perhaps one day it would be King Randel. As he daydreamed and allowed the horse to follow the trail, he did not notice the blood which was now dripping steadily from his wound. He did not notice that he was swaying in the saddle. He thought it was the motion of the pony.

Felix spotted the blood when it first began to drip. Loping ahead with Wolf he sniffed out the trail while the Decurion brought along the horses. On this rough trail Felix could run as fast as a horse and certainly faster than a man who could not ride very well. Running well ahead of the Roman cavalryman Felix saw the Votadini on the pony. He could see the blood almost pouring from the wound. Suddenly the rider lurched to one side and fell to the ground. The pony, freed from its rider, trotted a few paces and then began to eat the tufty grass which grew there. Felix drew his knife and ran up to the wounded man.

Caractus looked up. How had he fallen? He saw a young warrior there. He had with him a dog. The dog growled.

"Wolf, peace."

Caractus was relieved that it was not a Roman but why could he not feel his legs? It was not hurting any longer but he wished to sleep. He would ask the boy to take the message. He did not recognise the boy but the dagger he carried was a familiar one. Reaching up he grabbed hold of

Felix's tunic, "You must take a message to King Clutha. He is at Traprain Law. It is vital that he gets it."

Felix was a bright youth. He nodded, "Of course, elder, what shall I tell him?"

The urge to sleep was even stronger but Caractus dug his nails into his palms to keep himself awake. He had been given a task by Chief Randel and he would do it. "Chief Randel has gathered many clans. In two days he will attack the next Roman fort north. He begs the King to come and watch his victory. Do you understand?"

"I do, elder."

"You know which fort I mean? The one north of the one our clan destroyed."

"Aye, I know. Now sleep. I promise that I will make good use of this message."

As Caractus closed his eyes Felix was tempted to give him a warrior's death but the widening pool of blood on the grass told him all that he needed to know. The man was dying.

Marcus dismounted, his sword ready. Felix shook his head. "There is no need, Decurion. He will be with the Allfather soon. The barbarians intend to attack Bremenium in two days. This man was a messenger sent to fetch the King."

Marcus was nothing if not decisive. Despite what the First Spear had said it was unlikely that Bremenium would be able to hold out against such overwhelming odds. "Ride to Coriosopitum. Tell First Spear Brocchus that Bremenium needs relief."

"Will you not come with me?"

Marcus shook his head, "If you leave now you can be there by nightfall. Take the hill pony too. That way you can change horses if you need to. I will warn the garrison. They and the men at Alavna are exposed. I cannot desert them."

Felix nodded and ran to grab the halter of the grazing pony. He sprang on its back and trotted back to his own horse. He grabbed the reins. "May the Allfather be with you."

"And with you."

This time Marcus approached the fort during the last hours of daylight and was admitted sooner. First Spear Julius Sextus Sejanus hurried over to him, "I thought we had seen the last of you. From your face you do not bring good news."

"We intercepted a messenger. The Votadini are coming in great numbers to destroy you, your men and your fort. If I thought you might listen I would suggest abandoning the fort and heading back to Coria but I know that you will not. This time they have brought even more men. Their success at Habitancvm has drawn many hundreds of warriors here."

"Then your warning is timely. Will you leave for Coria too?"

"No, I have sent a message and I will not abandon fellow auxilia to the Votadini. One more warrior might make them bleed a little more."

"It would take a relief column more than two days to reach us. If one could be mounted then we would be in a better position."

Marcus smiled, "I know. How many men do you have here?"

"On paper six centuries but most are understrength. We can muster four hundred and twenty men. We have six bolt throwers and plenty of bolts. Go and stable your horse. I will get the men organised."

By the time the cavalry officer had stabled Raven and fed her the fort was a hive of activity. Men were in the ditch. They were emptying jars of night soil and night water on the lillia which lay there. Others were seeding the ground beyond the ditch with caltrops. It was an amazing sight to behold. Marcus noticed that there was neither panic nor distress. First Spear seemed to banter with his men rather than bark at them. He joined the men who were smearing the walls with grease to make it harder to climb. This would not be as easy as the Votadini expected. He saw the crews of the bolt throwers and the archers marking out the ranges around the fort. They marked them with white stones. They would stand out and give an indication to the men working the bows and the machines.

Felix spotted the column of men from a long way off. The barbarians were moving into position. He had planned on using the road but that was now impossible, he had to head east to avoid them. That would add time to his journey. He took shelter in a stand of trees and watched them as they passed. There were more than fifty of them. They were armed with a variety of weapons but he noticed that some had shields and, from a distance some had helmets and long swords. They were even more barbarians joining the warband. Felix knew how to identify a warband which was to be feared. They were the ones with long swords, helmets and shields. Before he could continue his journey, he had to wait while second warband of twenty warriors made their way from the south. He frowned they looked to be Brigante. A few Brigante still lived north of the wall. The biggest worry was the fact that south of the wall was still a hotbed of unrest. He needed to get to the fortress as soon as he could and that was not now as easy as he had thought.

By the time it was dark they had done all that they could in Bremenium. A messenger had been sent to Alavna and he had returned. He had seen signs of bands of barbarians wandering the countryside and they were armed. That was unusual. The half cohort there knew what to expect. First Spear Julius Sextus Sejanus nodded to Marcus, "Decimus Drusus Ambustus is a young centurion but he has his head in the right place. If he thinks they can't hold then he will slip out under cover of darkness and join us here."

"The message I intercepted was about Bremenium."

Julius Sextus nodded, "And what if they sent another messenger with a different message for another of their chiefs? They are sneaky and they are cunning." He pointed to the food. "Eat heartily. These are the last fresh vegetables. We were going to try to eke them out but we might as well give the lads a good meal and we will live on bread and porridge for the next few days."

"You will keep the bread ovens burning?"

"I do not thinks so, I will take a chance tonight and have the baker make a large batch. We have enough acetum to keep us going and there is a well here." He laughed, "The smell of the bread baking will have two effects. If they have scouts out it will make them think we suspect nothing and if the barbarians are close it will drive them mad. We have the best bread!"

Surprisingly Marcus slept well. He had no duties and he felt safe inside the fort. He and First Spear had walked the walls with the other centurions. Marcus was impressed with them. They all knew what they were doing. When he was returned to Marcus' Horse he would try to emulate this efficiency.

As they waited, the next day, the tension steadily grew. The auxiliaries went about their business. Mail and weapons were prepared, the last of the bread was taken from the ovens and stored, a forage party went out to collect wild greens and sentries stood their watch. As the afternoon watch took over First Spear asked, "Marcus, do you think you could ride abroad and scout? You can say no, no-one would blame you."

Marcus was relieved, "To be honest First Spear, I would rather be out there than worrying in here. My horse has a good nose. Not as good as my scout's but good enough. I will ride beyond the road although from what your rider said yesterday the Votadini are becoming more brazen."

"That they are. Thank you. I hate being blind and, like you, I hate waiting."

The Decurion left his helmet and shield. He would not need them. He covered his mail with a cloak but he would be marked as a Roman horseman by the saddle. He would have to use his wits. The sentries had a clear view of the road and he was confident that he would not find any signs of the enemy until he was out of sight of the fort. Raven's ears were pricked and that was a good sign. She was alert. After riding north along the road, for half a mile Marcus took a small side trail heading up into the hills. They were gentle slopes but they were covered in scrubby, windswept trees and rambling shrubs and bushes. Marcus was not taken in by the silence. There were barbarians around; he just could not see them. What he did see were the marks they had left. Broken branches and leaves as well as footprints told him all that he needed to know. They were surrounding the fort. Raven whinnied and that was enough for Marcus. He whipped his horse's head around and lashed his rump with his vine-rod. It was not before time. Four Votadini hurled their spears at the space he had just left. Lying flat along Raven's back he galloped back to the road. Confident that they would not approach the fort yet he headed along the road to Alavna. To reach it he rode directly across country. He had to cross the stream which gave protection to this side of the fort. It was as he clambered up the other side that he realised it would be a perfect place to hide men. As Raven made the top he reined in.

The auxiliary patted Raven, "Well done, girl. You have good ears and I have kept my skin whole." It was then he noticed a large tear in the left-hand side of his cloak. A spear had struck him. He had not felt it and his mail had protected him. He gripped the hilt of his sword. The past was protecting him.

He was unfamiliar with the road east. It was not a Roman Road. It was more of a greenway and followed the high ridge. He rode along it and searched for signs by the side of the road. When he spied the muddied prints, he turned and headed south. The fort was more than a mile away. He could still be seen but only from the east gatehouse. If danger came then he would be alone. What he noticed was just how desolate and empty the land was. He saw no farms and few animals. More alarmingly there was a great deal of cover for enemies. He stopped and dismounted. He pulled at a piece of heather. It was bone dry. He was about to investigate further when four warriors suddenly broke from cover. They were less than twenty paces from him and between him and the fort. They were armed with throwing spears.

Marcus did not panic. He vaulted himself into the saddle and pulled his sword in one motion. He dug his heels into Raven's flanks. In the time it had taken for him to mount and move the Votadini were just ten paces from him. He saw them pulling back their arms to throw at him. He had no doubt that they would aim at him and his horse. He galloped at the two to the left and then, as he swung his arm back he jerked the reins to the right. Raven bundled over one warrior and Marcus brought his sword down on to the neck of the other. They expected him to flee. He had used all of his luck up already. If he presented his back to the other two he was a dead man. He whipped Raven's head around, vaguely aware that there was a spear sticking out of one of the saddle horns. This time the two Votadini were taken by surprise. Marcus lunged at one and scored a hit along his shoulder. He swung his foot at the other and connected beneath the man's chin. He fell. Marcus had not time to examine the four for another five had broken cover and Marcus, wisely, headed back to the safety of the fort. He had learned enough.

As he reined in, just inside the gates, an auxiliary pulled out the spear from the saddle horn. "That was impressive sir. Taking on four barbarians like that."

"I was lucky."

First Spear strode over, "Well?"

"They have you surrounded. I found signs to the west, north and east of you. As their camp is to the south I think that we are cut off. In my opinion, they will use that stream for cover. It is only three hundred paces to the ditches. That is inside bolt thrower range."

"I know. We can change many things but not the course of the stream."

Marcus rubbed his chin, "There is one thing, sir, the heather to the east, it is bone dry."

"And?"

"If the wind was from the west it would not take much to fire it. As I discovered, they can hide in the stuff and be invisible. It is just a suggestion sir but if I were you, I would fire it as soon as an attack starts. Even if they are not attacking from there, I believe that there will be Votadini hiding."

"Good idea." He pointed to Raven. "Your horse is injured."

Marcus saw that a spear had scored a long wound down the shoulder of his horse. It was not serious but, without attention, it would be. He led the horse to the stable. He cleaned it with acetum. Raven protested but Marcus had her head tied to two rings so that she could not move easily. Then he smeared it with some honey. He put her nose bag on. He would not need to ride her for a few days but she needed all the help she could get to recover. Marcus had not ruled out the possibility that he might have to flee with news if the worst happened and the fort fell. He would fight as long as he could with the auxiliaries but he owed a greater duty to the army. He had been sent to gather information and that was what he would do.

Felix galloped wearily across the bridge into Coriosopitum. Tensions were running high and he was delayed until a messenger could be sent to the Principia for confirmation that they were expecting his news. Already delayed by the Votadini Felix was acutely aware that the attack would be taking place the next day. Knowing the Votadini it would be at dawn. First Spear was also unhappy with the delay. The unfortunate optio was berated by the centurion who came to fetch Felix.

"Where is your Decurion, scout?"

Felix was well used to the ways of the Romans. They liked to take charge and they did so with questions. The most efficient way would have been for him to simply pass on the message. He answered, "He is in Bremenium, First Spear. We discovered news that it is to be attacked and he needed to warn the garrison."

Before he could go on and give more details the impatient First Spear interrupted, "But the garrison knows of the trick which worked last time. They will be safe, surely? Why did the decurion not return?"

Felix hid the half smile, "The Decurion and I counted more spears than we have seen in a long time. I was delayed in my return by the weight of numbers who were surrounding Bremenium." He paused, "The decurion asked for help to be sent."

"It is that serious? What numbers are we talking about?"

When it came to large numbers Felix had to rely on those that both he and the First Spear understood. "I would say that there is the equivalent of two Cohors Milliaria."

There were other centurions present and one of them burst out, "Surely that cannot be right, sir! The clerk who escaped told us that there were less than two hundred involved in the attack."

46

Before First Spear could speak Felix said, "Sir, they have been drawing men from all over. I even saw some Brigante who live south of the wall heading there. The success in destroying a fort is drawing warriors from all over. This is not all of the warriors available to the Votadini. I spied some Selgovae. All who wish harm to the Romans are flocking to the banner of Randel."

First Spear looked at the map. On this coast there were just three forts north of the wall. One had been destroyed and the other two were surrounded. He cursed the Legate. Until a new Legate and Prefect arrived it was his decision to make and this was one which taxed him. He could not leave his comrades exposed. He would have to go to their rescue.

"Scout, you have done well but I need you again. Get a fresh horse." Turning to his number two he said, "Get the First Cohort ready we march north."

Felix smiled, "If you are marching then I need no horse, sir. I can keep ahead of you. I will go and prepare."

As he went First Spear said, "And that is my worry, gentlemen. Young Felix is right. Even at double time the barbarians can still move faster than we can. Whichever fool took Marcus' Horse south put the whole of the northeast of this province in terrible danger."

Randel had watched the Roman rider escape his ambush and head east towards the stream. The man was lucky. The men he had sent to take him had been too eager and too excited. That was the problem with their victory. His men believed that every Roman was an easy target. That was not true, Randel knew that and the Roman horsemen were their best warriors. He did not know how they could control their horses, use their shields and fight at the same time. This was when he missed his brother. Just talking to Baradh seemed to clarify his thinking. Creagh was there instead and he was no help.

"A little careless, chief, to allow the rider to escape."

"Where can he go? The fort is surrounded. If he heads to Alavna then there will be warriors to take him. Fear not Creagh, son of Agnathus, he was not important. Tonight, we get into position. They will be expecting us to fight in their borrowed mail. Instead, we will hide in plain sight. Our warriors will creep closer to them. Their bolt throwers are deadly but they cannot depress when you are close to them. Tadgh learned that. It cost him his life but we will benefit from that knowledge. They have six of them. By attacking from every direction and in a loose line we lose only six men. They can reload quickly but not that quickly. When we reach their ditches then they cannot hit us."

Creagh's face showed his disappointment. Randel had thought things through well and Creagh did not like it.

Randel lowered his voice so that only Creagh could hear him. "Until I fail then these men will follow me. You will have to bide your time to take control."

Creagh hated the way that the young chief seemed to read his thoughts. To cover himself he asked, "And where is your brother, Baradh? I heard he was always at your side."

"And he normally is but I had a task and he was the only one I could trust to do it."

"You do not trust the rest of your men?"

Randel smiled, enigmatically, "The ones I have fought with, those I trust."

The two of them watched the men as they began to slip acorns the road and into the stream. He had worried that the Romans might send bolts to discourage them but now he realised that the road was at extreme range from the fort. When the rider had been pursued across the road the bolt thrower had remained silent. The Allfather smiled on them. Had this been Baradh who had been with him then Randel might have shared that information. It was Creagh and Randel did not like the man.

"Creagh, why are your men not in the ditch with the others?"

"Look at the weapons my men carry. They are superior to those who wait in the ditch. Better to save them for the second assault when their weapons can be of more use."

Randel was angry and his voice, though quiet, showed this, "Put your men in the ditch with the others. When it is almost dawn you and I will join them and lead the attack."

Creagh looked appalled. He had assumed that they would watch the attack and then join in later on, "We go in the first attack?"

"That was the way of Tadgh and it is the way of my brother and I." He smiled, "You are not afraid to die, are you? I thought that death would be nothing to you. You have sent many men to the Otherworld have you not?"

Creagh did not like the way this young chief seemed to be able to get under his skin and see his flaws and weaknesses. "No, but I do not see any point in throwing it away."

"It will not be thrown away. We attack while it is still poor light. The bolt throwers and the arrows are the danger. The men who operate them will have difficulty seeing fast moving men who run without armour. We make the first ditch and we are safe from the bolts. Then we have to navigate the ditches. I confess that will not be easy and it is why we need your men. Many of them have shields. We have many we collected from the Romans but the more shields we have the fewer men we will lose."

Creagh was almost convinced and he nodded but he would make sure that he hung back. A shield was not a defence against a Roman bolt.

Baradh and his men were in position. They were south of the river and hiding by the road which led to the fort. The fort was five hundred paces from them. He dared approach no closer for the Roman commander had cleared the land all around. They had even cleared a killing zone for the three bolt throwers on that side. He had chosen the best place to wait. Hidden in a stand of trees they would be able to intercept any who fled the fort or join any refugees who fled after his brother's victory. He now had more men than when he had started out. They had found men heading for Otarbrunna to join his brother. He took it upon himself to order them to join him. His warband swelled to eighty. With forty equipped as Romans Baradh now believed he had more of a chance to take Alavna if the opportunity arose.

Cynwrig led the eighty men who waited in the heather to the east of Bremenium. Baradh had marched with his cousin on his way to Alavna. Cynwrig was eager to show his two illustrious cousins that he, too, knew how to fight and to lead. Although most of the men he led were new to him, he was confident that they would not let him down. As soon as it was dark they began to crawl through the heather and the gorse. The gorse was harder to negotiate. The spikes could take out an eye! It did, however, afford more cover than the heather. It was dark and Cynwrig knew that they would not be seen but even in daylight the movement would have looked like the wind blowing from the east. Cynwrig was like all of his people, he understood the land and the winds. Arianrhod, who gave them winds, was already shifting the wind for them. By the time they were within range of the bolt throwers the wind would be coming from the west and would take their smell away from the fort. The gods did not like the Romans! Even as they crept Cynwrig could smell the Romans. The food they ate was different. They ate something which smelled pungent, even from a distance and, as he crept, the smell came into his nostrils. He could also smell the faint whiff of fresh bread. If they were close to the wall with the bread oven then he and his men would have an easier opportunity to fire the fort. He and his men moved forward. They moved one arm or leg at a time to minimise movement. When Cynwrig made the noise of the owls which hunted at night they would stop. That would be just a hundred paces from the ditch. The Romans had cleared sixty paces from the ditch and Cynwrig and his men needed the cover of the heather and gorse to avoid exposure.

Agnathus was not camped as the others were. He and his men were at the camp of one of his chiefs. It lay to the north of Alavna. Agripanthus had been a mighty warrior in his time. His battles had been ended by the spear thrust at him by one of the dreaded horsemen of the Romans. His men had not joined those of Randel. He had awaited his chief. His village lay two Roman miles north of the fort although as there was no road and a river between the distance was more like three. He and Agnathus sat and talked, after they had eaten of their plans for the next day.

"I would not waste the one hundred men we have with us. My son will be with Randel. If they can attack and take Bremenium then we may be able to take advantage and reduce this fort which makes us cower."

"It is well positioned, my lord. It lies in the bend of a river. The river and the Roman ditches make it very hard to take. They have chosen a high part of the land so that they can see us coming from a great distance."

"And that is why I will be cautious. I will send some men to cut the road to Bremenium. There are woods north of the river?"

"Yes lord."

"Then the rest of us will wait there. If the chance comes, we attack and if not, we wait to see what happens further west."

Chapter 5

The message which Marcus had brought meant that First Spear knew when the attack would come. If they were outside the walls and ready to attack it would either be at night or at dawn. He had the men fed and standing on the walls well before dawn. The auxiliaries did not complain. Their centurions, optios and chosen men had told them all of the massacre just down the road. A little lost sleep was preferable to a lost manhood and head. The night drew on and still no attack materialised.

Marcus donned his helmet and made certain the Sword of Cartimandua was sharp enough to shave with. He picked up a handful of javelins and joined First Spear on the fighting platform above the road gatehouse. He sniffed the air, "They are out there. The wind has changed and I can smell them. They smell of sweat, pig fat and I can detect lime. There are warriors out there with limed hair."

First Spear nodded. The bolt thrower crew were peering anxiously into the dark gloom. He turned to them. "When they come it will be as fast as lightning. You lads will earn your extra pay today and that's no error." He shouted, "Everyone, stand to and keep watch. It will be dawn soon enough."

The optio on the bolt thrower asked, "Why don't they come in the dark, First Spear?"

"Simple, Optio Assellio, they are not as stupid as they used to be. They know that we have traps and stakes in the bottom of our ditches. They want to see where they are. They will avoid the bridge. They know it is a killing ground." Turning to Centurion Lucius Furius Calva he said, "Take charge here Centurion. I want to make sure that they have fire at the east gate. It seems our Decurion here has good senses. The wind has changed. We may be able to burn the buggers!"

Centurion Lucius Furius Calva was an older centurion. The grey at his temples told Marcus that the man had seen some service, "Could do with your lads right now, Decurion. Horsemen are the best deterrent to barbarians."

"I agree but there is never enough. There are three alae in the whole of the Province at the moment and two of them are now down at Deva. That leaves just one and they are heading north even as we speak. The good news is that they are twice the size of Marcus' Horse. The Ala Petriana have a good reputation. We just have to hope that that they can get a move on."

Well south of the wall Prefect Aulus Gemellus Glabrio was approaching Morbium. He was not a happy officer. He did not mind being prefect of Ala Augusta Gallorum Petriana. In fact, it was an honour for this was the most prestigious of all ala. What he was unhappy about was the haste with which they had been sent north. The Ala Augusta Gallorum Petriana had been at Lindum for three years. Depleted by the battles north of the wall the original Ala Quingenaria had been doubled in size. He had been with the ala for just three months, the original commander having died. Prefect Aulus Gemellus Glabrio needed more time to whip the wild Gauls and Britons into shape. He wanted them to be a disciplined unit. His success in this barbaric land might lead to a better posting in the east. That was a better climate and a life style which would be more agreeable than this little rock squatting at the edge of the world. The Governor had been insistent that they cease their training and go north of the wall to quell a rebellion.

He waved forward the Decurion Princeps, Marius Scaeva Pera, "You have served here before, Decurion Princeps. Does Morbium have barracks enough for us?"

"No, Prefect. The only fort on this coast large enough to house the ala is Coriosopitum. We cannot make that today. We will have to use Morbium. I believe that they have still to demolish the old fort. We can use that. The troopers will have a roof. It will be safe enough."

"I am more concerned about comfort. And this weather? Does it never get warm?"

The Decurion Princeps bit back the laugh, "Prefect, this is summer. This is as hot as it gets." It was on the tip of his tongue to tell him of the winter but that would be a surprise he would let the arrogant patrician discover himself.

"Then we must win a stunning victory and I will be posted to a decent clime."

"I fear that this will be anything but quick, Prefect. The land favours the barbarians and they are fierce fighters. Death in battle is an honour to them. They are no respecters of horses. They would as soon take an axe to a horse's leg as a sword to a trooper's throat. They know that once we fall then we are helpless."

"Barbarians! Why Emperor Hadrian does not exterminate them all I do not know. There is little in their land that we want! That is why he built the wall."

The Decurion Princeps was a native. He was Catuvellauni. The Prefect's views were not a surprise to him. "We need the forts north of the wall, Prefect, to control the tribes. Our very presence will keep the land quiet. Between us and Marcus' Horse we kept the frontier quiet while the wall was being built."

"Well they have gone and it is now down to us. We shall have to endure a night of discomfort then!"

Randel sniffed the air. It was still dark but it would soon be light enough to determine where the traps and stakes were in the bottom of the ditch. They had learned that to jump into a ditch resulted in a broken limb at best and an excruciating death at worst. While not glorious the best was to descend backwards having first ascertained where the stakes and obstructions lay. Climbing out on the other side was equally difficult and required collaboration between warriors. Tadgh had taught them that. The fact that they had two such ditches to cross made it doubly difficult. Randel gave a low whistle. Drustan, who led the eighty archers and slingers, nodded. His men and boys would be ready to support the warriors who charged the walls. Randel was aware of Creagh, hovering close by him. He had worked out why he was here. He wanted to learn Randel's secrets. If Randel fell he had no doubt that Creagh would lead and try to take all of the glory. Randel decided that would not happen.

To someone who did not know the land there would appear to have been no change but Randel knew that dawn was about to break. Putting the Roman helmet on his head he hissed, "Now, my warriors, now is the time." He turned to Creagh, "Let us see how the great champion of the Votadini manages in this attack eh?"

Creagh could not back out. He was surrounded by chiefs. He would have lost all face if he tried to sneak away. He nodded and, like Randel, began to crawl up the stream's bank. Like Randel and the others Creagh felt exposed. It was tempting to rush but he was aware that Randel appeared to be barely moving. The fort stood just three hundred paces away. Not a great distance but they were moving out of the long grass, nettles, dandelions and dock into the area kept free of undergrowth. Creagh was learning. He would, had he been leading, have jumped up and run to the ditch in an attempt to reach its safety. He saw now that would have been a mistake. It took some time but they were forty paces closer and no Roman shout had broken the night. All that could be heard was the murmur of sentries chatting to each other and oblivious to the disaster about to befall them.

On the walls Marcus pointed. "They are coming. I can see them."
Optio Assellio said, "I can see nothing."
Marcus said, "Look at the bank of the stream. The shadows there move." He had known that the Votadini would have darkened their faces. Some would have used the simple expedient of charcoal but the braver warriors would have used cochineal and other natural dyes to paint a war face on. Terror was part of their plan.
"I see them. Should we sound the stand to?"
Just then First Spear returned and growled, "You do Optio and you will be back to being a milites. We wait. They are crawling and the closer they come the more we kill."
Marcus knew he was right but he hated being idle. He hefted a javelin to assess the balance. One of the exercises he and his turma did was to throw a javelin from a moving horse at a tiny ring. The fighting platform did not move. He knew he would have an easier strike. He looked over his shoulder. Behind him he saw the grey sky which heralded dawn. As soon as the sun rose it would bathe the fort in sunshine. The bolts were loaded. The arrows were ready to be nocked. The whole of the fort was waiting for First Spear to roar out the command. Marcus was a good archer and it felt like a bow had been pulled back to its furthest extent; any further and the bow would break. First Spear judged it perfectly. The Votadini were still shadows but they were discernible shadows. More importantly, the majority were within the two hundred paces marker. Some were in javelin range. From their elevated position the archers would hit.
"Release!"
The simple one word unleased an apocalypse of bolts and arrows. Even as Marcus' javelin pinned a crawling figure to the ground he heard the triple cracks of the bolt throwers as they hurled their rods of death.

One warrior had heard the Roman command and had been unable to restrain himself. He had leapt forward screaming a war cry. The bolt hurtled through him, throwing him backwards into two others before burying itself in the head of the Votadini who was just emerging from the stream.

Marcus picked up another javelin aware that the Votadini were only just rising. He heard the cries and saw that the Votadini who had first stood to run at the wall, had discovered the caltrops. The first warriors would clear them for the ones that followed but the ones spiked by them would be crippled. Marcus saw the chief who had been speaking at the camp. He was a brave one. He was leading his men. Slightly behind him was another huge warrior with limed hair. The easier target was the lime haired warrior but he knew the value in killing the chief. He pulled back and hurled. It was a killing strike. Or it would have been had not a Votadini risen inexplicably before the chief and took the javelin in the chest. Even so the force of the javelin took it through the warrior and it grazed the chief's leg. As he pulled a shield around, he stared at the Decurion and their eyes met. They would know each other again.

The Votadini now sprang forward. They hopped from side to side in an effort to throw off the aim of the arrows and bolts. Their own archers and slingers began to take their toll. One of Optio Asselio's men was struck by a stone and fell dead.

First Spear shouted, "Relief crew."

A voice shouted from the east wall, "First Spear; they attack!"

He nodded and shouted, "Then it is time for fire!"

Marcus could not help watching as ten fire arrows rose in the sky along with a flaming ball from one of the two stone throwers. The other would not be needed but the one on the east wall did enough for the two of them. Suddenly a wall of flame leapt so high in the sky that the Votadini attacking on the west, south and north stopped to look. Marcus took the opportunity to send his third javelin into the chest of an archer. The rest were out of range but one had been bolder than the rest. He had paid for his boldness with his life.

"Archers, aim for their slingers and archers. Our spears can handle the barbarians."

When the Roman cavalryman had almost ended Randel's life, the Votadini chief took it as a sign that the gods were with him. They had lost men but he was now within a few paces of the ditch. He had just reached it when a wall of fire appeared above the fort. What kind of magic was this? He forced conjecture from his mind. Speculation would gain him naught. They had two ditches to conquer. He peered over. There were stakes sticking up and there were also fixed crosses. The crosses had spikes in them. Everything was covered in excrement. A wound infected with it would result in death. The Romans had to be admired. They knew more ways of killing than Randel had even considered.

He saw that there were twelve dead warriors close by and all had borne shields. He shouted, "Use the shields to make a bridge!"

Holding his own above him he grabbed Ninian's shield and placed it on top of the stakes and jammed against a cross. Morcant placed another two next to it and Randel lowered himself on to the three shields. They were remarkably stable and the stakes which were fire hardened wood, did not penetrate. More shields were passed to him. At first it was hard to work for he had but one hand. Then Morcant joined him and they had a bridge. The two of them hurried to the second ditch. The arrows and bolts were still aimed at those following. It was spears and javelins they had to worry about but more men flooded across. Sheltered beneath the shield he held Randel looked back. His men were joining him but, of Creagh there was no sign.

When the javelin almost hit Randel then Creagh realised it was too risky where they stood. The sudden fire convinced him. He shouted, "Oathsworn! Back!" He saw that two of his men were dead. One had been struck by a bolt and Creagh knew how close he had come to death. The remaining oathsworn sprinted back to the stream.

A warrior asked, "Is the attack over?"

"No, I go to fetch more warriors for a flank attack! We are winning." It was a lie. Creagh and his father had been fooled by Randel and his lies. The trick they had worked only succeeded the once. The Votadini were being slaughtered. The only good part was that when Randel and his confederates lay dead then Creagh would lead the survivors.

When First Spear saw the two warriors make the second ditch he became a little concerned, "Persistent aren't they?"

The Decurion saw that the chief and some of his men had used shields to cross the ditch while holding Roman shields over their heads. As Marcus hurled his spear and impaled a warrior who had ascended the first ditch but was without a shield he said, "The one who managed to cross the ditch is their chief. Kill or capture him and the rebellion is over."

"And that is easier said than done. You may not have noticed, Decurion, but we are losing men."

Marcus had noticed but they were slowing down the attack. Marcus noticed that the lime haired warriors had gone. Two lay dead. Were they up to something else?

Cynwrig heard the command from the walls and the twang of the bolt throwers. The cries from the west told him that his people were dying and yet the bolt throwers on this side had remained silent. He waited and still there were no arrows or bolts. He had been given a task and he would do it. He whistled his men forward. The sky was lighter but they would still be hard to see. Suddenly he heard three loud cracks and three of his men fell. Then a rain of arrows descended. Ten of his men died, pinned to the ground.

"Votadini! Attack!" He stood and, holding the Roman shield before him, ran at the walls. He had eighty men to lead. They would succeed. Two things happened at the same time. He watched as three more of his men fell to the deadly bolt throwers and then he saw archers with smoking arrows. When they rose in the air and then descended, he knew that his life was over. Mercifully for Cynwrig, the Roman bolt tore a hole in his head and all thoughts and life left his body. He did not see the flames rise and, fanned by a wind from the west, sweep through the heather, grass and gorse. He did not witness fifty of his men being burned to a crisp. His body crackled as the fire ignited the bolt and burned him from within and without.

The Fates are unpredictable creatures. The fire heralded a Roman victory. The battle was not over but the defenders of the east wall could join those in the west. Far to the east, at Alavna, Centurion Decimus Drusus Ambustus frowned when he saw the smoke to the west. It appeared to be Bremenium. He forced himself to stay calm. Perhaps the garrison there were fighting the fire. If it continued to burn then that would be bad news for it would mean that it had fallen. He knew he was surrounded. The Votadini had been seen. As the fire raged and black smoke filled the sky so Decimus Drusus Ambustus began to plan ways out of his predicament.

He waved over Optio Vitellius Nerva Maro, "I want our two best men. After dark I want them to slip out and head for Coriosopitum. They need to tell the garrison there that I think Bremenium has fallen."

The optio looked at him, "Surely not, sir?"

"Look west, Optio, what do you think the fire means?"

He nodded, "First Habitancvm and now Bremenium."

"But we will not be next! Find the men!"

The Votadini outside the walls were also confused. Agnathus and Baradh knew that the other was there but they had not yet spoken. The fire in the distance could mean many things. Agnathus decided that he would speak with Baradh and, with his oathsworn, he went to the young Votadini. When Baradh saw the chief approach, he became suspicious. His men had told him of the arrival of Agnathus but he had not done him the courtesy of coming to his camp and speaking to him.

"What think you Baradh, brother of Randel the Roman killer?"

Mollified by the tone of the High Chief Baradh nodded and answered, "It could be that my brother has managed to capture the fort and set it on fire."

"Your voice tells me that you do not think so."

"No. He would fire the fort but it is too soon after the attack has begun. I am at a loss to explain it."

"And what of this one, could we take this one?"

Baradh was about to say it would be a waste of life and then an idea sprang into his head. "We could try a trick, Chief Agnathus."

"A trick?"

"We both believed, for an instant, that the fort at Bremenium has fallen."

"We know it has not."

"And yet my first thought and yours was that it had. Do you not think the Romans will think so? This has a small garrison. My men have captured armour. If you and I, with say ten men took the armour to the fort we could say we had destroyed the fort and garrison."

"They would kill us."

"The Romans are a strange people. They will listen to us. You offer to let them go free. Say something about enough blood being shed already."

"They would not fall for such a trick."

58

Baradh shrugged, "It matters not if they do or not. There will be doubt in their mind and, when we do attack, they will fall quicker. I am willing to take the risk. Are you?"

Agnathus was astounded by the audacity of the young warrior. He was far cleverer than his own son. If this succeeded then Agnathus knew he would be the next King of the Votadini. It was worth the risk.

"I am."

Centurion Decimus Drusus Ambustus was briefing his two messengers. At the fighting platform of the gatehouse, the optio shouted, "Sir, there are barbarians approaching should I send bolts their way?"

"How many?"

"Ten sir. Eight bear auxilia weapons and mail."

"Have the archers ready and the bolt throwers loaded but do not release until I am there." He turned to the two messengers. "I may have a further message for you. Wait."

He hurried to the fighting platform. He had thought he was ready for command. The fort seemed perfect. He was close to the sea and the Classis Britannica, he commanded just a large cohort and the tribes who lived close by the fort were known to be harmless. What had gone wrong?

He saw an older warrior, by his torc he was a chief. The other was a younger warrior and he wore a mail shirt taken from a dead Roman. The rest bore arms.

"I am Centurion Decimus Drusus Ambustus. I command here. Speak quickly or you will die."

He was uncertain if they spoke Latin but he was not about to risk making a fool of himself.

The older man spoke, "I am Chief Agnathus of the Votadini." His words were accented but Centurion Decimus Drusus Ambustus could understand them. The chief pointed behind him to the west. "As you can see we have destroyed your fort at Bremenium. We attacked it in the night and surprised the defenders. We slew all within it."

Baradh could not help smiling. The old chief was embellishing the story they had concocted. It sounded even more realistic.

"We bring some of their arms and armour to prove that we do not lie."

Centurion Decimus Drusus Ambustus nodded, "Try to attack us at night, old man and you will see that I am made of sterner stuff."

Agnathus nodded, "There has been enough bloodshed. All that we require is that you leave this last fort in our land. We give you safe passage south. Just leave."

"You think me a fool, old man? The moment we leave you will massacre us."

"I give you my word."

"And what is the word of a barbarian worth?"

Agnathus looked at Baradh who nodded, "Then take us as hostage. We are surety to your good health. It is less than forty miles to your wall. Take us fifteen miles south. There is a straight trail which leads to your road. You will be safe upon your road will you not?" Centurion Decimus Drusus Ambustus said nothing. He was already looking for flaws in the plan. "Then you will know that you are safe."

Centurion Decimus Drusus Ambustus realised that this was a tempting offer. Alavna was untenable alone. If the other two forts were lost then he would be praised for saving the century. "I must speak with my officers. Stay where you are. My men have their weapons aimed at you. If there is the slightest hint of treachery then you will die!"

With just two other officers it would not take long. He waved them over. "What do you think?"

Both were as young as Centurion Decimus Drusus Ambustus. The other auxiliaries were also young. The half a dozen who had served on the frontier for more than ten years had been sent here because they were troublemakers.

Optio Vitellius Nerva Maro said, "We could destroy everything of value in the fort and fire it before we left, sir. They would not gain anything from it and if we have their chiefs with us we would be safe."

The optio had almost made the decision for the Centurion. He needed balanced counsel but Optio Vitellius Nerva Maro was just speaking what was in the centurion's mind. "You are right but the problem will come once we release our hostages. We will have to double time down the road."

"The lads can do that, sir. That is one advantage of being such a young century."

The disastrous decision was made.

Chapter 6

Quintus Licinius Brocchus led the double century of legionaries up the road. He had no auxiliaries as scouts. There was just the Brigante youth, Felix and his dog, Wolf ranged ahead. He was confident they would not be surprised. He had had to leave the auxilia on the wall in Coriosopitum. The horsemen had not arrived and he could ill afford to take men from the wall. With his vine rod in his hand he led the First Cohort north. On paper he should have had eight hundred men. With retirements, wounds, injuries and even deaths he just had six hundred men. He deemed that was more than enough to deal with this little rebellion. The two garrison commanders had been forewarned and he knew they could both hold out for a couple of days at the very least. As he watched the sun pass its zenith he knew they would have to make a marching camp. His men were veterans. They could erect and dismantle a fort in a short time. The would reach Habitancvm during the afternoon of the next day and First Spear intended to double time them up to Bremenium.

One of Cynwrig's men escaped the inferno. Seisyll had been at the rear. If truth were told he had been afraid. He had seen the effect of the bolt thrower. That was not a way for a warrior to die. He did not mind going sword to sword with a Roman. There was honour in that death. He ran around the fort to reach Randel. He waited in the stream. Wounded were being brought there and the clan's healers were tending to their wounds. "Where is Randel?"

Judoc pointed to the wall. Randel and a dozen of his men had made the wall of the fort. With shields held above them they were hacking at the wooden walls with wood axes. More of the tribe were hurrying across the flimsy shield bridges. Victory appeared close at hand but Seisyll knew different. Randel was expecting pressure from the east wall. There

61

would be none. He picked up a shield. The warrior who had run back from the wall had bled to death before Judoc could tend to him. Running from the stream was the bravest thing that Seisyll ever did for there were three bolt throwers and they were still sending their missiles of death over with monotonous regularity. He was saved by the fact that another eight warriors had joined from the failed attacks in the north and south gates. Two of them fell to the bolts as they rose and that spurred the rest on.

Seisyll was fast and he jinked from side to side. With the shield held above him his eyes scanned the ground for danger. Tripping over a dead comrade could be as disastrous as taking an arrow. As he clambered over the first ditch he saw some of the clan lying spread-eagled on the stakes. They had fallen from the shields. There were fewer at the second ditch. The ones who had reached there had learned how to run. In many ways being so close to the wall was the safest place to be. Randel had his men picking up the javelins thrown by the defenders and hurling them back. It was a deadly duel but most of the men with Randel wore a Roman mail vest.

"Chief Randel!"

Randel turned and frowned. He recognised the man who stood there but could not remember where he should be fighting. He had been struck in the helmet by the haft of a spear. He now understood why the Romans wore them. If he had not then he would have been dead. "What is it?"

"I bring dire news. Cynwrig and the rest of his men are burned to death. The Romans fired the heather and the gorse. All are dead. The Romans are shifting men from the east wall."

In that moment Randel knew that they had failed. Eighty men had disappeared in a flash of fire. That was too many for them to bear. He needed his brother and his men. He knew that they would lose men when they fell back but they could keep their grip on the fort as tight as ever. He even saw a way that they could use this to their advantage. They now had bridges across the ditches and they could attack again but at night.

"Fall back to the stream!"

When the fire had taken hold and they had heard the screams of the burning First Spear Julius Sextus Sejanus had pulled the men from the wall and the gatehouse to reinforce the west wall. The two bolt throwers on the corner towers turned their bolts on the attacks which threatened the north and south gates. The centurions there were confident that they could hold easily. It was the west wall where the danger lay. The Decurion had been right about the Votadini chief. He was a tough warrior. He heard the axes as they tried to break through the fort's walls. Had they had better axes they would have had more success. Now the barbarians were hurling javelins back at the walls. Five of his men had already been hit. None had died but they were no longer on the walls. They had been wounded and the capsarii were dealing with the increasing flood of casualties.

Suddenly he heard the Decurion shout, "They are pulling back!"

With his shield held before him First Spear Julius Sextus Sejanus peered over the wall. The Decurion was right. "Is this some sort of trick?"

"They have lost a lot of men, First Spear. I am guessing they need to lick their wounds. The fire must have cost them a lot of men."

"I intend to use the respite! One man in two bring food to the walls. Every wounded man, no matter how minor, needs to be taken to the capsarius."

Despite the damage they had suffered they were still able to defend themselves. The enemy had lost far more men than they had. The problem lay in the two ditches. There were now bridges across them and they needed to be removed.

"Assellio, we need to do something about those bridges across the ditches. Any suggestions?"

"You would have to shift the bodies first, sir and then the shields. I can't see the barbarians taking too kindly to us undoing all their work sir."

First Spear was about to snap at him when the Decurion said, "Of course, First Spear, you could leave the bodies and the shields there. Just cover them in oil and pig fat and then, when they attack again, set fire to them. That way you will get rid of the bridge and thwart an attack."

First Spear smiled for the first time that day. "I like the way you think, horseman. Well don't just sit there optio. Go and get oil and fat!"

"Sir."

Marcus nodded and began to head to the ladder. "I will go and fetch more javelins too."

"You work hard, Decurion. Most officers just sit on their backsides and let others do their fetching and carrying."

"And we both know that they don't last long up here on the last frontier!"

"Truer words were never spoken!"

Marcus went down to the armoury. There were plenty of javelins still left but a few more days like this and they would have to resort to reusing damaged ones. When he returned what he noticed was good humoured banter between the auxiliaries. First Spear was a good officer. His men knew that if they obeyed orders then they would come through the experience. By the time he returned to the walls the dead had been cleared and the wounded replaced.

There was a skin of acetum and some bread on the fighting platform. First Spear was eating, "Dig in." He gestured with his knife. "I dare say they will be indulging in some sort of magic eh?"

"They aren't much different from you, First Spear. They will replace weapons. The druids, healers and witches will attend to the wounds and their chiefs will go around to tell them how close they came to victory and that one more effort will succeed."

"They will be back."

Marcus nodded, "I would think that they will return after dark. They know where their bridges are and they know that the bolt towers and bows are less accurate in the dark. The difference will be that we know their attack will be on this wall. They have weakened it and they have bridges."

"I agree. I have pulled one man in two from the other walls. I have also sent for the bolt thrower from the east gate."

On the far side of the stream Randel and his chiefs were assessing the damage. The loss of Cynwrig had hurt them as had the attack on the west gate but they still had more than two hundred men. Others were coming from the abortive attacks on the other walls. Randel waved over one of the younger warriors, "Aodh, go to my brother. Tell him that I need his men here."

"I will, my chief, but I will not reach him before dark."

"It matters not. Just so that he is here." As his young warrior ran off Randel said, "Where is Creagh? Was he hurt?"

He saw some of the men Creagh had led. He saw the men of Ammabile. The leader of them, Cynbel, shook his head, "I am sorry, chief. He did not follow us to the attack. His father is our chief but Creagh is not the man we thought he was. He ran. We will not let you down. I swear that we will follow your commands.

"You cannot change the nature of a man. Creagh might have feared death today but tomorrow he will discover that there are worse things than death. Men will shun him. You do not flee from battle." Cynbel nodded. "Rest and when it is dark we will attack once more."

Cynbel said, "Chief Randel, allow my men the chance to atone for the dishonour of Creagh. Let us lead the attack."

"You do not need to. The wounds your men suffered are testament to their courage."

"Nonetheless we are honour bound to do so."

"Then you shall have the honour."

As the afternoon drifted towards evening Randel gathered his chiefs around him. Men who had fled had returned during the afternoon. Men with minor wounds had had them attended to and they also wished to fight. The result was more men than Randel had expected.

"Cynbel and his men will lead the attack. There are two bridges. We know where they are and we have watched. The Romans have not removed them. Many of our dead brothers also lie in the ditches. They will not be unhappy if their bodies are used to bring death and destruction to the Romans. I want every archer and slinger to be ready to rain death on the walls. The dark will aid us. They cannot see in the dark. We know where the fort lies and we can send our arrows and stones blindly towards the walls. So long as we hit some of their men that will aid Cynbel. My brother will be bringing eighty fresh men by dawn. Their numbers will swing the battle in our favour."

As both sides prepared for battle they noticed, in the growing dark of the east, a glow. The glow grew until it became obvious that it was a fire. While the barbarians were perplexed First Spear had no doubt what had happened. "That is Alavna. It has fallen. They must have had more men than we thought. Perhaps that is why they have not attacked yet. They must have sent men there."

Decurion Aurelius shook his head, "I doubt it First Spear. A horseman could easily have reached it but a man on foot? You may be right. The fort might have fallen but I do not think they were aided by men from here. This is a bigger rebellion than we thought." He shook his head. "I have no idea who the Legate was who ordered Marcus' Horse south but he has opened the flood gates to insurrection. Horsemen can control large areas. A turma of cavalry can watch a section of road and prevent enemy movement. These forts are well made but they only control that which you can see. If my turma was with me we could ride to Otarbrunna and raze it to the ground. I have seen it. There will be few men guarding it and the gatehouse would not stop my horsemen."

"You are right but it is ever the way. Leaders like Agricola and Hadrian are rare. Most are pampered nobles who have read too much and campaigned too little. You will never change them. All that we can do is the best that we can."

Randel was beset by doubt. Had the fort fallen or had the Romans there used fire to their advantage? Was his brother a charred corpse? He forced himself to put the image from his mind. He had to see his plan through. If they had no reinforcements in the morning then it was the will of the Allfather. He had his men smear charcoal on their faces and hands. They needed night's cloak to aid them. He sharpened both of his swords. He would not take his shield. The mail shirt and the helmet had both proved adequate during the first attack. He and his men made their way to the stream and then, as darkness fell they crept from cover. In many ways it was now easier. They knew the ground over which they were moving. The caltrops had gone and the Romans would not see them until they reached the first ditch.

It felt strange to Randel. He was not in the fore of this attack. Cynbel and his men were the screen before them. He had his own sword in his hand. The Roman one was better but this one felt somehow, luckier. As he passed the bodies of those who had died in the first attack he touched the amulet around his neck. He did not speak. Their spirits would understand. In many ways it made him feel stronger knowing that their spirits were so close. As they neared the ditch he rolled in to the back slope and held his sword aloft. That would be the signal for the archers and slingers. They had to cause as many deaths as they could. They all knew that the Roman bolt throwers and archers had the ranges marked out. Once the arrows fell they would send their missiles. They would be releasing blind but men would die. As soon as his sword came down Randel heard the noise of snapping strings and whipped slingshots. As he rolled on to his front he saw a shadow fall from the wall. A Roman had died. He heard the Roman voice and knew that retribution would be swift.

"Stand to!" First Spear turned to the soldier with the two covered pots of coals. "Now, Murena, remember, the far one first."

"Yes, First Spear." The auxiliary began to blow into the two pots to make them hotter. When the hot coals struck their fire would spill and the fat and oil would burn. As Marcus knew, there was also a great deal of fat in human bodies. When they caught the fire would be out of control.

"Release bolts and arrows." He hefted his shield up as the arrows flew from the dark. The barbarians had managed to hit three men in their first shower of missiles but only one man had died. It could have been worse.

Marcus kept his clipeus up to protect him but he had a javelin ready. The fire would work but there was still a risk that someone might risk climbing the walls. He glanced down and saw men rising to race across the first ditch. The bridge was indistinct from the walls but Marcus knew that the barbarians would still be able to see it. He pulled back his arm. The first warrior was already approaching the second ditch when Marcus spear struck the third warrior across. His body tumbled to the side. Others were now sending their javelins into the men charging across the bridge of bodies and shields.

First Spear had nerves of steel. He allowed forty men to cross. They had begun to use their shields to make steps up the wall when he shouted, "Now, Murena!

The auxiliary had been chosen because of his strength. He whirled the ropes holding the pot of white-hot coals. Fate intervened. The first pot struck a warrior in the head. He fell into the ditch and the falling coals spread over a larger area. The first ditch suddenly flared. It looked like a volcano had erupted. The ditch was so close that the second burning pot was almost dropped. In the burning light the Votadini were easy targets. As the flames leapt around the warriors they had no time to defend against javelins. Even without the fire many would have died. The screams of the dying were terrible. Their falling bodies merely spread the fire so that both ditches were impassable.

Marcus heard a voice in the dark. "Fall back! Fall back!"

He turned to First Spear. "We have broken the back of their attack."

At the Roman camp twenty-five miles south of them the glow of the fire at Alava had been seen and Centurion Brocchus informed. He had no idea what it meant and that disturbed him. It was bad enough heading north to fight barbarians but to do so without intelligence was even more worrying. He needed scouts.

"Felix, head north. See what you can discover."

Felix shook his head, "It is a waste of time First Spear. That fire is many miles north. If I started now I would not reach it until dawn."

First Spear shook his head, "Just go as far as you can and then come back and report eh? There's a good lad. I want to know if there are a bunch of hairy arsed barbarians close by."

"There are no barbarians close by First Spear. Wolf would have told me."

"Just go!"

The boy was probably right. He had skills and abilities which Brocchus could not even begin to understand. First Spear just shook his head and took another turn around the sentries. The last thing he needed was for a sneak attack.

Felix and Wolf knew how to move both quickly and silently. They headed up the road for that was in the direction of the light in the sky. Felix had not liked to say that he thought it was in the direction of Alavna. He had learned not to make guesses which might be wrong. Most Romans were desperate to find a barbarian making a mistake. That was why he preferred scouting for the Decurion. He did not judge and he understood the land. Drugi had told him that the Decurion was special. It was not just the sword, he was descended from greatness. The power of the ancestors and the spirits lived in him.

He stopped after counting five of the Roman mile markers. He listened. Wolf listened and Wolf sniffed. When he lay down on the road then Felix knew there were no barbarians close to hand. He sniffed and he sought out the strange sounds. In the distance he heard feet and he could smell Romans. They were to the north and east. He loped off along a trail. It was a wide trail. He guessed the Votadini used it. As he ran he saw no sign of iron studded caligae. He was not aware of how far he had travelled but when Wolf stopped and put his ears back he knew someone was close. He stopped. The sound of running feet was cleared. He stepped off the trail and into the woods. He saw, in the distance the glint of moonlight on metal. It was some way away. There were Romans. Felix had worked with the Romans long enough to know what to do. He turned and ran back towards First Spear. This was news that he needed to know.

The first hint of dawn was in the eastern sky as Felix ran into the camp. He smiled for he had passed the first one before he was recognised. The duty optio recognised him, "Now then Felix, what have you discovered?"

He pointed north east. "There is a column of Romans heading here. They are running."

"Romans running at night? Have you been drinking unwatered wine?"

Felix stood patiently. First Spear would not be happy if the scout was right and Felix knew what he had seen.

Eventually the optio realised that he would have to wake the centurion. "You come with me. When I wake First Spear you can brave his tongue!"

First Spear was awake before they reached him. He stood and stretched. He looked at Felix, "Well?"

"There is a column of Romans, First Spear. They are headed from the north east." First Spear said nothing, he just cocked his head to one side. "If I was to guess I would say that it was the garrison from Alavna."

There was a moment's pause and then First Spear looked to the east. "It will soon be dawn. Let's wake them up. Well done Felix. Get your head down while we take down the camp!"

The legionaries were not surprised with an early break of camp. They were professionals and First Spear rarely made mistakes. With Felix awoken after an hour of sleep they headed up the road. They met Centurion Decimus Drusus Ambustus and his weary men just five miles up the road. They were close to the burned-out fort at Habitancvm. It seemed appropriate. The centurion snapped to attention. "First Spear, Centurion Decimus Drusus Ambustus reporting with the garrison of Alavna. We have burned and destroyed the fort. Bremenium has fallen!"

If he thought to be praised he was wrong. First Spear looked at him with a slightly cock-eyed expression. Decimus was not sure if it was a smile or grimace on his face. "Impressive, Centurion. You march from Alavna to Bremenium and discover it has fallen. You manage to march back to Alavna, fire your fort and escape the barbarians who destroyed Bremenium."

The centurion endured his first doubts. "The barbarians told us that it had fallen."

First Spear turned to the Signifier, "Ah, the barbarians told the centurion. Well, that is fine. I shall put that in my report to the Governor. Well done Centurion. Just to be clear, what happened to the barbarians?"

"They were brought as security until we left them at the road." Even as he said it Centurion Decimus Drusus Ambustus realised that it sounded weak. He knew he had been duped but he had seen the fire. He had seen the mail, weapons and helmets. What else could he have deduced?

First Spear wanted to say more but he knew that the young centurion had made a career ending decision. He would not survive the enquiry. He had deserted his post. He had destroyed a fort and all on the say-so of a barbarian. At best his career was over and at worst he would be executed. On the positive side First Spear now had some auxiliaries. "Right, lad, what say we march up the road to Bremenium. We can, at least, bury the bodies of the poor buggers who were killed there, eh? Have your men fall in behind us and try to keep up."

Centurion Decimus Drusus Ambustus noticed that his optios kept as far from him as possible. The only one who was loyal to him was the signifier.

Aodh arrived back when the sun was beginning to warm the land. He was exhausted. Randel and the clan were having their wounds tended. Aodh dropped to his knee. "Chief Randel, your brother and Chief Agnathus have had a great victory. They have tricked the Romans into abandoning and burning their fort. The Romans are heading south. Chief Agnathus and your brother will follow with their men some time later today"

That was the moment when Randel knew that they might win. Creagh had proved weak but his brother and Creagh's father has shown them the way. When they had fallen back from the walls he had thought that they had lost. They had not. They would make the Romans think that they had been defeated and when their reinforcements arrived they would attack once more. He turned to Drust, "Go back to the hill fort. I want every man who can bear a weapon. Take the wounded back with you. They can defend our home. We have almost broken the back of this Roman beast. It is but a little battle that we need to fight."

The warrior loped off and Randel began to believe once more.

Inside the fort everything had been put back into fighting order. First Spear knew that the fire had not destroyed the enemy's will to fight. They were still out there. They could be seen in the distance. In fact, there had been a great deal of movement. Warriors had been seen joining from the east. They were beyond bolt and bow range. Others had been seeing approaching from the west. However, the ditch was now clear of the human and wooden bridges. The stakes had been burned but it would be hard to climb out of it. They still had plenty of javelins. They had killed more than two hundred that he knew of. They had not counted the bodies in the burned fields to the east. The garrison had suffered fifty casualties. Thirty had been fatal. They still had food and they had hope. In a battle of wills there could be but one winner, Rome.

As the men began to join Randel so he started to get a picture of what had happened. When his brother and Agnathus had gone with the Romans as hostages the rest of the warband had followed at a discreet distance. They had not trusted the Romans but the Romans, it appeared, had kept their word. Agnathus had shown his wisdom when he had forbidden the hot heads to follow and fall upon the auxiliaries. "This defeat is so shaming that when we fight them next we will have already won. They will be expecting us to attack and we can afford few casualties. The loss of Cynwrig and his men is a blow. Chief Randel will need us!"

Agnathus and Baradh were the last to reach the camp which was now swollen with more men than Randel had started with. A clan of Brigante from the west had come to join them. Randel began to believe. Before they could plan properly Randel had to clear the air with Agnathus. He took the Chief and his brother to one side. "Your son brought men from Ammabile. Cynbel and his men were brave. Most of them perished in the last attack. They were burned." Agnathus nodded. "By then your son and his oathsworn had fled. He spoke neither to me nor Cynbel. I tell you this for I do not wish bad blood between us. You aided my brother and have brought us hope but I cannot forgive Creagh. When next I see him then I will challenge him."

Agnathus shook his head, "That would be foolish. He has killed many other champions and we can ill afford to lose you. You have shown that you are a true War Chief. It has been many years since the tribe had a War Chief."

"And I would be honoured to lead the tribe as War Chief but I have seen little evidence that your son is the warrior he claims to be. He ran before we even crossed the ditches."

"Then I shall punish him. I will spread the word that he is to be brought to me to account for his actions."

Baradh said, "That would be the best for the tribe, Randel."

"Very well."

"And how do we reduce this last Roman fort in our land? I do not think that this will fall to a trick such as your brother and I managed."

"No. They are well led. I think that you and your warriors need the day to rest. We have little need to surround the fort. The only escape for them is south. We will block the road to the south and camp between the hills to the east and the place where the road crosses the stream and runs next to the river. It is six hundred paces wide. That is large enough for a camp and out of the range of their bolt throwers."

Agnathus smiled, "You are a War Chief."

Far to the north Creagh and his men were heading for Traprain Law. He now knew that he had made a major mistake. They had met warriors who were heading for the battle and they spoke of Chief Agnathus and Baradh brother of Randel joining forces to defeat the Romans. Creagh had counted upon reaching his father and getting his version of events in first. Now that could not happen. Creagh was taking a bold decision. He would go to King Clutha. He would use words to defeat Randel and his father. He knew that he could play upon the King's insecurity and lack of an heir. He would not need to lie. He would just suggest that, perhaps, they had ulterior motives. They sought the crown. The alliance of Baradh, Randel and Agnathus would back it up. It was a gamble. If it failed then Creagh would have to seek shelter amongst his mother's people, the Brigante. That would mean travelling to the west and crossing the wall.

Decius Brutus Maximus marched with First Spear and the signifer, Sentius Laevinius Potita. Only Felix was ahead of the three of them but First Spear was confident in the scout's ability to detect danger. The Ala were lucky to have him. The centurion turned to First Spear, "Should the auxiliary centurion and his optios not be under arrest? They abandoned a fort."

First Spear just stared ahead. "He may well be arrested when we return to Coriosopitum. By then the new Legate may be there or a Prefect at the very least. It will be their decision. Right now, we need the auxiliaries. We can use them as a screen when we attack. At least the man had the good sense to bring all the javelins from his fort. I am just concerned that Bremenium has fallen. In my heart I cannot believe it but, if it has then we could be heading for a trap such as befell Varus in the Teutonberger Forest."

"The man was a fool." Sentius Laevinius Potita rarely spoke but when he did then it was sense.

"I take it that you mean I am no fool. I am not certain about that. Would a wise man have left the safety of Coriosopitum on the off chance of saving a cohort of auxiliaries?" He glanced down at the mile marker as they passed it. "Just five miles to go. I think we will send the scout ahead of us. He can be at the fort and back in no time." He cupped his hands and shouted, "Scout!"

Felix trotted into sight. "First Spear?"

"We are getting close to the fort. Find out if they still hold on and where the barbarians wait." He just nodded, turned and loped off with the dog, Wolf, next to him.

Decius Brutus Maximus shook his head, "They are a funny pair. That is a good-looking dog though."

First Spear chuckled, "Don't make the mistake of trying to stroke it. The beastie will have your hand. The only person who can touch it is Felix. Even the Decurion would not try to touch the dog unless Felix allows it."

The auxiliary shook Marcus awake. "You are needed, sir." The young Lingone handed Marcus a wet towel and waited while the horseman cleaned his face. He then handed the officer a beaker of acetum and a piece of day old bread. The young man said, "Sorry about the bread, sir."

"Don't worry. I have eaten older." He dipped the bread in the acetum for a moment or two and then ate the softened bread. "How goes it out there? Is it still quiet?"

"Yes sir but the barbarians have all gathered to the south of us. They have cut the road."

"I wouldn't worry about that. It means they won't risk another attack. We can just sit here and eat stale bread and porridge until they get tired of waiting."

"Will they get tired sir?"

"These are not like you or me. They don't get paid for fighting. They follow their War Chief because of their clan and the chance to fight. If they just sit and wait they will get bored. There will be fights inside their camps. Blood feuds will begin or men will become reckless and hurl themselves at our walls. We are not fighting regulars. We are fighting barbarians. They are wild and they are brave but they do not know the meaning of control."

When he joined First Spear on the main gate he said much the same to him. "Aye, Decurion. That is much as I thought. What is happening yonder?"

He pointed to where some barbarians were labouring close to the road. They looked to have crude mattocks and shovels. "From what I can see, First Spear, they are digging."

"That is what I thought but why?"

Marcus leaned out and shaded his eyes. The afternoon sun was sinking. It would be some hours until sunset but it was past its zenith. He saw men hauling logs from the nearby wood. As he stared he saw what was now obvious. "They are damming the stream and the river."

"But that means that they cannot use the stream for cover."

"They do not intend to attack that way. They mean to make the river and the stream burst their banks. The road north will be flooded. Eventually, your ditches will fill with water. They are using Nature to defeat us."

"Nature?"

"The cult of the Mother is strong in this part of the world. The witch, Caronwyn, and her sisters were part of it. They believe that we offend the goddess by building permanent structures like roads and bridges. This fort has some stone and that, too offends them."

"Well it won't hurt us but it might cause a problem for a relief force."

"If there is a relief force."

"There are two garrisons isolated up here. I cannot see them abandoning us. First Spear Brocchus sent you and your scout to aid us. Even if your scout had Mercury's wings it would have taken him some time to get to Coriosopitum. If they are not here by this time tomorrow then I will be worried but, for the moment they can dig all they like. A bit of damp ground will not hurt us."

The Votadini were not building the dam to hurt the fort. Some of the Brigante who had joined them had reported Romans heading up the road. They had no idea of numbers but Randel was not a fool. By damming the two streams and the river they narrowed their frontage to just three hundred paces. No matter how many Romans were heading north they would be able to hold them. For the first time the Romans would face men who were armed and armoured much as they were. Randel knew that his men did not have the discipline of the Romans but they had something the Romans did not have. They had raw and reckless courage. He had also chosen a place where the Romans would be attacking uphill. This time he had his brother and his men. They had rested and they were fresh. The presence of Agnathus also gave Randel more authority. Agnathus would stand behind the main battle line with the clan and tribe's standards. Randel and Baradh would be in the heart of the battle line. Already men were pleading to fight alongside them. The warriors in the centre would be the best that they had. They just had to wait for the snake of metal clad Romans to reach them. Then the slaughter would begin.

Chapter 7

When Felix reported that a Votadini army blocked the road First Spear had a dilemma. His men were tired. The Lingones were exhausted. He needed to make a camp. Felix had said that the walls of the fort were still manned. His heart said to attack but his old head told him to camp. He ordered the camp to be built two miles south of the Votadini. While it was being erected he sent for the centurions, including the unfortunate Lingone.

"Tomorrow we will relieve the garrison at Bremenium. Ambustus, you and your auxilia will be a screen in front of us. Use your javelins and stop them from disrupting our men."

Centurion Ambustus took in the fact that the fort and its garrison had not been slaughtered. He said simply, "The barbarians tricked me."

Brocchus nodded, "So it would seem. That is why we have standing orders so that we do not put ourselves in a position where we can be tricked. The men inside Bremenium are doing just that." The other centurions avoided looking at Ambustus. He knew better than any that he should have held out.

"We will use a three-deep line. Ambustus, your wounded can guard the baggage. I will send the scout to warn the fort of our attack. It may help them."

"Yes, First Spear."

Brocchus allowed a moment of silence and he stared into the eyes of the young centurion. He was giving the young officer a chance to redeem part of his reputation. The centurion understood and gave the slightest of nods.

"Any questions?"

There were none and First Spear went over to where Wolf slept next to Felix. The youth had done well and deserved his rest. He had prevented the Romans from marching into battle with the barbarians. The

Roman was about to leave when Felix opened an eye, "What is it, First Spear?"

"Can you get to the fort and tell them when we attack?"

"Easily but I will have to wait until I can attract the attention of the decurion. You Romans like to use your bolt throwers on barbarians!" First Spear laughed. "When do you attack?"

"Tell First Spear in the fort that we will wait for him to signal three times with his standard. That way we will know that you got through."

Felix nodded, picked up his sleeping cloak and water skin and loped off through the woods. He would head east before turning north. He did not need the road to make good speed.

As he watched the sun rise in the east Marcus was disturbed at the increase in numbers of the barbarians. He pointed at one large warband of a hundred which had arrived during the night. "They are Brigante!"

"Does that make a difference, Decurion?"

"It makes this a bigger insurrection than we first thought. Something has happened to make the barbarians so confident. Perhaps Alavna has fallen. There are more than a thousand barbarians out there."

"And they have a sizeable number in mail. If there is a relief force, they will need plenty of luck in addition to their skill."

"You are hoping for the VIth?"

"I am. For work like this you need the steel of the legion. My lads are good but the legions are something else. Even better would be an ala on the flanks."

"If Marcus' Horse had been here we would not be in this situation."

Just then a sentry on the east wall shouted over, "First Spear."

First Spear shouted, "If you have a report then get over here!" As the auxiliary ran First Spear shook his head, "Some of these lads haven't got the sense they were born with." The man stood to attention, "Well?"

"Sir, I have to report that there is a barbarian staring at the east gatehouse sir." Even as he said it the soldier realised that it sounded a little lame.

"Soldier there are a thousand of the buggers on this side. I'll tell you what, you watch the barbarian, he is yours, and we will watch the rest."

Marcus said, "Does he have a dog with him?"

The man's mouth dropped open, "Yes sir. How did you know?"

Without answering Marcus began to run along the wall walk, "That is Felix, sir!" His identity was confirmed when Marcus reached the other gate. "Keep your hands off your bolt throwers and your bows. He is one of us." Marcus began to wave. He saw Felix stand and wave back. Then he and the dog trotted towards the gate.

First Spear and Marcus met him at the gate. "I take it you got through Felix?"

"Yes sir. First Spear has the 1st Cohort. He also has the garrison from Alavna. He is bringing the cohort up this morning. He said he will attack when you wave the standard three times."

"That is the best news I have heard in a long time. Well done Scout."

Marcus asked, "What do you know about Alavna, Felix?"

Felix had no guile and he just answered honestly. "The Centurion there was tricked by the Votadini. He was told that this fort had fallen and the garrison slaughtered. The Centurion burned the fort and then headed south. First Spear has his men with him."

Centurion Sejanus shook his head sadly at the news, "Then the Centurion had better hope for a glorious death on the battlefield. He has committed treason. I thought better of him, Decurion, but he is young. Sometimes the young are beset by doubts. Us older ones do not have that luxury." He shook his head, "Assellio, leave a couple of men in the gatehouse and in the towers. I want the rest of the cohort on the south and west walls. Now we will see what the Votadini are made of."

As First Spear ran off to bark orders Marcus said, "You and Wolf get some food and some rest."

He nodded, "There are many Brigante, sir. I heard them speaking as I made my way through their lines."

"I know. We have much work to do south of the wall when this is over." The Romans believed that the wall was a barrier to the Brigante and Votadini. Both Marcus and Felix knew that was an illusion. At night time it was possible to climb over the wall in many places. The milecastle forts were only manned by a handful of men and between them were just isolated turrets with a couple of men watching. They were not a barrier to determined warriors.

Marcus went to the south west corner of the fort. The bolt thrower was now aligned at the centre of the barbarian line. The Votadini and their allies were busy building themselves up for the battle. Marcus knew they would be drinking their strong beer. They would smear their bodies with designs and they would wear every magic amulet that they possessed. They would tell each other of what they would do to the Romans. The barbarians were just out of bolt range. Marcus saw that the hundred Brigante were at the centre of the line facing the fort. He had begun to get the measure of this Randel. The flooded fields had been an act of genius. He was forcing the legion up into a killing ground. He saw serried ranks of slingers and archers who were just waiting to rain death on the advancing Romans. But the Votadini chief was not ruling out the possibility that the garrison might sally forth and join in the battle. That was why there were more than a hundred Brigante along with some Selgovae and a handful of Votadini lining up to stop a breakout.

First Spear came along. "We have seen the standards in the distance. They are coming." The signifer waved the standard three times. He saw a strange look on Marcus' face. "Do you have something in mind, Decurion?"

"Do you mind if I try to make these barbarians attack us?"

Centurion Sejanus laughed, "That would be a neat trick if you could do it. Why not? Anything which upsets the enemy plans helps us." He turned, "Lads the Decurion here thinks he can make the barbarians attack us prematurely. Get ready to give them a hot reception eh?"

The auxiliaries all banged their shields and shouted, "Yes, First Spear!"

The shout made all the barbarians turn. Marcus had their attention. He unsheathed the Sword of Cartimandua and held it aloft. He shouted, "I am Decurion Marcus Gaius Aurelius of Marcus' Horse. I wield the Sword of Cartimandua. I command the Brigante to lay down their swords. I forbid you to fight our allies!"

First Spear asked, as the barbarians began to shout and argue, "What did you say?" Marcus told him. "And that will start an attack?"

"Firstly, I have insulted them. Secondly, I have put doubts in the minds of the Votadini. There are blood feuds between the tribes. Thirdly, and most importantly, if the chief leading them can get the sword from my dead fingers then he can rule the tribe. At the very least he will be the most powerful warrior."

"So your plan is to make them come for you?"

Marcus grinned and nodded, "It is a plan. I did not say it was a good one!"

In the time it took to tell the tale the Brigante had made up their mind. They ran up the slope towards the fort. The men who had been with them, Selgovae and Votadini followed. Others who had been waiting to fight the legion joined them.

"Stand to! Archers draw!"

Marcus heard the click of the bolt throwers and the creak of the bows.

"Release!"

Four bolt throwers hurled their missiles towards the reckless warriors. Thirty arrows sailed in the air. All along the wall the auxiliaries stood ready with javelins. Marcus kept the sword held aloft. It was a beacon, drawing them to their deaths. Behind them he saw that the 1st Cohort of the VIth was arrayed for battle. Auxiliaries spread themselves out becoming a screen before the legionaries. Randel, Marcus recognised him by his horsehair crested helmet taken from a dead Roman, tried to put order into the lines. The Votadini plans had been upset. Some of the warriors he had wanted to use to face the legionaries were now racing recklessly towards the fort.

Men were dying. The Brigante wore no mail. The bolts went through three and four of them. Still, they came. The arrows began to thin them out.

First Spear shouted, "Signifer, wave the standard three times." He wanted to make sure that the Legion knew they understood the orders.

A stone from a Brigante slinger rattled off the decurion's shield. One of the auxiliaries next to him laughed, "Looks like their lads want that sword, sir!"

As much as Marcus wanted to pick up a javelin and to throw it he knew he had to keep the glinting, gleaming sword aloft. As the Brigante and Selgovae reached the ditch they fell not only to the arrows and bolts but also to the defences of the ditch. The southern ditch had not been damaged in the fire and there were screams as barbarians had their ankles broken. The Roman archers now began to target the slingers and Brigante archers. Without mail they fell. In contrast many of their stones and arrows found helmets or mail in the Roman ranks. Even so there were casualties. The capsarii were kept busy.

Still holding the sword aloft Marcus saw the Lingones as they advanced to meet the barbarians. He saw the Centurion leading them. First Spear said quietly, "There is a man going to his death. I had high hopes for Ambustus. I should have kept him here with me,"

Even as he spoke he saw the Centurion, optio and signifer carve their way through the Votadini. Behind them the others hurled javelins over their heads. Then the Centurion and his handful of men met Randel and the mailed Votadini. Even though six of the Votadini fell Centurion

Ambustus, his signifer and optio fell. They had died well. Behind them Marcus could see the legionaries as they prepare their pila.

First Spear chuckled, "Now they will see the mincing machine that is the legion."

From the viewpoint of the gatehouse Marcus and First Spear could see that the sacrifice of the auxiliaries allied to the Brigante attack had seriously weakened the integrity of the Votadini line. The Brigante and Selgovae, however had managed to reach the second ditch. Like the first attacks the barbarians used the bodies of the dead as stepping stones. Their lack of armour made them fast and they had shields too. The javelins of the defenders were still hitting them but fewer were dying.

"Hold on! We will have to weather the storm." First Spear turned to Marcus, "I reckon I had better stand by you. This will be the hottest part of the wall."

The deaths in their approach to the Roman fort had just infuriated the barbarians. All thought of victory had disappeared. All that they wanted was the glory of getting the sword and killing the Roman who had taken it. As men fell at the foot of the wall others used the dead bodies to spring up and grab hold of the top of the wooden palisade. As their slingers and archers were still whittling down the defenders, inevitably, some made the top. With First Spear at his side Marcus stepped towards the three who had made the top. All three were bloody. It was hard to tell whose blood. They had short swords and each held a shield.

One spat at Marcus, "I will gut you like a fish and take back the sword which belongs to our people!"

First Spear just stepped forward, punched the man in the face with his shield and then rammed his sword up through the Brigante's groin. The blade came out of the man's neck. As he threw the body over the side Marcus blocked the blow from one Brigante with a shield as he swept the Sword of Cartimandua across the middle of the other. The Decurion had time to turn and head butt the first Brigante off the fighting platform to the ground below.

"You can use the sword then. I wondered."

As they turned back to the wall Marcus saw that the VIth had broken through the Votadini line. Now the flooded ground they had made came to haunt them. They had nowhere to flee. Marcus saw what First Spear had meant about a mincing machine. Gladii and scuta punched, slashed and stabbed, seemingly with impunity. First Spear saw that they had broken the Brigante. They were fleeing. He shouted, "First Century! Form up! Let us go and help our comrades."

Sheathing his sword Marcus followed the auxiliary centurion down the steps to the gate.

He looked at Marcus, "You coming to join us?"

Marcus picked up a couple of javelins, "I can identify the chiefs. We need them, remember?"

"Aye. Optio, close the gate behind us."

There were just forty-six men left from the first century. They formed a column which was four men wide and eleven men deep. As First Spear led them across the body littered bridge Marcus joined the signifer and optio at the rear of the column. Marcus' crest and the fact that he bore the sword drew attacks from Brigantes who sought a glorious death. Marcus was flanked by two of the best men in the century. The signifer and optio were fighters. The wild attacks of the barbarians ended in their death. Now that the Votadini were being attacked in two directions the end was in sight. The two groups of Romans closed in on the last of the mail covered Votadini. These were the hard core. They would not die easily. They would take as many Romans with them as they could.

"Skirmish order!"

Now that there was no need for a column First Spear allowed the auxiliaries to break formation. They knew how to use their weapons. Marcus found himself facing the young chief he had seen in the camp. He was bloody. It could have been Roman blood or his own but the man had a wild look in his eye. He recognised that Marcus was an officer and he shouted, "I am Baradh brother of Randel. We have destroyed two Roman forts. Your time is over Roman. You will die at my hand."

He had the hexagonal shield used by the auxiliaries. Marcus had the oval clipeus. Where he did have an advantage was his sword. The Votadini's was notched and scored. It had bent. The barbarian had used it like an iron bar. As he swung it at Marcus the Decurion saw that it did not swing true. He blocked the blow on his shield and then surprised the barbarian with a sweep below the shield into the knee. He felt his blade scrape off the man's kneecap. It must have hurt but the man did not cry out. He tried to lunge at Marcus. A true blade might have hit but it slid over the mail on Marcus' shoulder. The blade rasped but did no damage. Marcus then punched with his shield. The barbarian's nose broke and blood splattered his face. The wound to his knee was now weakening him and the blow to the nose disorientated him. Even as he raised his

Roman Courage

sword for one more blow Marcus hacked sideways tearing through mail
which had been weakened by the fighting. The Votadini wore nothing
beneath the mail and the Sword of Cartimandua tore across his middle.
Baradh looked in horror as his guts spilled out. He tried to lift both shield
and sword but he was dying. Life was leaving his eyes. He fell at
Marcus' feet.

As Marcus lifted his eyes for his next foe he saw that it was over.
First Spear Brocchus shouted, "Take prisoners! The bastards will all die
but I want to find their chiefs."

Marcus raised his sword, "This is one of their chiefs."

One of the Lingones who had survived said, "He is one of the two
who tricked the Centurion!" He ran at the corpse and began to hack at it.

First Spear Brocchus held the man's arm, "That can't help the
centurion. Search the other bodies and if you find the second chief, the
older one then let us know." He sheathed his gladius and took off his
helmet. He held out his hand, "Well done, Decurion, First Spear. I am
sorry we took so long."

Centurion Sejanus waved his sword at the dead Lingones. "They
have redeemed themselves."

"Perhaps. I am not certain what the new Legate will think but if we
keep them here with you, Centurion Sejanus then perhaps they will be
forgotten and can begin again."

There were fifty prisoners. More than two hundred men had escaped
but the insurrection was over. Agnathus' body was not discovered. He
had escaped as had Randel. The two men were as slippery as eels.
Marcus identified the chiefs by their torcs. Their torcs were taken as were
their warrior bracelets. They would identify the clans who had rebelled.
Their families would now suffer.

First Spear Brocchus had the prisoners lined up. "Lingones go and
make crosses. First Cohort VIth Legion. Break their ankles!"

The legionaries made short work of using the barbarian's own swords
to break their ankles. They were not delicate and the broken wounds
bled. One by one the men were hung on crosses. The last were the eight
chiefs who had been captured. As the last one was hoisted on to his cross
First Spear Brocchus shouted, "This is the Fate of all those who defy
Rome!" The fifty barbarians began their long slow death. It was not a
glorious death and their corpses would be seen for months. It would be a
reminder to the Votadini of the price of failure.

Randel and Agnathus were both wounded but alive. Somehow, they had managed to avoid capture. There were just forty men left to the two of them. As they stood and watched their fellows being crucified Agnathus said, "This was not a defeat. We came within a heartbeat of victory. Had that Roman not lured the Brigante to the walls we would have won."

Randel was not certain but he nodded, "What now?"

"We use this to our advantage. This is the last fort in our land. We will travel to Traprain Law and speak to King Clutha. He must furnish us with arms and men to complete our victory."

Randel nodded, "You may be right. We do not have enough men now to destroy the fort. Others will return but it will take time."

The two of them led their men to the Roman Road and headed north. Randel had been tempted to go to his hillfort and fetch his family but by doing so that would bring more danger to them. This way was better. He would disappear and when they had seen the King they would return at the head of an army. Agnathus was right. They had learned much and next time they would win.

First Spear Brocchus was anxious to return to Coriosopitum but first he intended to re-establish Roman rule. While the auxiliaries and one of the legion centuries repaired the fort, he took the rest of the cohort to Otarbrunna. Felix and Marcus went with them. Marcus rode Raven. The horse did not like to be confined. The ride in the open would do her good now that she was recovered from her wound. The hillfort did not have enough men left to defend it. The ones who had fled there had no heart left for a fight. As the column wound its way to the fort people, mainly warriors, were seen to be fleeing.

Brocchus was sanguine about their departure. "It matters not. We will destroy the hill fort. Their symbol of power will be gone."

As they passed through the gates Brocchus ordered one of his centurions to take his men and destroy the gates. When they reached the middle of the huts he sent another century to destroy the palisade and another to empty the huts. There were just forty people left in the hill fort. Marcus saw the wife of the chief approach Brocchus. He knew her from the torc. She began to berate Brocchus. The bemused First Spear turned to Marcus, "What is the harpy going on about?"

Marcus dismounted and walked over. "She says she is Olwen wife of Randel chief of the clan and warns you that her husband will soon return with a mighty army."

Brocchus rubbed his chin. "Then I should be petrified, Decurion." Laughing he turned to his optio. "Have her bound and a halter put around her neck." He saw four children. "I take it that they are her brood. Take them too. They will make good hostages. Decurion, find out who else is in the chief's family. We will take them as hostages. The rest will be sold as slaves."

Once Olwen realised what was happening she fought. The Optio was having none of it. He cuffed her hard on the side of the head and she fell in a heap. That cowed the rest and they submitted. Their warriors had abandoned them. The fight in them was gone. Marcus found six more members of Olwen and Randel's family. The emptied huts were burned. The animals from the hillfort were driven, along with the captives, back down the road to Bremenium. The legionaries had not only destroyed the gates of the hill fort they had also destroyed the two huge ramparts which had supported them. It could be rebuilt but it would take time. The smoke rose in the sky behind them as they headed back to the fort. Randel's stronghold was gone. Marcus doubted that it would be rebuilt. Only the ramparts and ditches remained and they would not be an obstacle to a Roman army. Stanwyck, close to his home, had been the mightiest hill fort in the north of the province. Now it was a series of mounds and ditches. It had long been abandoned as a defence. When the Romans destroyed something, it stayed destroyed.

They left Bremenium the next day. The Lingones and the legionaries had repaired all the damage. The dam had been removed and the road reopened. Some of the crucified men still lived but the last would be dead in a day or two. All the dead had been burned. It would not do to encourage foxes and rats.

Marcus stayed behind to speak with First Spear Julius Sextus Sejanus. When you faced death with another warrior there was a bond there. You became shield brothers. The two men had kept the fighting platform clear during the battle. Marcus and Julius clasped arms. "Will your ala be returned here soon?"

Marcus shrugged, "I am detached to a new ala so I dare say I will be seeing you."

"You are a good man and you can think. You saved men's lives and for that we are indebted to you."

As Marcus rode through the gate the garrison made a guard of honour for him and banged their spears against their shields. Marcus was touched. He dug his heels into Raven and trotted after the Roman snake which wound down the road. Felix and Wolf trotted behind.

Chapter 8

When they reached Coriosopitum, three days later, they found that the new ala had arrived. Marcus' days of freedom were about to come to an end. Prefect Aulus Gemellus Glabrio watched the Cohort as they marched through the gates. When he had arrived and found only a cohort of auxiliaries guarding this most important fortress he had become concerned. His annoyance at his posting was alleviated by the fact that the legion had returned. There was also a question of authority. Until the Legate arrived, who would command? In theory, as a Prefect, he outranked First Spear, but Prefect Aulus Gemellus Glabrio knew that was not always the case. He decided to play it by ear. He also saw that they had prisoners with them. He had learned that forts had been destroyed. The prisoners suggested that First Spear had been successful.

First Spear Brocchus smiled at Marcus, "Looks like your days of freedom are over. Your new Prefect has shiny armour. I am guessing this is his first time out of Rome. You will have your work cut out."

Marcus was well aware that he had been lucky. Rufius and Metellus had told him of the Prefect in command before his father's time. He had been an arrogant officer who had almost destroyed the ala. He hoped that this one would listen. He saw the ala as they groomed their horses. They had been in the province for some time. Until they had been sent south for a refit they had been based at Omnun, The Rock. He wondered if they would be returned there or would they be based at Cilurnum, Cauldron Pool? Both were better suited to an ala than Coriosopitum.

The Prefect waited for them to approach him. First Spear spoke first, "Prefect, I am sorry we weren't here to greet you. We had a little bother to the north of here. To be honest, Prefect, we could have used your horsemen."

The Prefect nodded. "We arrived the day after you had left, First Spear."

Brocchus frowned, "It is a pity that you did not send a turma north to let us know. We might have saved lives."

The Prefect coloured, "My orders were to report to the Legate at Coriosopitum and not risk the ala chasing foot sloggers."

First Spear just stared at the Prefect and then he smiled, "Well, we managed it without you. I take it the Legate is not here yet?"

"No First Spear."

"Then you are welcome to share my fort until he arrives." Marcus hid the smile. First Spear had established that he commanded the fort.

"Thank you."

"And this is your liaison officer, Decurion Marcus Gaius Aurelius of Marcus' Horse. He and his scout were most useful. In fact, his conduct was exemplary. I shall be saying so in my report for the Governor."

The Prefect turned his gaze to Marcus. "I have heard of your ala. It has covered itself with glory although why it was deemed necessary to transfer you to my ala is a mystery."

It was a mystery to Marcus too but he knew enough to keep a straight face and a diplomatic answer. "Perhaps it is the fact that I know the land for I was born close by Morbium and I can speak the language of the tribes. Sometimes that is useful. Besides, sir, Marcus' Horse will return north eventually."

"Hm." He pointed to the officer next to him. "This is Decurion Princeps Pera. He will assign you your duties. Now we just await the new Legate, whoever he is." He then turned and walked back to the Principia.

Marcus saw the look on First Spear Brocchus' face. The Centurion shook his head and then said, "When you have finished your duties, Decurion, come to my office and we will share a beaker of decent wine."

Decurion Princeps Pera came over, "I hear a fort was destroyed and the garrison slaughtered?"

"Two forts were destroyed. But for the arrival of the legion it might have gone badly for us. There were more than a thousand Votadini. They had allies with them. You know how dangerous that can be."

"I tried to explain to the Prefect on the way north. He seems to think that the wall will stop all thoughts of insurrection." Marcus nodded. The Decurion Princeps said, "You were inside the fort? I thought you were with the legion?"

My scout and I were sent to assess the problem. When we discovered that an attack was about to take place I sent Felix here for help and I joined the garrison at Bremenium. That is now the only fort north of the wall."

"I am guessing we will be back at the Rock. Who is there now?"

"Just an understrength cohort of auxiliaries. If the Legate does not arrive in the next day or so I can see First Spear sending them to reinforce Bremenium. They lost a lot of men."

"I am not sure how we use you yet. A lot of my officers speak the local languages and we know the area. You may end up as a glorified messenger."

"Sir, I don't want to seem pushy but one of my skills is as a scout. I was trained by a couple of Explorate. I know the land and I have a Brigante scout. If you wanted to use my skills and keep the ala safe you could use me to scout for you."

"I heard that there were Explorate in Marcus' Horse. Did I also hear that they had Frumentarii too?"

"They were one and the same. The Emperor sent them on a detached mission. They taught me a great deal."

"Then we will try to use those skills."

The new Legate was at Vinovia. Flavius Celer Fullo had been sent by Emperor Hadrian himself. He had served as a Tribune with the VIth when they had helped to build the wall. The Emperor had taken him back to Rome when his time as Tribune was over. He had been quite explicit in his orders. The Legate knew that the Emperor wanted the frontier stabilising so that the VIth could be withdrawn and used elsewhere in the Empire. To that end he had with him a mixed cohort, the Vangiones from the Rhine, and a cohort of infantry, the Frisiavones also from the Rhine. The fifteen hundred men would allow him to fully garrison the understrength forts and to begin to stabilise the land. The loss of the fort at Habitancvm was a worry and he had already requested another cohort. He had requested another part mounted force.

He knew the strengths of his command and he knew the weaknesses. The wall was not a barrier. It was just a means to slow down an enemy. That was why he had requested more horsemen. He could not understand the wisdom of withdrawing the best ala on the frontier to Wales. When he had met with Legate Demetrius they had agreed whole heartedly on that matter. The Legate of the VIth, Quintus Antonius Isauricus, was also at the meeting. Flavius was happy that Legate Demetrius was there for Quintus Antonius Isauricus was a little resentful of the promotion of the tribune. Part of his displeasure was shown in that he stayed in Eboracum. Flavius had managed to get another two cohorts sent north. He wanted forts building in stone!

The arrival of the new Legate had an energising effect on the men of the wall. The recent attacks had made them feel abandoned. The heavy losses brought home to them how perilous was their existence.

Prefect Aulus Gemellus Glabrio and First Spear Brocchus had their men paraded to welcome their new commander. When Legate Fullo dismounted he strode, not to the Prefect but to First Spear. The Prefect felt snubbed and his attitude to the Legate hardened in that instant. Of course, neither snub nor insult were intended. The Legate held out his arm and Centurion Quintus Licinius Brocchus grasped it in a soldier's handshake.

"Quintus. I am glad to see you still command here."

"Thank you, sir. And congratulations on your promotion. It is well deserved."

"I hear we lost a fort."

There was no way of hiding the disaster. Centurion Quintus Licinius Brocchus would not cover up the mistakes which had been made. "No sir. We lost two. Alavna was destroyed as well."

The Legate knew First Spear well enough to keep any questions until they were alone. "But Bremenium is held?"

"Yes sir but they need reinforcements."

The Legate seemed to see Prefect Glabrio, "Prefect, you and your men have been here for a few days I understand?"

"Yes sir. We were just awaiting orders."

"Good, then you and your command can head north. Until I can get the Second Cohort of the VIth there to rebuild Habitancvm your ala will have to keep the road patrolled. Have them prepare and you can leave at dawn. I will hold an officer's meeting as soon as I find my office."

"Let me show you, sir."

Of course, the Legate knew where the office was. He had been based there for some time. This allowed First Spear to give the Legate the full details of the disaster. "Does the Prefect of Lingones know what happened?"

"No sir, Prefect Gaius Cinna Maro suffered a wound some months ago. It needed treatment. He is still in Luguvalium. I wanted to tell the Prefect to his face. The Centurion, optios and signifer are all dead. The handful who survived are with the 1st Cohort at Bremenium."

"But you have written a report?"

"Yes sir. One is there on your desk and the other awaiting a messenger to take it to Eboracum."

"Good then I will read the report before I have my meeting. Anything else I should know?" The Legate knew his First Spear well.

"I took hostages. It is the family of the chief, Randel. He is still at large and we think he is still dangerous. I have them under armed guard. It may not do much to control the barbarians but it will have annoyed them if nothing else."

"What do you make of Prefect Aulus Gemellus Glabrio?" Brocchus was silent. "Quintus, I want your honest opinion."

First Spear sighed, "Sir. Too full of himself sir. He arrived here and found that I had taken the Cohort north. He didn't even think to send one Turma to see if we needed any help."

"Thank you. I shall rely on you. Your knowledge of the cohorts will be vital."

The three prefects and First Spear Brocchus stood while the Legate gave them his vision. He had offered them seats but standing showed more respect to their new commander. "The Vangiones will be based at Cilurnum, Prefect Decimus Porcius Sura. The Lingones who are based there can go with the Ala Petriana to Bremenium and reinforce the garrison at the last fort. Cohort Frisiavones will take over Onnum, Prefect Titus Albus Bucco. The century who are there can also go to Bremenium. Prefect Aulus Gemellus Glabrio you will build a temporary fort close to Bremenium. Your liaison office Decurion Aurelius has good local knowledge. He can choose the site. Your task is to keep the road north and south of Bremenium clear and safe. We will have plenty of supplies and men using the road and we want them safe. When the rest of the VIth Victrix reach us, I intend to build another fort north of Bremenium as well as rebuilding Habitancvm and Alavna. The road which Legate Agricola built is vital to this province." He sat back and spread his arms, "I know this is a hard and hostile environment. Along with First Spear I have endured both the land and the barbarians. We will prevail. That is all."

When Prefect Aulus Gemellus Glabrio remained behind First Spear groaned. He wondered if he ought to stay. The Legate gave the subtlest shakes of his head and Brocchus left. Smiling, the Legate said, "Yes Prefect? Did I omit something?"

"I assumed that we would be based in a fort."

"You will be based in a fort, a marching fort. The auxiliaries will allow you to use their bread oven."

"And how long do you expect us to stay in such conditions, sir?"

"Until we have built the new forts, rebuilt the old ones and made Bremenium from stone."

"But sir that means we will be in the marching camp over winter!"

"Then you had better make it as comfortable as you can. You leave in the morning. I will send the wagons with the wood for the buildings later on in the day." The Legate looked up and stared at the Prefect. "You are now dismissed. I suggest you organize your baggage."

The Prefect was incandescent with rage but he could not argue with a superior. That really would be the end of his career. His officers were waiting. "Decurion Princeps, we are leaving at dawn tomorrow. We have to build our own fort. There will be some wagons following us. Make certain that we have all that we need. We will be wintering up there."

"Yes sir." He turned to the other officers, "Come on let's get started."

"Not you, Decurion Aurelius, I need to speak with you."

"Sir."

When the others had gone the Prefect said, "The Legate appears to have great faith in you."

"I am honoured."

"I, on the other hand, am less easily impressed. I know that Marcus' Horse had a good reputation. I intend the Ala Augusta Gallorum Petriana to exceed and eclipse Marcus' Horse. You are now with my ala and I expect your loyalty to be to me and the ala. Is that clear?"

"Yes sir."

"Good. Now the Legate says you might know of a good site for the fort. We need to be close enough to Bremenium to use their bread ovens and I do not want to be totally isolated. Is there such a place?"

Marcus closed his eyes to visualize the fort.

"Are you tired Decurion?"

"No sir, I am just picturing the ground. When the barbarians attacked, they took shelter by a stream. There was a large piece of ground there. It was protected on one side by the stream and it overlooked the road on the other. It would be about six hundred paces from the fort. Their bolt throwers would prevent an attack from that side and we would have a good view of the road."

"I would have to view it but you seem to know your business; I suppose that comes from growing up in this province. You will be attached to the Twentieth Turma. The decurion has little experience. In helping him to learn how to lead you may be of some assistance."

Marcus sought out Felix. "It seems we are heading back to Bremenium. Take a couple of horses and ride there. Warn First Spear that we have been ordered to build a fort close by. I have picked the flat ground to the west of the stream."

"I remember."

"We are likely to be there until next year. You had better make sure that we have all that we need."

Marcus knew that he could rely on Felix. He then hurried to join the other officers. Decurion Princeps Pera saw him approach. "I understand you are in charge of finding our new billet?" There was the hint of amusement in his voice.

"Yes sir. I have picked out a spot. If I am to be honest I think it is a better site for Bremenium but who am I to question the ones who built it?"

He gestured to a young officer, "This is Decurion Servius Hirtius Stolo. He commands the Twentieth Turma. You may have heard of his uncle, Legate Stolo."

"I fear that unless he has served in Britannia then I do not know him. Sorry Decurion."

The young officer was aghast, "You have only served here?"

"I was born here. My mother is a Brigante."

Decurion Princeps stepped forward, "And before you say anything you may regret, Decurion Aurelius outranks you in addition to which the sword he bears was once presented to the Divine Claudius. You listen to Decurion Aurelius and we may make a half decent officer of you." The officer nodded, "Now we have two days of riding to reach our new home. I doubt that we will be well supplied up there which means we need to be resourceful." He turned to Marcus. "I take it they don't have any decent horses there."

"Their stock is getting better. They are hardy enough and they are stocky enough but they are too small. Even my scout, who is not the tallest of riders, scrapes his feet along the road when he rides."

"You have a scout?"

"I sent him north to see that the road was clear. He is good. It was he brought the legions to the aid of Bremenium."

It was dark before they finished. Marcus had plenty of everything, including grain for his horse but many of the others in the ala had to scrabble around to find what they needed. When they left, with the first hint of dawn behind them, Marcus felt the first chill which marked the end of summer. The Prefect had Marcus and the Twentieth Turma as the van guard. It showed that he did not rate Decurion Stolo. He and his turma were expendable.

As they rode north Marcus kept his eyes on the sides of the road. They had killed many barbarians but others had escaped. They were in dangerous territory. When the gates at Onnum had clanged shut it had made Decurion Stolo jump. To cover his embarrassment he said, "I did not mean any disrespect when I asked about serving in Rome. It is so unusual. That is all."

"I am not offended. I know that many high-born Romans look down on those born to natives." To ease the tension he said, "Which is your Chosen Man?"

"Chosen Man? I do not have one."

"You need one. You have the vexillarius but you need another who can be as your second in command. As I am attached to you it does not matter for the moment but you will need one. Command can be lonely. Often you have to split the turma. Who leads the other half when that becomes necessary?"

"I had not thought of that. Will my turma be operating alone?"

"This is a large ala but the odds are that you will. We are now in land which does not pay taxes to Rome. They still see themselves as free. It is an illusion, of course. An ala can cover a larger area than a cohort. This road is a luxury. Most of the time you will be operating there." He pointed to the woodland to the west of them. "It is perfect ambush country and also very easy for you to become lost. That is why you need to know the skills of your men. You may not be the best at spotting trail. Find the one who is. Being a leader is harder than just riding at the head of a column of men."

Manius Balba Ralle, the vexillarius, nodded to his shield brother Sextus Verdius Naso. He said quietly, "That is what the young patrician needs; advice from someone who knows what he is talking about. I can tell you now, Sextus, that I feel a great deal happier with the new officer."

"I would still rather be south of the wall. We lost a lot of good men last time. You and I are the only two left from the original turma."

"You know what they say, if you haven't got a sense of humour, don't sign up."

They made their first marching camp at the ruins of Habitancvm. The Prefect frowned. "This seems an odd choice for a marching camp, Decurion."

Marcus shrugged. "The fort was built here for a reason, it is a day's march from Coriosopitum and from Bremenium. The camp is already laid out. We just use the blackened marks where the palisade stood. The ditch is deeper than we normally need."

"Yes but Romans died here."

"Sir, Romans have died all over this land. You won't find many places close to the road where some trooper or auxiliary didn't come to an early end and went to the Otherworld."

He could see that the Prefect had not really understood what he said but the camp was built on the ruins of the old fort. Marcus stood his sentry duty with the turma. Two turmae stood watch at any one time. When it was the Twentieth and Twenty First turmae's turn it meant they had three officers. Decurion Stolo was nervous. This was his first sentry duty in hostile territory.

"Servius, do you want some advice?"

"Do you think I need it?" He was defensive.

Marcus sighed. He had his work cut out. "You are as nervous as a house cat. If you are nervous then you can't use your best weapons."

"What are they?"

"Eyes, ears and most importantly, nose."

"Nose?"

"We can also be smelled from a long way away. It is the horse leather and horse sweat. Add to that the acetum and a barbarian can smell us a mile away. They smell too. Barbarians smell differently to us. The first thing you do is sniff the air. Smell each side of the camp. Try to identify what you can smell. When you look then listen. Keep your head still and, while you listen for sounds which are there and shouldn't be or noises which are noticeably absent then look for shadows which move. They shouldn't."

"That sounds like a great deal to think about."

"It is but remember, you have the responsibility of guarding your comrades who sleep. If you get it wrong, then they die."

As they approached the fort Marcus saw that First Spear Sejanus was still improving the defences. All signs of the battle had now gone but he had his men making more traps for the ditch and obstacles between the two ditches. The Votadini had managed to get to the second ditch far too easily. The crucified bodies remained where they had been planted. The birds and the rats had got to them. Marcus had no doubt that First Spear would have them taken down soon. The point had been made.

Prefect Glabrio rode next to Marcus as they approached the fort. He had with him Decurion Princeps Pera. "Where would you have us build the fort then?"

Marcus pointed north. "Where the road begins to turn you can see a piece of flatter, higher ground to the west of that bush line. There my scout, Felix, is sitting atop it on his horse."

The Prefect turned, "Your scout?"

"To speak correctly he is the scout of Marcus' Horse but as his skill would be wasted in Wales the Prefect attached him to me before he left. I sent him two days ago to ensure that it was as I remembered it."

The Prefect nodded and mumbled, "Resourceful." He turned in the saddle, "Come Decurion Princeps let us see if our liaison offer has done well."

As they trotted up the road Marcus looked around. If it were not here then it would have to be close to the river and that would mean flooding. Autumn rains could turn the small river into a torrent overnight. Felix and Wolf diplomatically headed away from the approaching officers. The Prefect rode all around it. Marcus had remembered well. It was flat and the floods made by the dam had made the soil easier to work. It was as close to perfect as possible. It was also large enough to accommodate the nine hundred strong herd of horses that they needed.

"Very good, Decurion. Decurion Princeps, begin the construction. Decurion Aurelius, you can introduce me to the commander of the fort."

The Prefect was going to ride down the road. Marcus said, "Sir, the stream is not wide, we can jump it."

The Prefect shook his head, "If you think I am going to risk the ignominy of falling from my horse in front of a cohort of Lingones then you are mistaken. However, I am more than willing for you to try."

It was a challenge and Marcus accepted. He dug his heels in and Raven took off. Marcus did not break stride and his horse sailed over. Marcus heard a cheer as the Twentieth Turma watched him.

He reined in next to First Spear, "You showing off, Decurion?"

"I offered the Prefect the chance to do it and he declined. I am sorry about this First Spear. You will have more than eight hundred men and horses for neighbours."

"I am not complaining. It will keep the Votadini from us. What is he like, this Prefect?"

"He doesn't want to be here."

Sejanus laughed, "None of us do." First Spear stood to attention as the Prefect dismounted. "Sir, welcome to Bremenium. My officers and I would be delighted if you and your Decurion Princeps would dine with us this evening. It is nothing special but we do have fresh bread." He gestured with his left hand, "And we do have a bathhouse. It is not the biggest but it does have hot water."

That convinced the Prefect. Marcus had not been able to enjoy the facility when he had been there. He had been too busy fighting. Conveniently it lay to the north of both forts next to the small stream. "Most kind. Decurion be so good as to send over Decurion Princeps Pera. This fort is more civilised than I first thought."

I nodded my thanks to First Spear. He had made my life easier.

Chapter 9

Even as the Prefect was entered the hot room in the bathhouse a council of chiefs was meeting at Traprain Law under the stern gaze of King Clutha. Agnathus and Randel had taken days to reach the north. The lack of horses and their wounds slowed them. Four men died on the journey. Riders found them and told them of the assembly. When Agnathus walked in he was surprised to see his son sitting close by the King. Randel's eyes narrowed. It was more than surprise which he felt. It was raw anger and hatred. All the way north he had brooded about the death of his brother and the capture of his wife. His home was destroyed and, for some reason, Randel blamed Creagh. He knew it was irrational. Creagh had just taken a handful of men from the battle but it was the dishonour which rankled. Now he saw the man sitting close by the King. It was unfair.

Agnathus saw that they were the last to arrive. The other senior chiefs were already there. When he had met with Góra, Witan and the others it had been a closed meeting. The chiefs there had all been unhappy with King Clutha. Now the rest of the tribe's chiefs were there and Agnathus realised that they were in the majority. He wondered about his son's part in this. What was he doing here?

"You are the last to arrive, Agnathus and Randel. Sit that we may begin our council of war."

They sat between Góra and Witan.

"We now have a war against the Romans. It was not a war I chose." The King jabbed a finger at Randel. "It was Tadgh, Randel and Baradh who began it. Two have paid with their lives. We need to consider if there is a punishment due to the third."

Randel's hand went to his Roman sword. It was under the table and Agnathus gripped it. He hissed, quietly, "Peace. Think with your head and not your heart."

Randel nodded and placed both hands on the table.

Vinicius stood. He had been at the council at Din Guardi, "King Clutha, Randel and his brother, aided by Chief Agnathus have destroyed two Roman forts. They came within a heartbeat of a third. Chief Randel deserves praise and not condemnation."

"What retribution will it bring forth? My father told me of the legions who marched north and laid waste to our land. The Romans have built a wall and left us alone. We have poked the sleeping dog. It will bite."

Drest was a chief from the north of the land of the Votadini. "I support you King Clutha but I agree with Vinicius. Randel has shown the Romans that we can fight and we can win. There is but one fort left. If we could take that then our land would be free from the boot of the Romans. They have built a wall. Let them keep the land to the south. Their forts show that they still have ambitions to rule us. Are we free or are we subservient to Rome?"

Men spoke to their neighbours and Agnathus saw a chance. He had thought they were in the minority but it was not necessarily true. He spoke. "King Clutha, when we fought many Selgovae and Brigante joined us. Surely, we can be the tribe who leads this revolt. We can become greater as a result of this."

This time even more chiefs agreed with Agnathus. King Clutha frowned and then looked at Creagh. "Chief Agnathus your son has come to me and told me of your ambition to be King of the Votadini." There was a ripple of conversation and outrage around the room. The outrage was that a son had betrayed his father. "Do you deny it?"

Agnathus shrugged, "You believe a man who deserted the warriors he led to battle and fled to you. Why should anyone believe a word he says? He is no longer my son."

Creagh leapt to his feet, "I told King Clutha when I first reached him that I was not your son." Randel noticed a strange smile on his face. "As we are both agreed on the matter then there is nothing more to be said."

A strange silence fell over the meeting. Randel had not yet spoken. He chose that moment to do so, "Is this a council of war or a place for men to speak of petty grievances> I have lost my family in this revolt and for me it is not over. I would be War Chief of the tribe. I believe that I have earned the right. I tell every chief here that Randel will continue to fight the Romans until the last breath has left his body."

This time there was no doubt that Randel had the full support of almost every chief. Yet Creagh continued to smile. Agnathus stood too and looked at Randel. Agnathus put his hand on the young chief's shoulder. Randel sat. Agnathus was known to be a wise chief. When he spoke then men listened. "You are High King of the Votadini. None here threatens that position but it seems to me that almost everyone here wishes Randel to be War Chief of the Votadini." Every eye was on King Clutha. "Is there any who oppose Randel as War Chief?"

Surprisingly, even Creagh remained seated.

King Clutha spoke, "You all think I am old and weak. Just because I have no children you conspire against me. Know this, I have spent my life making the land of the Votadini safe from our enemies. When I go to the Otherworld I will continue to do so." He jabbed a finger at Agnathus, "But you, Agnathus the snake, will never be King. I announce here, tonight, in this sacred hall, that my heir will be Creagh. I have adopted him as my son. I presented him to the priests two days since and he has been anointed. He is now Prince Creagh. If Chief Randel is War Chief then he serves Prince Creagh!"

The announcement was greeted with disbelief. Randel had got his way but it was for nothing. If he failed then Creagh would have won and if he won then Creagh would reap the rewards. He had been outwitted.

As the hall erupted Agnathus turned to Randel. "My son is as slippery as an eel. He has no honour but this changes nothing. You are War Chief now."

Randel nodded, "Aye but this is not the time for war. Warriors will need to provide for their families and with so many warriors dead it will be a hard winter."

Agnathus shook his head, "I am not talking of the whole tribe. We brought with us forty men whose families are either dead or hostage. I now have no family. We will not farm this winter. You are War Chief. Can we not make war on the Romans when the snow lies hard upon the ground? Can we not be as the wolf and use stealth to hurt our foes? What we need we take from the Romans. And there will be others without families. There will be young warriors who seek to follow you."

Agnathus was right. Randel nodded, "They may have stopped my home from being a fortress but, in winter, it is still a refuge. The forest to the sunset side of the road can be a home for many warriors. It is still a place of safety for men. We will do this."

"Then while you plan the war I will speak with others. My son thinks he has outwitted us. We will show him that there are more in the tribe who do not want him than support him."

100

The Prefect showed that he knew how to organize. Two thirds of the ala were tasked with building the marching fort. He left Decurion Princeps Pera in charge and as soon as the wagons arrived they were able to erect the buildings. They would, perforce, be rudimentary but they would give shelter from the elements. Pera divided his men in two so that one half erected the walls and gates while the other worked on the stables and barracks.

The Prefect led the other eight turmae and he had Marcus show him the surrounding area. They rode, first, as far north as they could. The thick forests which threatened to engulf the road showed the Prefect that they were not in cavalry country. As they returned south the Prefect questioned Marcus, "Do people live there? Surely there cannot be many."

"The Votadini are not like the Romans, sir, nor even the Brigante. Apart from the coast they do not live in large settlements. The valleys here are steep and narrow. What might constitute a town further south will be spread up a valley. Some will even eke out a living in the forest. It teems with game." Marcus turned in his saddle. He waved at the turmae behind him. "That is why the Legate sent an ala. A single turma can control a whole valley. There will be no hill fort to subdue nor walls to breach. A single turma will outnumber the warriors in any settlement they find."

"Then how did they manage to destroy two forts? That is unheard of."

"They have a good War Chief and he did have a hill fort. It is now thrown down but he is still at large. Until we have him we will have no peace."

"But we have his family as hostage."

"That will not matter to him. It is a blood feud now. We slew his brother and destroyed his home."

"Surely we destroyed their army. Who can he lead?"

They were approaching the forts. "The land of the Votadini stretches south to the wall. To the north? On our ride today, we barely made inroads into their territory."

"Tomorrow I would see this hill fort."

The next day when they went to Otarbrunna Marcus sent Felix to ride around the hill fort in case anyone fled at their approach. The Prefect did not question Marcus' decision. He was beginning to understand that his liaison officer knew his business. Otarbrunna was not deserted. Marcus had not expected it to be. The ramparts, however, were undefended and no one had attempted to repair the gates. What the survivors of the clan had done was to repair their huts and to begin to rebuild their lives. As they rode up the valley Marcus saw that there was not a single man of warrior age. There were the old and the lame but most of those who toiled were women or children. With summer coming to an end they were working urgently. Even in a normal year winter was hard. With no men to hunt for them this would be even harder. There would be deaths.

As they entered the hill fort smoke rose from a building and Marcus heard the unmistakeable sounds of metal being worked. He saw that it meant nothing to the Prefect who merely looked at the wrecked defences.

"I can see that this might have been hard to take but the VIth did an effective job of rendering it indefensible."

There were more people in the centre of the fort than Marcus had expected. When it had been razed, any animals they had found had been taken. Marcus now saw goats, cows even a family of pigs. There were fowl too. A cohort of legionaries did not approach quickly and they had taken their animals to safety. Had the ala been there then they would have had nothing to begin their rebuilding.

As they reached the centre Marcus saw the source of the smoke and the banging. There was a blacksmith. He was one armed. His left arm was a stump. Two boys looked to be doing the work of his left arm. His right arm was like a young oak. He was the youngest man Marcus had seen. He looked to be about thirty summers old. He was coming into his prime. When they reined in Marcus saw that the wound had not been inflicted in the recent battle. The scars had healed but they were still visible. Marcus looked at the man's face. His eyes burned with hatred as hot as the fire his boys fanned.

The Prefect said, "Ask him where is this Chief Randel."

Marcus knew that it was pointless but he did as he was ordered. "Smith, my Prefect would know where is your Chief Randel?"

Judicael hated the Romans but he was no fool. The other warriors had fled as soon as the Romans had approached but, with his one arm, it was thought that Judicael would not be seen as a threat. It would be foolish to annoy the Romans. He also recognised that the Roman officer who spoke to him knew his language. As he glanced at his weapons he saw that this one did not carry a Roman sword but one with a decorated pommel and hilt. This was the Brigante who carried the Sword of

Cartimandua. He was known to be a clever man. Judicael decided to be as honest as he could be without giving away too much. The word was that Chief Randel was on his way south, but in secret.

"After the battle, lord, he left and headed north. We think he went to King Clutha's court."

Marcus could tell that this was partly the truth. However, the man's eyes had not held his. He was hiding something. "The man says he has gone to the King. He has a home in the far north of the land."

The Prefect nodded, "What is he making? Swords?"

Marcus had already worked out what the smith was making, "No sir. They have no need of swords for they captured more than a hundred from the dead Lingones. He is making animal traps. With so many warriors dead they will have to trap animals for food. There are mainly women and children here."

"No warriors then."

"Oh yes, sir, there were warriors. They will have fled when we arrived. Felix will tell us how many there were."

The Prefect led the turmae around the hill fort. It was a statement of power. Over two hundred horsemen told the Votadini that the ala was back. Felix met them at the end of the valley as they returned. Marcus nodded for him to report to the Prefect.

"There were eighteen men who might be warriors, sir. They headed into the forest as you approached. They were watching you as you rode around the fort."

"Eighteen eh? Not enough to worry about."

Marcus warned, "Yes sir but Chief Randel is at large. If he can convince the King to give him more men then they might be enough to worry about."

"Then the sooner the fort is built the better. That way we can send out twice the number of men. I can see what you mean about a turma operating alone. Tomorrow we will ride to Alavna and then the coast. By the time we return Decurion Princeps Pera might have my quarters ready."

The next day, as they approached Alavna Marcus realised that despite his mistakes, Centurion Ambustus had done an effective job of destroying the fort. Romans could rebuild but the Votadini would never have the skills to do so. The Prefect shook his head. The Legate had told all of his prefects of the disaster. "What possessed the man to destroy the fort. Surely it was more dangerous to be out in the wild."

"He had hostages and he genuinely believed that Bremenium had fallen. I spoke to some of the survivors and they told me. This was a century fort sir. Coriosopitum is the nearest help and he knew that there was no cavalry."

The Prefect gave Marcus a sharp look. "It was my fault?"

"No sir. It was the fool who ordered Marcus' Horse south before you had come to replace us. If there had been an ala here then it would not have fallen."

Mollified he nodded, "I appreciate your candour. We have a great responsibility."

Ammabile was also without men although, as Marcus pointed out that was probably less sinister. "These are fishermen too sir. They will be out in their boats. When the weather worsens they will not be able to fish. They catch while they can. They will be out from dawn to dusk."

For the next patrols the Prefect divided the eight turmae into groups of two. He had seen nothing to suggest numbers which might overwhelm them. He had thought of sending one but his officers were just becoming accustomed to the land. This would allow them to become familiar with small trails and paths.

When Randel and his men reached the hillfort it was three days after the Roman visit. Judicael was pleased to see the chief. He liked the young warrior. They had been unlucky. Everyone knew that luck changed and he and his brother had destroyed two Roman forts.

"The horsemen are back."

Randel could not hide his disappointment. Horsemen would restrict their activities. "How many were there?"

"More than two hundred here but twice that number are building another fort."

Randel frowned, "They are not rebuilding the one we destroyed?"

"No Chief Randel, they are building another one between the stream and the road. The horsemen are here to stay. They came west, went north and then east. Today they have smaller patrols out, perhaps forty or fifty horsemen in each group. They also sent more men to man the fort we attacked. Our sheep herders counted more than two hundred of them. And there is one more thing. The warrior with the Brigante sword was with them."

"He is the one who killed my brother. Then the gods still smile on us. I can have vengeance for Baradh." He turned to the men who had come with him. "We do not risk bringing the Romans here. We will make shelters in the forests. We are warriors and we will endure."

Agnathus was not with them. He was busy raising more warriors in the north and the east. Randel's lieutenant, Teutorigos asked, "Will these horsemen and the reinforced garrison change our plans, Chief?"

"If anything, they help us. They think the road south is secure. We can strike there and cut off their supplies. There are many valleys to the south of us where we can hide. We know the small trails over the ridgelines. Even their horses will struggle. We will not win this winter. We make them bleed while we gather strength. Agnathus is now an ally. He hates his son so much that he will do all in his power to raise us an army which can beard the Romans! My brother and the others did not die in vain." He turned to the blacksmith, "We have many short swords?"

"Yes War Chief but they are not much good against Roman swords."

"But if we tied them to spear hafts, what then?"

Judicael grinned, "You would be able to reach up and use them as slashing weapons. The Roman horsemen do not wear armour on their legs. We have many spear hafts. You brought back great quantities from the fort you burned. I will make this weapon for you and we will defeat the horsemen!"

In Coriosopitum the Legate had not been idle. He had ridden the length of the wall as far as Magnis and spoken to all of the commanders. He had sent more requests for troops. There were reports of unrest in the land of the Brigante. It had long been a quiet part of Britannia but there was always a glow of insurrection. The Votadini had fanned it. There was a mixed cohort of Gauls promised to him. They would be able to build a fort at Habitancvm. Most importantly, another cohort of the VIth was on its way. The Prefect was not with them. The Legate did not mind. He would lead them. Until they had a fort a day's ride north of the wall the garrison at Bremenium was in danger. Alavna would have to wait. Until the road north was secure then Alavna was a luxury. What was arriving, in great numbers, were wagons with stone and other building material.

When he had arrived the Legate had appointed Centurion Spurius Caelius Vata as Camp Prefect. He was just two years short of retirement and his optio was ready for promotion. The fact that the Prefect, Quintus Antonius Isauricus was not involved in the decision was immaterial. Both the Legate and Brocchus agreed. The new camp prefect was having the stone stored. No one wanted to risk the precious stone being stolen before the walls could be erected. There were also cart loads of seasoned timber. The Roman Army was nothing if not efficient.

The three of them sat in the Principia. "The moment the cohort arrives I want them sent north."

"Sir, if we ask the Prefect at Morbium to send a rider when they reach him we can ask the Prefect of the Ala Augusta Gallorum Petriana to send a couple of turmae to escort them."

"I wonder how the new Prefect is making out?"

"The First Spear at the fort and Decurion Aurelius are both good officers. So long as he listens then he should be alright."

The new Camp Prefect said, "We have some supplies for them. They came north without winter cloaks. Should I wait until we send the stone?"

"No. Haven't we a century of Lingones due to head north?"

"Yes sir."

"Then send them up as an escort."

Six days after they began the fort it was habitable and two days later it was finished. It was, by Roman standards, crudely built but it would last the year and that was what counted. The Prefect was happy that he could bathe and his men have fresh bread. He would have to live with the crude quarters. Gathering his officers about him he gave them their instructions. "I intend to have half of the ala in the fort. The other half will spread out in every direction on patrol. We swap each day. The turmae will not have the same patrol area." He pointed to Marcus, "Our liaison officer has pointed out that having the same patrol can induce complacency. I agree. By changing each patrol, the men will be forced to look at their surroundings. When Decurion Princeps Pera and myself ate with the Lingones officers they told us how it was complacency cost us the first fort. Sixteen turmae give us sixteen patrol routes. Decurion Princeps Pera has a list of the routes. The maps may not be the best. I suggest that you improve them."

Marcus and Decurion Stolo had a patrol south and slightly west, towards Broccolitia on the wall. They would not actually reach the wall but it would be a long hard ride. Next to them Decurion Vibius Seneca Dives was a happier man. He had the road patrol. They had ridden up the road and the Decurion was confident that he knew where the danger might lie.

Marcus was pleased with the progress Decurion Servius Hirtius Stolo had made. He had listened. Although he had yet to appoint a Chosen Man everything else Marcus had suggested had been done. Marcus had overheard Manius Balba Ralle, the vexillarius, talking to another of the older troopers and it was obvious that they had a new-found respect for the young officer. Marcus had seen many like them. They came from privileged backgrounds and looked down on the troopers, many of whom had chosen the auxilia for its higher rate of pay.

As they rode Marcus looked over his shoulder and saw that the troopers' bodies looked relaxed but not their vigilance. Even when they talked their eyes were scanning the ground for sign and for danger. Felix was ahead of them with Wolf. They had all learned to keep their distance from Wolf. Only Felix could approach him.

"We haven't seen any signs of Votadini on any of our patrols, Marcus, perhaps they are beaten."

Not necessarily true, Servius. We may not have seen signs of armed Votadini but their scouts have dogged our trails and they have been close to our walls."

"How do you know?"

"After I have made water I walk around the walls of the fort. I look for signs. It is there to be seen."

"But the sentries have not reported any barbarians at night."

"That is because they did not want to be seen."

Decurion Stolo looked anxiously around him, "Are there any close by? Should I order a stand to?"

Marcus laughed, "Wolf would have told us if there were any barbarians lurking."

Just then Felix wheeled his horse around and galloped back to them, "A warband headed east. It was before dawn. They are disguising their numbers by walking in each other's footsteps."

Marcus nodded, "Go find them."

The scout slid off the pony and hurtled off east. "What about his animal?"

"He will whistle when he wants it. The Votadini can smell horses. A man on a horse stands out. Felix knows what he is doing. Now you can tell the men to stand to!"

Turning in his saddle the young officer shouted, "Stand to. The scout has spotted barbarian sign heading east."

Marcus was pleased. Servius' voice was calm and measured. That was what the men wanted. "We had better head further east too. Decurion Dives is on the road and he will have no idea that war band is to his right."

As they made their horses go faster Servius said, "Surely the Decurion will be able to handle a few barbarians."

"Decurion, a warband can be anything from ten men to a hundred. Did you not hear Felix? He said they ran in each other's footsteps. That disguises the numbers."

They hurtled through scrubby bushes and stunted trees. The ground rose and fell. He knew the road was ahead but he could not see. Already Marcus feared the worst. They would have been in position along the road before the patrol had even set off. Decurion Dives would be further down the road. Even as they rode to his aid he could be under attack. Suddenly Felix appeared from the undergrowth. "Decurion, the turma is under attack. They are half a mile away. There are eighty Votadini!"

Marcus turned, "Our brothers are under attack. Form line! Use your javelins first." Marcus was aware that Stolo should have given the order but this was not the time for niceties. Raven was laden with equipment: a spear, three javelins and his shield. This was one of the times when it was worth it. He slid a javelin from its quiver and held it aloft. Suddenly they burst over the top of a small rise and Marcus saw the ambush. Three horses lay writhing; they had been gutted and were in their death throes. The vexillarius stood protectively over the Decurion who had been wounded. The other troopers were fighting valiantly but they were surrounded. Marcus saw that the Votadini were using long pole weapons.

As soon as Marcus and the turma were seen one of the Votadini shouted a command and the sixty warriors who remained suddenly split up and ran. Marcus shouted, "Capsarius, help the Decurion. The rest, get as many as you can. Vexillarius Manius Balba Ralle, stay by me and be ready with the buccina!"

"Yes sir!"

Marcus wheeled his horse to the right. Most of the Votadini were heading west. He pulled his arm back and hurled his javelin at a barbarian who was thirty paces away. The javelin impaled his arm and went into his chest. Marcus had another one out before Raven had taken another three strides. Raven, like all Roman cavalry horses was strong. Her powerful legs pushed hard up the slope. The barbarians could run quickly but they would tire. Marcus saw one turn and prepare his pole weapon. Marcus second javelin took him in his middle. The barbarians were now harder to see. This was obviously a pre-arranged strategy. Marcus was suddenly aware of a man who had been hiding, rising up and swinging his pole axe at Marcus. Had it struck he would have been dead. A javelin pierced his head, killing him instantly.

Marcus turned and saw a grinning vexillarius, "You said to stay close, sir."

"Thank you, I owe you a life."

Marcus and the vexillarius caught and killed two more before the rest disappeared from sight. "Sound recall."

The buccina's strident notes rode up the valley. Marcus turned Raven and headed back down the slope. He saw that Trooper Labeo had fallen foul of an axe man. His body had been almost cut in two by the weapon. Marcus saw the trooper's horse. "Vexillarius, fetch the horse. We will take him home to bury him."

"Yes sir."

Marcus realised he had called the fort home. It was not much of a home but while they were here on the wild frontier then it would be their home. Marcus dismounted and wrapped the trooper's body in his cloak. It would help to keep it together. He laid it between the saddle horns. He handed the reins to the vexillarius and then mounted Raven. He headed back to the road. Later Manius Balba Ralle, the vexillarius, would tell the troopers of the ala the story. "An officer and he looked after poor Labeo like he was his son. I tell you lads, we have a gem here. I am not sure it would have happened had Decurion Stolo been in command."

When Marcus reached the ambush, he saw that Decurion Dives was heavily bandaged. The capsarius, Numerius Helva Licina, said, "He has lost his leg below the knee sir. I have cleaned it and applied a dressing but if we don't get him back he will die."

"Who is the Chosen Man?"

The vexillarius pointed to a cloak covered body, "That would be Spurius, sir."

"Right Vexillarius. You take the turma and your Decurion back to the fort. We will clean up here."

He nodded, "Thank you sir. You arrived in the nick of time."

"We were lucky." Just then Marcus saw Felix arrive, "Felix ride to the fort and tell them we have seriously wounded men."

"Sir!" He galloped off. "They will be ready for you."

As the depleted turma headed north Marcus dismounted. He saw Decurion Stolo. He was only just returning. His javelin quiver was full. He would say nothing. He turned to the troopers. "Search the dead barbarians. You are looking for amulets, torcs, rings; anything made of metal or bone. They will tell us more about our enemies. Collect the weapons too. We don't want them using them again."

"And the bodies sir?"

"In a perfect world we would burn them but we have neither the time nor the manpower. We leave them. Tomorrow's patrol can deal with them."

Later, as they headed north, Marcus could tell that Decurion Stolo was brooding about something. It did not do to brood. "Vexillarius, give the Decurion and I some space."

"Yes sir."

"Spit it out Servius, what is it?"

He almost whispered his answer, "It is you, Marcus! You have taken command of my turma. I should have given the orders. I should have had the vexillarius riding with me."

"And the fact is, Servius that you are right. Yet if we had waited for your order how many more men might have died? Here you are either quick or you are dead. I am sorry if your feelings are hurt or you are offended but you and I are merely tools. We do not have any right to have feelings."

Stolo said nothing.

Marcus said, "Why were you late responding to the recall?"

"I am an officer. I do not need to heed a recall."

"And that is where you are wrong. Even the Prefect responds to such a command. We are successful here because we know how to obey orders. Every order. Even the barbarians are learning that. Did you not notice how quickly they dispersed? Yes, we killed more than twenty of them but in times past the number would have been much greater. You are improving, Servius but you are not yet ready to be let off the leash. Sorry. I am your senior and I will continue to give commands,"

Chapter 10

By the time Marcus and the patrol reached the fort all the other patrols had returned. As he dismounted Decurion Princeps Pera came over to the two officers. "Decurion Dives will live but he cannot command any longer."

Marcus nodded, "Will he leave the ala?"

Decurion Stolo burst out, "How could he stay in with one leg?"

Pera and Marcus exchanged a look. They had served much longer. Decurion Princeps Pera said, "What would he do out there? Run an inn? He will probably stay in. He is a good officer. We need an adjutant and a camp prefect. He could do either or both of those jobs. The problem is that we are an officer short."

"You want me to take over until you get a replacement?"

"The Fifteenth Turma is senior to the Twentieth. The Prefect thought you might like the promotion, Decurion Stolo."

"Promotion? It has fewer men to command!"

Decurion Princeps voice hardened. "It has veterans in its ranks. The Twentieth has two veterans. The rest are young. Troopers Drusus, Fimbria, Piso and Nerva have only been with the ala for four months. When I said the Prefect thought you might like the promotion I was being kind. You are now the decurion of the Fifteenth!" Stolo flashed a look of pure hatred in Marcus' direction. He saluted and stormed off.

Marius Pera shook his head, "I thought he was getting better!"

"He is but this has not been a good day, sir."

As they headed to the mess Marius said, "A bit worrying this, Decurion. I mean barbarians who ambush normally fight to the death. The fact that these managed to escape shows planning and their choice of pole weapons: six troopers lie dead and four wounded; three horses were killed. This was our first full day of patrols."

"I told you, sir, this Chief Randel is a thinker. They used to be rare in the tribes but now bright young warriors are learning from us. At the moment, they have the advantage. They can strike wherever they choose. Until Habitancvm is up and running there is too big a gap between the wall and us."

Marius nodded. "The Prefect is pleased with you. He was not happy at your appointment but he has come to see that you are an asset."

As they approached the Principia he saw First Spear Julius Sextus Sejanus emerging. "Good to see you, Decurion Aurelius. I have just been to see the Prefect. Now that we are at full strength again I intend to have my lads patrolling the road north and south of the forts. We will also head to Alavna. It means you donkey wallopers can ride further afield. My lads want to make up for…" He looked at Marcus, "Well you know better than most."

Marcus nodded, "They have nothing to make up for. Centurion Ambustus and his officers did that. They were the reason we won!"

The ala clerk, Vibius Calpurnius Alba, gestured to them, "If you gentleman would come this way, the Prefect wants a word."

The Prefect had a map of the area. He was studying it intently. He waved them to two chairs. "Today was disturbing, gentlemen. We almost lost a turma of troopers on their first patrol and I had to replace a decurion. I am less than pleased!"

Decurion Princeps Pera said, "We hurt them more than they hurt us sir. It was to be expected."

"The trouble is they do not fear us enough. Decurion Aurelius, where are the nearest big settlements?"

Marcus looked at the map. Pera peered over his shoulder. Both knew the area quite well. "Close by there is just Otarbrunna. Then there is Ammabile along the coast. There must be five or six fishing villages. The majority of them are between here and the coast."

"Then tomorrow I want every settlement searching. Confiscate any weapons that you find."

Decurion Princeps Pera asked, "Axes too? Most of the people here need them for timber,"

Marcus nodded, "And most have a need for a skinning knife or a bow."

The Prefect sighed, "Do not be pedantic gentlemen! A weapon is a spear, a sword or a shield. That should be clear. Tell the decurions who ride out tomorrow of our new orders."

Marcus was not happy about the order. It would just further antagonise the Votadini. Just as Marcus had buried that which was valuable when he had left his home so the Votadini would not risk leaving weapons in their homes. However, they would resent the intrusion and it would make hostile those who were, at the moment, ambivalent.

He said so to Decurion Princeps Pera. "You have served up here before, you know that this is a mistake. Further south the tribes have forgotten how to fight. Here they do not think that they have lost."

"I know. I will ask the Decurions who ride tomorrow to use tact."

Marcus was uncertain of the efficacy of that but it was better than nothing. He was now in sole command of a turma and the next day would give him the chance to get to know them even better. A day off was a luxury.

Far to the south in the land of the Brigante a meeting was being held. This one was in secret. The Brigante chiefs knew that there were Roman spies who watched the moves of those chiefs who were known to be less than friendly. To that end they had chosen a meeting place which would not attract attention. There was a sacred grove of yew trees which grew close by the whirled hill in the land to the south of the river. Druids had lived close by and although the cult had been destroyed by the IXth Legion the Romans knew that Brigante would travel there to seek help from the gods. It was not considered a threat. Most chiefs and their advisers would travel there in the spring and again in the time of the harvest. They would make offerings and pray to their gods. Ten chiefs were meeting in the yew grove.

All ten had brought but two bodyguards. Any more would have attracted attention. Some had travelled from north of the Dunum. One had come from the land of the high divide. One had come from the east but the rest were all from the rich farmlands of the vale which supported the garrison at Eboracum. While the twenty oathsworn stood watch the ten chiefs first made an offering to the gods and then they began to speak. It had been some time since this council had met. The Roman heel was planted firmly on this land. This was not the frontier. The only garrison that was needed was the legion at Eboracum.

The leader was Haerviu. He was the nearest man they had to a king. When Venutius had tried to have Queen Cartimandua killed he had taken a second wife, Fedlimid. She had borne but one son. Haerviu was the issue of that son. Briac was his sire. He was chief of a tribe who lived in his ancestor's old heartlands. He was of the Carvetii. Now, having seen forty summers, he was a bitter man. Two of his sons had been lost in battle and now he had just a daughter remaining. She had married a Brigante chief, Belenus who ruled the land by the Roaring Waters. It had been the birth of his first grandson that had spurred him to call the meeting. He wanted his grandson to grow up free in a land which was not ruled by foreign invaders. More than that, he wanted his grandson to be King of the Brigante and Carvetii.

He looked out from beneath his hooded cowl. Only he knew the identity of all the chiefs he had chosen for this secret council. All of them were powerful and could still command many hundreds of men. None had succumbed to the Roman way of life. They had neither villa nor bathhouse. They lived as their ancestors had done. Their roundhouses had not changed since the beginning of the tribe. The difference was that they now knew how to fight the Romans. Their ancestors had bled on the spears, swords and shields of solid lines of soldiers. They had been hunted down by horsemen.

"You all know me. I am Haerviu. I have the blood of the last King of the Brigante in my veins yet I do not seek to rule this land. I seek to free it." That was not true. When the Romans were gone Haerviu would claim the crown and rule as Venutius had done, with a rod of iron. "All of you here are unhappy with the taxes you pay the Romans. Why should we pay taxes to live on our own land? They say it is to keep the peace. Whom do we fight? Our enemies in the north have a wall between them and us. I say it is time to fight. I would hear your words. I do not mind that you keep your heads covered for, until we make a decision we do not need to know the identity of any chief here. You may speak openly."

The chief from the land close by Streonshal spoke, "We cannot fight the legions. My father and half the tribe died in the last revolt. We followed the witches and it brought us ruin."

"And that was our mistake. Warriors do not follow women. Look what happened when we had a queen. Cartimandua gave the land to the Romans. We know the strengths of the Romans and we know the weaknesses. Marcus' Horse left the land of its birth to head south. That was a sign. The Legion sent more than half of its men north to the wall. At the crossing of the Dunum there are less than two hundred men. The land is ripe for revolt. Their tax collectors become more insufferable each season. The soldiers abuse our women when they come. How much longer can we endure such pain?"

The chief from close to Cataractonium nodded, "Haerviu is right. The garrison from the fort close by my lands left seven days since to head north. There were just two hundred or so of them but now there are none. I have many young men who wish to fight. I have restrained them for their deaths would be pointless. We must all have young warriors who wish to be blooded."

Iodocus had travelled a long way south. His clan lived north of the Dunum. They had fine land along the waters of the river the Romans had named Vedra. That was not the Brigante name. They called it the river of life. They had had a hill fort in a bend of the sacred river. The legions had thrown it down. However, he and his tribe were close enough to the road which led to the wall to see and hear much of what went on in the lands close to the frontier. "The Romans have lost two forts north of their wall."

Even Haerviu had not heard that. "Is that rumour or Votadini boasts?"

"It is true. Some of the warriors of the clan north of us went to join them. They were defeated in a battle but they told us that two forts had been burned and only one remained in the north."

The chief from the land close by Streonshal shook his head, "As you said, they lost."

"They lost the battle but not the war. The War Chief who led them, Randel, escaped. They still fight. We know the Romans sent men north from Cataractonium and I can attest to the fact that we counted more than a thousand fighting men heading north."

The chief from close to Cataractonium asked, "How does this help us?"

Iodocus shook his head, "I am not the War Chief. I am a warrior but it seems to me that if the Votadini can draw more Romans north then that makes this land ripe for revolt."

Haerviu began to see hope. He addressed the chief from close to Cataractonium. "You are the closest to Eboracum. How many of the legion remain there?"

"No more than fifteen hundred."

"Then what we need is to make them head north."

As men spoke with their neighbours Iodocus said, "There is one more thing. The Sword of Cartimandua did not travel south with Marcus'

Horse. It is in their last fort north of the wall. It does not have the protection of the horsemen."

There was a stunned silence in the grove. Everyone knew that Marcus Horse had been the bane of the Brigante. Not only had it kept the Dunum quiet it had guarded that most holy of swords. If the sword could be returned to the Brigante then the gods would return their favour.

Haerviu sensed a shift in the mood of the chiefs. "I have a suggestion. I will travel north with Iodocus. We will travel to the land of the Votadini and we will speak with this Randel. As one of you said we all have young men who wish to fight the Romans. Ask those who wish to do so to meet at Iodocus' old hill fort on the sacred river at the feast of Eostre. I will find a way to lead them north and join this Randel. When the Legion leaves Eboracum then the rest of you can rise and destroy the Romans. Without the legion and without Marcus' Horse they have no defence. Do you remember the story of Boudicca? They almost drove the Romans from this island in just such a revolt. The difference now is that we will be more than one tribe. I will visit the Novontae and the Selgovae when I have spoken with the Votadini. We can light a fire now which will grow and engulf the frontier."

He had the agreement of the chiefs. The initial danger was not to them. It was to Haerviu and Iodocus. It would help make their lives easier for it would rid their clans of the hotheads who would hasten to fight the Romans. There were plenty of young warriors. Haerviu and Iodocus left for the journey to the land of the Votadini. It would not be easy but both men saw that it was an opportunity for them to reclaim their former glory and for them to rule the land north and south of the Brigante river.

Marcus was right. The heavy-handed tactics of the Prefect resulted in few weapons but an increase in resistance. Even amongst those clans which had accepted Roman rule there was now a resistance. It manifested itself in small ways. The road would be blocked. Human faeces would be dumped around the two forts. Their own caltrops would be scattered to maim and lame horses.

When Marcus and his new turma were given the road patrol they saw an even greater example of revolt. A messenger had come to say that a convoy of wagons with winter cloaks, cereal and javelins was on its way north. The Prefect had given Marcus the job of meeting them south of the old fort at Habitancvm. He had given Marcus the Fifteenth to help him. It was an uncomfortable journey south. Decurion Stolo was still resentful. They made a marching camp at the old fort. The Brigante in Marcus could feel the spirits all around him.

With sentries set the two officers sat around the fire. The nights were drawing in. The chill which preceded the falling of the leaves was in the air. Marcus broke the ice, "How is the new turma?"

The Decurion shrugged, "They are all veterans. They seem to think that they know what to do."

"Surely that is a good thing. They will not let you down and when your new troopers arrive you will have experienced men to guide them."

The young Decurion was silent for a while and then he said, "I thought that an auxiliary cavalryman would be safe from the barbarians. It was what we were told when we were training. When I saw Decurion Dives and the dead horses I was shocked."

"They have learned how to fight us. We must learn too. When we attacked the Votadini the other day why did you not use your javelins?"

He lowered his voice, "To be honest Decurion I am not that good. I prefer the spear. It is harder to miss."

"And it is easier for the enemy to close with you. These Votadini wear no mail. A javelin will stop them. I was not very good with a javelin when I first joined. Rufius, my mentor, made me practise each day. It is free advice but you will kill more if you learn to use a javelin."

Decurion Stolo nodded. Marcus wondered if the young officer had actually managed to kill any during the skirmish at the road. The young officer pointed down the road. "This should be an easy patrol should it not? The wagons have one escort already. They would not dare to attack two turmae and a cohort of auxiliaries."

"You will live longer if you expect the worst. I will not relax until we see the fort once more."

Marcus made an early start and they broke camp before dawn. It meant that some of the sentries had had little sleep but Marcus was anxious to join up with the wagons. Their early start meant that they met them fifteen miles down the road. The Centurion looked pleased to see them. "I am Centurion Appius Domitius Gurges of the Fifth Lingone Cohort. I have half the cohort here and the other half will be coming along with the Legate. They are going to help rebuild the fort at Habitancvm. I am glad to see you."

117

"Decurions Aurelius and Stolo of the Ala Augusta Gallorum Petriana. There is a marching camp we just left. It is another fifteen miles."

"We can push on further if you don't mind. We had a night in Coriosopitum. We are not yet weary."

Marcus sent Felix back to the fort to tell the Prefect that they were on their way. He knew that there would be another turma ready to meet them after they broke their next camp. He placed the Fifteenth Turma to the east of the road and he rode with the Twentieth to the west. Keeping four hundred paces from the auxiliaries they were protecting meant that there was a good buffer should they be attacked. The further north they went the more that Marcus felt that they were being watched. It was the absence of birds. As they rode through the bracken, heather and gorse no birds suddenly took flight. When they passed through the elder and bramble bushes there was a lack of animal and bird noise. The animals and birds had been alerted before they arrived. The Votadini were around.

He turned in his saddle, "Vexillarius, are you getting prickles at the back of your neck?"

"Yes sir. The buggers are out there."

"Who is at the rear?"

"Trooper Naso, he is the most reliable man in the turma sir. Only I have more time in. He won't panic."

"Good."

Nothing happened despite their fears. They camped just ten miles from Bremenium. Although it was just three or four miles from Otarbrunna Marcus was not worried. With almost three hundred men, including the wagon drivers, they had plenty of men to use as sentries. He allowed Decurion Stolo to have the first watch and he took the middle. He went first to the horse lines to make sure that Raven and the other mounts were secure. Although he did not fear an attack he worried that they might try to cut out the horses. One of the Lingone centurions had also drawn the worst of duties. It was the one where you were woken up, you did your duty and then you had to try to get back to sleep.

"Quiet sir."

Marcus nodded and pointed east. There is a hill fort there. It is the centre of the rebels. There could well be over a hundred barbarians within bow range of our camp. If you hear a noise assume the worst."

After Marcus had walked the perimeter and seen that his turma were in place he returned to the horse lines. When passing through the scrubland he had found a stunted apple tree. Although the apples were small and sour, he had picked a dozen. Raven liked apples. He gave a couple to the horse. Raven munched them. She was a noisy eater. When she stopped Marcus was aware of a noise. He sniffed. He could smell grease. There was a barbarian close by. He slid his sword from his scabbard. He headed for the nearest sentry. It was the Vexillarius. He saw the drawn sword. Marcus made the sign for danger and pointed left. The Vexillarius drew his sword and headed right.

The barbarian, Aedh, was good. He had managed to sneak into the defences and slit the throat of a Lingone sentry. He had been about to cut the horse lines when he sensed the Roman searching for him. His greased, half-naked body was covered in charcoal. It made him a moving shadow. He was still. He saw the crest on the helmet and knew that the Roman who sought him was an officer. It was too good an opportunity to miss. He waited until Marcus turned to search. The other Roman would soon find the body of the dead sentry. Aedh did not have long. Aedh was good but, in his haste to garner the glory of killing an officer, he made a mistake. He moved too swiftly.

Marcus smelled the grease and knew he was getting close. He almost made the classic mistake of assuming he had his foe. Then he heard a noise. It was barely a noise. It was the sound of a freshly fallen leaf being crushed. It was a whisper of a noise. Marcus heard it. The noise was behind him.

At that moment Vexillarius Ralle found the body of the dead sentry. He knew standing orders. He yelled, "Stand to!"

Marcus whirled around. Aedh had tried to use the noise of the shout to close with the Decurion. His body was in the air with a wickedly sharp dagger ready to strike. Marcus lunged. The Sword of Cartimandua impaled the barbarian. He died with a snarl on his face.

Centurion Gurges ran up, "Are there any more of them?"

Marcus shrugged, "I am not certain. This one was good. He almost had me."

"He did for Milites Flava. He was a good lad too."

They searched the camp but found no others. Marcus found it hard to sleep when he was relieved. That was as close to death as he had come. He ran over in his mind the sequence of events. He had barely heard the leaf yet he had. Was that luck or was it skill? As he tossed and turned he knew that it was neither. It was the sword. It was protecting him.

As the camp was broken Decurion Stolo was in high spirits. "We have almost done it. Ten more miles and we will be home. When we were woken in the middle of the night I feared the worst."

Marcus nodded, "It will not be over until the last wagon enters the fort. Remember that!"

Marcus was worried when no turma arrived to escort them the last few miles. He wondered why Felix had not returned after delivering his message. It was a worry. Had the Prefect also assumed that they would be safe so close to home? They were just four miles from the fort when they were attacked. Arrows flew from cover. One wagon driver was hit and four auxiliaries struck before their shields were hauled into position and lines formed. The arrows continued to fall. Another wagon driver was too slow to take cover and he fell.

Decurion Stolo shouted, "Charge!" and led his men up through the thin line of trees in which the barbarians were sheltering. Marcus would not have charged but the Decurion had made the right decision. He saw the barbarians break cover at the top of the hill. There were just fourteen of them.

Something about this felt wrong. Marcus shouted, "Twentieth, watch the hills to the east. Vexillarius, sound the recall!"

As the buccina sounded Marcus scanned the hill side. It was a patch of black which caught his attention. It was a barbarian with a charcoal covered face. He had made the mistake of hiding by some gorse and it stood out. Marcus shouted, "Attack from the left. Twentieth, skirmish order. Javelins."

He drew a javelin and urged Raven up through the bracken and undergrowth. He knew where at least one barbarian was and he galloped towards him. The barbarian must have thought that if he stayed still he would be invisible. The javelin flew straight into his charcoal covered face. As soon as he fell the Votadini knew that their attack had been seen. They rose and hurled stones, threw javelins and released arrows at the horsemen. Trooper Lanata fell from his horse, struck in the head by a stone.

Centurion Gurges shouted, "Second Century, skirmish order. Support the turma."

Marcus' next javelin hit a Votadini squarely in the chest. He heard a Votadini voice shout, "Fall back!"

Marcus knew that they were trying to lure them into an ambush. "Sound recall! Capsarius, see to Lanata."

The centurion from the Lingones looked up into the undergrowth. The barbarians were leaping like mountain goats. "Seems a strange place to attack. I mean we are almost at the fort. Looking at the numbers who are running they would have been slaughtered."

Marcus shook his head, "They expected us to send more men after their archers. When we didn't it spoiled their surprise. I am guessing they would have waited for us to move and then attack the rear." He pointed up the hillside, "Unless I miss my guess there is a warband up there. We were the target."

When they reached the fort Marcus saw the reason for the lack of support. There were ten troopers laid beneath their cloaks. As he dismounted Decurion Princeps Pera came over, "Decurion Potita was ambushed by a handful of archers. He led his men up into the hills after them. Fifty barbarians sprang from cover. Four of the turma are still up in the hills. Only ten are without wounds and we are short another Decurion."

Marcus told him of the night time attack and the ambush. "I think, sir, we can take it as a compliment that they think we are more of a threat than the Lingones. Where is the Prefect?"

"He took six turmae up to collect the bodies and to see if he could find the Votadini. He took your scout with him."

"If they are up there then Felix will find them but I think they will have headed further west. There is a forest there so deep and dark that horses can barely pass between the trees. As the crow flies it is just thirteen miles or so. A Votadini could run that in half a day. It would take us the same time just to reach the forest. I think that the Prefect will return a very unhappy man.

Marcus was correct. They had tried to follow in the midge and fly infested forest and had come away empty handed. All that they had for their trouble were arms legs and faces covered in angry red bites. Even Felix looked unhappy. When Decurion Princeps Pera told the Prefect Marcus' theory the Prefect had nodded. "I fear you are correct. We would need an army of barbarians to go in there and even then they might fail. I do not like these tactics."

Decurion Princeps Pera pointed to the cohort of Lingones. "If it is any consolation, sir, we will soon have a fort at Habitancvm. The centurion has orders for us to escort them back south to the fort. They have been given the task of doing the ground work. The VIth are on their way to make it a stone fort. By this time next year Bremenium will be made of stone too."

The dead troopers had been buried in the ground between the two forts. "And how many more of us will occupy that ground do you think, Decurion Princeps? This is a war we cannot win."

Chapter 11

Randel was pleased with the attacks. His men had obeyed orders and they had hurt the horsemen. Lessons had been learned. They needed a combination of slingers and archers along with men with pole weapons. The last attack had almost destroyed a whole column of horsemen. Having set up the plan he was confident that he could leave further attacks with his lieutenants. The Votadini had more than a hundred and fifty men sheltering deep in the forests to the west. There they were safe. The grease and herbs they wore stopped the insects biting and there was plenty of game. Even the horsemen could not follow them. Randel had a journey to make. He was heading for Blida. Roman ships had been seen at the river close to the burned fort of Alavna and the horsemen sent a daily patrol towards Ammabile. Blida was far enough to the south to be considered safe. Agnathus had sent a message summoning him to a council of war. Some of Randel's men had taken exception to this. Randel was the War Chief after all. Randel did not care so long as the meeting moved the whole of the tribe further down the route to war. He took with him just four young warriors. It would be a good test of their skills for they would have to cross the Roman Road and avoid the patrols which radiated from it.

They were helped by Roman efficiency. They left the fort at the same time each day. By waiting close to the fort then, as soon as the twelve patrols had left and passed them, they could head east. They would be safe until noon which was the earliest any patrol might return. Randel watched the horsemen ride south. The first turma passed within forty paces of the five men but none saw them. They were not even looking for them. They were so close to the two forts that they were almost within sight of the watchtowers. Randel led them across the road. He had timed it perfectly for he heard the crash of hob nails on the road as the foot soldiers patrolled. Many days of careful watching had taught them the routine. They were ready for a rest by noon and they found a place to hide, sleep and wait. They found a place close by the small village of Morthpath. Randel did not wish to risk the village. He did not know the chief there or his allegiances. Besides he had no desire to bring the wrath of the Romans down on any other village.

They watched the turma as it galloped north and east. They slept briefly and left late in the afternoon. They reached their destination after dark. Agnathus had hidden sentries. Randel spotted them first. They were taken into the chief's hall. Ragdh was an old warrior. He had lost an eye in an earlier war but he was a supporter of both Agnathus and Randel. There were just four other chiefs there. There were Witan, Góra, Vinicius and Old Baglos.

Agnathus looked relieved. "You are safe. We wondered."

"I hope the journey was worth it." There was a hint of criticism in his voice. "We have begun to hurt the Romans."

Agnathus looked pleased with himself. "And we have an opportunity to destroy them. Some Brigante chiefs wish to speak with us. They are travelling north, even as we speak. This is as close as we could manage to make the meeting."

"How will they get beyond the wall?"

Agnathus shrugged, "Their messenger found us. Perhaps they will too. We wait a couple of days. If they do not turn up we have lost but two days. If they aid us then we have a powerful ally."

Even as they waited the five Brigante were in Arbeia. It was a risk. There was a Roman fort there. When they crossed the river they might have to pass a second one but Iodocus was confident that they could manage it. They had bribed some of the Arab watermen who worked the river. The settlement was nicknamed Arbeia because it contained so many brought from the Tigris to work the river. They hated the land as much as they hated the Romans and the gold provided by Haerviu was all the temptation that they needed. The journey east had not been as hard as Haerviu had expected. Iodocus was a resourceful man. They had had safe places to stay each night and during the day had masqueraded as traders of wool. It explained their arrival in Arbeia. They were seeking a ship. The boatmen who would take them would take them after dark and land them on the beach on the north side of the Tinea. They had had to arrange a time to be picked up before they left. They had three days to find the Votadini and make their proposal.

The Tinea was wide and it was tidal where the boatmen crossed. It was rougher waters than they normally risked but the gold in their purses made the risk worthwhile. The white flecked waves would hide them from the brooding fort at the end of the wall, Segedunum. Iodocus handed over half of the gold. "When you return in three days you can have the rest." The boatmen were more than happy to slit throats but the five Brigante looked like they could handle themselves and the leader nodded.

With less than nine miles to go their journey was almost over. They had brought just enough gold with them to pay the boatmen. When they met they would present an idea and a promise that the Votadini would have support in their rebellion. They pulled up their hoods and followed the beach north.

In Coriosopitum the Legate was pleased that he had been promised reinforcements. The Fourth Cohort of Gauls, part mounted, were already across the Dunum. The Lingones had begun work on Habitancvm. The Gauls would finish the work and then the Lingones would regain their honour by rebuilding Alavna in the spring. The Legate could not understand why the river Alavna had not been used before. He had sent two ships from the Classis Britannica to explore the area and they reported that ships could tie up almost next to the fort. Alavna would never fall again. The Classis Britannica would see to that. What was worrying was the scale of the unrest in the land of the Votadini. Already the ala had lost the equivalent of a turma and a half. Two decurions were dead and wagons had been attacked. Normally that would have resulted in a large number of dead barbarians but from the reports it seemed it was just a handful. The most disturbing news came from the two Explorate he had sent south. He had actually sent six but four had been found with their throats cut. The two who returned spoke of an alliance. The Brigante were becoming restless.

The Legate was across the table from First Spear, "Just one little thing like a fallen fort can trigger an avalanche, Quintus. The Votadini have always been seen, by the Brigante, as inferior warriors. They have seen them trounce us and it has encouraged them. Worse, their leader, Haerviu, has not been seen for some time."

"Perhaps one of his family has killed him sir. You know what the barbarians are like."

The Legate laughed, "That is a nice thought, Quintus but I fear a misguided one. When the Fourth Cohort of Gauls arrive, we will send the Third Cohort of the VIth to help them escort the stone wagons. Two thousand men should be enough to build a fort and protect it from the barbarians."

"It will be winter sir, when they begin to build."

"I know, I know. I intend to travel with them but I shall want an escort of horsemen. Send a messenger to Prefect Glabrio. I want their liaison officer, Aurelius, isn't it?" First Spear nodded, "He appears to know what he is doing in this part of the world, at least."

Randel kept quiet at the meeting. He was trying to weigh up the Brigante and their motives. He and his family had lived close enough to the Brigante to be less than happy about allying with them. His grandfather had had a blood feud with them. Consequently, he just listened and allowed Agnathus to conduct the negotiations. Haerviu was speaking, "We are keen to help our brothers in the north. We have more than five hundred swords who are willing to fight with you."

Agnathus asked, "Veteran warriors?"

"Not as such. They are young warriors who are keen to kill Romans. When we begin our own revolt then we will need our own veteran warriors."

"And how will these boys reach us? We are north of the wall."

Iodocus interrupted, "Chief Agnathus there are ways and there are means. I live by the sacred river and I swear that all of them will reach your land." He looked at Randel. "I believe it is the land to the west of Otarbrunna where you are gathering?"

Randel nodded. It was no secret. The Romans knew where they were but could not get close.

"Then that is where they will come. Their allegiance will be to you."

Agnathus said, "Then their presence will be welcome but, from what you say, they will have a short life."

"They are happy to exchange their lives for this land to be free from Rome's iron grip." Agnathus nodded. He knew that there was more to come. "Once you begin your revolt we will rise in the south. We will cut off their supplies. Their warriors may be armoured but we will starve them to death."

Randel knew that they could not promise that. He had seen the Roman warships sailing up and down the coast. It was a recent phenomenon. No one would starve to death. He remembered talking to an old warrior who had spoken of a warrior called Agricola who had conquered the whole of Britannia. He had kept his men supplied from the sea. They would not starve the Romans out.

"There is one more thing. One of the Romans has a sword which is precious to the Brigante. It is the Sword of Cartimandua. If it could be taken and returned to its rightful home then we would pay a chest of one thousand Roman gold pieces."

Even Randel was impressed by that figure. Agnathus could not believe that they were willing to pay such an amount for a sword. Randel said, "And the rightful owner would, of course, be you Haerviu or should I say King Haerviu?"

"You are astute, Randel the Roman Killer. I would be king but I cannot be without the sword. The sword would unite every clan in the land of the Brigante."

Having begun to speak Randel made more suggestions. "Perhaps if you began the revolt first then it would be easier for us. We would break through the wall at Coriosopitum."

"I fear we are not as ready as you are. We have a larger number of warriors but they are spread out over a greater area. Besides I intend to travel to the land of the Selgovae and the Novontae. I wish them to join us. If they rise in the west then we will break the back of the Romans."

Iodocus said, "Do not think we lack courage, Randel. We have fought the Romans since the time of Venutius. The blood of the Brigante is deeply embedded in the lands around the wall. We fought when the Votadini sat in their hill forts."

Haerviu whipped his head around but he saw that Randel nodded, "You are right. When the wall was being built we were complacent. We thought it marked the end of Roman ambitions. Had we fought alongside you, Iodocus, then the wall might not have been built. For that I blame King Clutha therefore I will not rise to your insult for it is deserved. But I tell you Haerviu and Iodocus, we are the tribe who are fighting and if the Brigante do not keep their word and rise then know this, there will be a reckoning and a blood feud. Our enemies will become not the Romans but the Brigante. Do not betray us."

The two Brigante stood. To Randel's ears Iodocus' words sounded sincerer than Haerviu's but he accepted them, "We swear that we will rise and we will support the Votadini."

Two days later as they crossed the Tinea on the riverboat Iodocus said, "You have the gold?"

"I will have it. I have a spy in Eboracum. He has promised to tell me when the next pay wagon is heading north. The Romans have sent more men north and they need payment."

"And your trip to the Selgovae and Novontae? I cannot help there. I do not know the land."

"I know the land but I also know the wall. The western part of the wall is not made of stone. I have men who can slip over. The clan who live there use hide boats called coracles. We can cross without using mercenaries. Fear not. I have much to do but I can now see a light at the end of this long tunnel the Romans have buried us in. Get me home and I will begin my work."

The Prefect summoned Marcus. He held a wax tablet before him, "It seems, Decurion, that you have friends in high places. The Legate himself has asked for you and your turma to escort him north."

"I have not met him, sir, at least not to my knowledge."

The Prefect waved an airy hand as though it mattered not, "I ask you to use your favour to get us more officers, troopers and remounts." More turma had been attacked. Another eight men were either dead or wounded and two horses had been lamed.

"When do I leave?"

"You had a patrol today and tomorrow would be your day off. Why not use tomorrow then you can have an evening in Coriosopitum? The Lingones' bathhouse is adequate but no more."

The turma were delighted to have a night in Coriosopitum. There was a vicus there and an ale house. As much as they enjoyed wine most cavalrymen enjoyed beer too. They were also honoured to have been chosen. Marcus did not like it but he knew that they preferred him as Decurion to Decurion Stolo. It was not the young officer's fault. He was still learning. One day, Marcus would leave the ala and rerun to Marcus' Horse. Hopefully, the frontier would be safer. Marcus was acutely aware that the security of the frontier hung in the balance. The Votadini had learned. If they spread their knowledge to the other tribes then the task of the Romans would be so much harder.

They left with the road patrol. Leaving at the same time as the Lingones as well as the Sixth Turma meant a great deal of banter as the three units met at the road. As much as the foot soldiers appreciated the presence of the horsemen they also resented the piles of horse dung which inevitably marked the passing of the beasts. Marcus scanned the slopes to their right. The Votadini would be watching and they would be wondering why there was a double patrol. Anything which upset the barbarians worked in the ala's favour.

Decurion Scaura was a long-serving officer. He had been with the ala for ten years. He was calmness personified. He was also the Decurion with whom Marcus had had the least conversations. He glanced down at the sword hanging from Marcus' left side. "That is the famous, or should I say, infamous sword."

"It is."

"I heard that the Brigante want it so much that they tried to destroy the ala just to get it."

Marcus could see what the Decurion was getting at. "Marcus' Horse regarded the sword as a sort of badge of honour. In many ways it helped us. Whoever had the sword would always be the target of the Brigante. Knowing where an enemy will attack is half the battle. Oft times the sword was used to lure the enemy into an ambush or a trap."

"I also heard that it could be used as a rallying point."

"That is true. Raising it and shouting, '*Sword of Cartimandua*' somehow made the troopers fight harder. I do not think it will have the same effect here and to the Votadini it is just another sword."

The Decurion smiled, "I was not being critical, Decurion, I like the idea of a sword which has a life of its own. I am a Gaul. My father served as an auxiliary and was rewarded with citizenship. I heard that the sword was Gallic in origin."

"Perhaps. Certainly, the design and the manufacture both have Gallic elements but to the Brigante it was the sword handed down from ruler to ruler until the last one, Queen Cartimandua perished and Ulpius Felix, to whom she had given it gave it to my father. It is a blessing and a curse."

They had reached the point at which the sixth would return north. Marcus intended to ride for the wall and reach it before dark. "Take care Decurion. Your sword is going home. Pray that the Brigante do not know!"

That was a worry. There were no patrols this close to the wall. The garrison of the wall stopped intruders. That was their whole purpose. It was with some relief that they spied the fort at Onnum. They would have safe beds for the night.

The fort at Coriosopitum was full to bursting but First Spear Brocchus made certain that there were beds for Marcus and his men. He greeted Marcus warmly, "Call it a favour for a worthy comrade. You and I have fought together and we do not forget. The Legate wishes you to dine with him and the other prefects who are in the fort. He was anxious for you to meet Prefect Decimus Porcius Sura, Prefect Titus Albus Bucco and Prefect Aelius Plancus Tulla. It is why he asked for you to escort him north rather than Prefect Glabrio. You have something they need: local knowledge."

Marcus groaned, but he did it inside his head. He just wanted a quiet reflective night of peace. His troopers would eat in the mess and then enjoy a night in the vicus. He would have to watch what he ate, drank and said. First Spear smiled, "It will not be that bad. The Legate is a real soldier. He is not here for the politics or for the rich post when it is over. Emperor Hadrian rates him and you know how hard he is to please. If you get drunk and say something stupid, who cares. We are at the last frontier here." He lowered his voice. "Make the most of this time. I have heard that the Brigante are becoming restless. We could soon be between two tribes both of whom want our jewels as decorations!"

The Legate had made it as informal as he could. The six of them had couches and the slaves and servants brought in delicacies and dishes which both tempted and rewarded the palate. The wine flowed freely and had not been heavily watered. It was, perhaps, a measure of the confidence the Legate had in the men around him.

"Well Decurion Aurelius, Marcus, you have three prefects here who are about to step into a world they know nothing about. Start by telling them about the Brigante."

Marcus had had enough wine to be relaxed without being drunk. He nodded and addressed the three prefects, "You know when you passed Lindum, heading north?" They nodded, "Brigante land began just north of there. You have still to reach the northern edge of it. Where we dine was disputed by the Brigante and the Votadini. Brigante land went as far west and north as Luguvalium and the Itauna Aest. It was a vast land. The sword I was given belongs to the last ruler of the land. There is no king and that is in our favour. If there was a king and he had the sword then the whole of the land of the Brigante would unite behind him and our men would be swamped."

Prefect Tulla said, "That is a vast land. There is no king or royal family?"

"Not that I know of and my mother was Brigante but Queen Cartimandua had sisters and her husband, Venutius, had other wives so that there may be. Without the sword they would have no chance of claiming the throne. The sword is seen as a symbol, a magical symbol."

"And the ones who are rebelling at the moment, the Votadini, what of them?"

"They have a King, King Clutha but he will not fight Rome."

"Yet they are rebelling."

"He has no children. This is a fight to rule the tribe. Even if this Randel does not defeat us by hurting us he will be in a position to rule the tribe when the old king dies. Then he could unite the tribe."

The Legate nodded, "In the days of the Divine Claudius someone would have paid a healthy stipend to him and get him to leave the land to us in his will. That is how we acquired the land of the Iceni."

Prefect Bucco had not spoken yet. He was quietly spoken and thoughtful, "You say they are not numerous yet?"

"No. The largest force we fought was a thousand strong. I would say that Randel has no more than two thousand men at his disposal and I think they are all spread out over a large area."

"Then we will outnumber him by almost three to one. We are used to fighting against odds of three to one. I cannot see the problem unless there is something you have yet to tell us."

"The problem is the land. There is one road to Bremenium. It carries on north to the land of the Picts. In the west there is one road heading north. Everywhere else is raw and wild. I know precisely where Randel is hiding. It is within twenty miles of the fort."

Perfect Sura said, "Then go and get him!"

Marcus laughed, "Would that we could, sir. It is a forest so vast that I suspect the Teutonberger is parkland by comparison. In the winter it is covered by a blanket of snow and at other times of the year by clouds of biting insects. Prefect Tulla, I consider myself a good horseman yet I would struggle to get my horse between the trees. There is a partly paved road to Alavna and that is all. There is nothing between the two roads which run from the wall north. Between is a high ridge and trees. If the Selgovae and the Novontae join forces with the Votadini every single member of both tribes could enter this land and we would have no warning. That is why we can't get Randel and his rebels. The best that we can do is keep the road open and restrict his movements. The road and the wall are the two main reasons they rebel. They cut through their land and stop them moving, raiding and trading. Their lives have been changed by Rome and they have had enough."

The Legate banged the table in delight, "I knew you would be a good choice to explain it. Well done Decurion. The Decurion has given you the problems. Now you come up with the solutions!"

It was a large column which wound its way north. The Gauls led and the Cohort of the VIth brought up the rear with the wagons loaded with stone. It was not a long journey to Habitancvm but it would take them most of the day. The Lingones who were waiting for them there and had begun the preparations would leave as soon as the Mixed Cohort and Legionaries arrived. They had work to do at Alavna.

Prefect Tulla looked relieved that the hard work had been completed by the Lingones. The ditches had been cleaned out and the edges sharpened. The foundations for the stone and timber walls were all prepared. At the meal he had confided in Marcus that he feared the fort would still be incomplete when the days became non-existent. The Lingones would share their crowded camp for one more night and then head to Alavna. After the Legate had satisfied himself that the Lingones had done a good job he said, "Come Decurion. I hear you and your men are good horsemen. It may well be that an old foot soldier can keep up with you. Let us see if we can make Bremenium before dark."

Marcus laughed, "Sorry sir, even riding Pegasus, you wouldn't make it before dark but if we put on a spurt we will be there soon after."

"Good."

"However, sir, I want you between me and the vexillarius. I am not going to risk the Legate being hit by a barbarian arrow."

Those last miles were tense. Marcus' troopers all rode with their shields on their arms rather than on their horns. The Decurion and his men were taking no chances. As they reined in at the fort the Legate said, "Ask the Prefect if he can furnish me with an escort of four turmae. Tomorrow I would ride up the road and identify the site for another fort." He saw, from Marcus' face that the horseman was surprised, "Decurion, the Emperor sent me here to make the wall safe so that he can withdraw the Legion. The more of our road that we control the better. I was listening when you spoke. The Votadini are unhappy about us dividing their land. We have two choices, we either abandon the road or we tighten our grip. I choose the latter. Too many of my comrades died in this land to dishonour their memory by abandoning their work."

The Prefect had seen the Legate arrive and was waiting, somewhat anxiously, when Marcus and his weary troopers arrived. As they dismounted the Vexillarius said, "I'll look after Raven, sir. I think the Prefect wishes a word."

"Give all the horses a double ration of grain. I have the feeling that we will be riding again tomorrow."

"Sir."

The Prefect looked annoyed, "The Legate preferred the Lingones' fort to ours, Decurion?"

"It was not that sir. The Legate has decided to begin work on Alavna sooner rather than later. He wishes to speak with First Spear about the building of the fort. He asked you to furnish him with four turmae. He intends riding north to find a site for another fort."

"Another fort?" He shook his head in disbelief. The Prefect could see nothing in this land worth fighting for.

"We have more company now sir. The Gauls are rebuilding Habitancvm." Marcus told him of Prefect Tulla and his men.

"But they are just a Cohors equitata quingenaria. They have but one hundred and twenty horsemen!"

"Yes sir but it means they can patrol the road to Coriosopitum. We will not have as far to watch and the Legate has sent for replacements for us."

Mollified the Prefect smiled, "Thank you for that, Marcus." He led the Decurion to the mess. "I have amalgamated the two depleted turmae into one. The Fifteenth is now almost at full strength. We will use the replacements to form a new turma when they arrive."

Deep in the forest Randel and his men had lit fires. The herb infused grease they wore was only partly effective against the biting insects. Fire was a better deterrent. There were now four hundred men living in the fly-infested forest. Agnathus was tireless in his efforts to recruit more. Like the ones who had been promised by Haerviu, they were all young. None had families as yet. Randel was being careful to protect the inexperienced ones as much as he could. Each raid made them more experienced. They attacked the patrols from ambush. They had learned that if they could lure the horsemen into the woods then they could use cord tied between bushes and trees to bring down horses. A horseman on foot was an easier target than one on a horse.

The ones seated around the fire were his leaders. They were warriors who had shown that they could fight and lead. As a mark of that they had all been given one of the captured mail shirts and a helmet. The shields they had captured were kept safe. They did not need them for ambush. They would be needed when the war came with the new grass.

Ieucher had been with the men watching the fort. He now spoke, "Chief Randel a chief of the Romans has arrived."

"A chief?"

"He rode a white horse. His cloak was red and he had a larger red crest than the horseman who rode with him."

The Votadini had identified officers by their crests. The fact that this one was a larger crest, to the barbarians, suggested a leader. They were right.

Ieucher said, "You remember when the horse warriors came? The first thing they did was to ride up the road and inspect it. Perhaps this chief on the white horse might do the same."

"On the other hand, he might return south tomorrow. But you have given me an idea. We will take half of our men and watch the road north and south of the fort. If we have the chance we will take this leader. I will take my warband to the north. We will wait by the river where it is close to the road. Ieucher you take your warband and watch south."

"What if they head east, Chief?"

"Then we will have to hope that Aedh son of Aedh is also keeping a good watch and can make the right decision."

There were still warriors close to Otarbrunna. The woods there were not as much an obstacle to horsemen but Aedh son of Aedh and forty warriors lived in and around the hill fort. They kept a watch of which the Romans would be proud. A stream ran parallel to the road and the line of bushes there were both a barrier and a shelter. Aedh son of Aedh had a road watch of four men who waited close by the junction of the stream and the road. There was a route to the hill fort which kept them hidden and which would be difficult for horsemen. It meant that forty warriors still protected the hill fort but if the Romans came all that they would find would be old men.

Randel and his men lived much as the Romans did. The main difference was that the Votadini had to supply themselves with both food and with weapons. When half left the next day, the other half would either hunt or make weapons. They had learned that long spears were useful against horsemen. They searched the vast forest for long straight branches that they could use. They made arrows. The heads were made of flint, when they could find it or sharpened stone when they could not. The boys they had with them paddled in the icy streams to find pebbles that they could use with their slings. Randel had an army. When the war came his four hundred would be the core which would break the Romans.

He and his men were sheltering in the Rede, the narrow and shallow river which ran alongside the Roman Road. The river was an obstacle to horsemen for its sides were steep and its course had dictated the line of the road. Consequently, it was not as straight a road as the Romans normally built. Randel spread his men out but he had twenty men with him where the road passed within twenty paces of the road. It was not far from the fort but the river was just eight paces wide and they could ford it. He placed four boys with slings and two men with bows on the bank to the west and waded across, in the thin light of early dawn, to the east bank. Like the men he had with him he had a long spear with a fire hardened tip. It was three paces long and they would use them to keep the horsemen at bay. Four of his men also had bows. All of them had a good Roman sword. Randel and his men were patient. Often, they waited for an opportunity to kill Romans and were disappointed. They crouched in the undergrowth which was five paces from the road. The garrison kept it cut back.

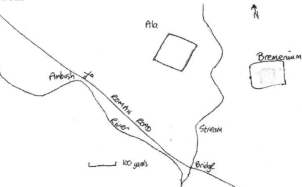

The Prefect had the four turmae waiting outside the fort. Marcus and his men had been given a day to recover. The Legate had risen early. To the Prefect's surprise First Spear Sejanus was also mounted and accompanied the Legate.

"Prefect, I thought it might be useful to have First Spear's views. The site for the fort will be one for a Cohors Quingenaria. He will know, better than any a suitable site." He noticed the other turmae who were preparing for their patrols. "Having seen the land from the back of a horse I am now aware of the problems facing you Prefect. I know the task you have been given is not an easy one."

The Prefect smiled. Like all men he enjoyed praise. "We do our best sir."

"Let us go then."

Unlike Marcus the Prefect did not surround the Legate. He had ten of the troopers from the first turma ahead while he rode next to the Legate and First Spear. Decurion Menenius Drusus Galeo and his vexillarius rode behind. The rest of the first turma followed. There was an autumnal chill in the air. The troopers were not yet using their winter cloaks but it would not be long. The coats of the horses were becoming longer. The Prefect preferred the shorter summer coats, they looked smarter. Prefect Glabrio kept turning in his saddle. He wanted to make a good impression on the Legate and he needed his men to look as smart as possible.

The Legate turned to Centurion Sejanus. "Your men seemed in good spirits the other day. They have recovered from the loss of the fort?"

"They were just pleased to be given a second chance Legate. When you lose so many men in such a short time it affects warriors. When we beat back the barbarians, that began the recovery and the news that we were going to rebuild the fort has completed it. But Legate, we need more than a century to be based there."

"I agree. I intend for it to be half a cohort initially rising to a full cohort as men become available."

Prefect Glabrio said, "And when do we get a permanent fort, Legate?"

"When this trouble is over there is a fort already for you on the wall. The Vangiones are part mounted. They occupy Cilurnum. When the Prefect here has finished the fort at Alavna then the Vangiones can move into Bremenium and you will be based at Cilurnum."

Before the happy Prefect could answer there was a whizz of stones and arrows as Randel began his ambush. They had waited until the ten troopers had passed them. Their targets were the officers. In that they were lucky. One stone struck the Legate on the side of the helmet. The extra expense he had incurred having it especially made saved his life. He was knocked from his horse. He did not have the four horns of the auxilia. Two stones and an arrow hit First Spear and an arrow struck his arm. He would not have fallen had his horse not reared. Decurion Galeo was hit by two arrows. Prefect Glabrio escaped injury but his horse was struck by an arrow.

Prefect Glabrio was no coward. "First turma, stand your ground, protect the Legate, the rest of you, charge!"

The vexillarius sounded the charge and Prefect Glabrio dug his heels into his wounded horse's flanks. His horse leapt and impaled itself on a Votadini fire hardened lance. The tip pierced its heart and its head fell. The Prefect flew over the animal's head. He landed face down in the river. All along the river bank the troopers suffered the same fate. Arrows and stones pelted them and they could not get near to the hidden, invisible Votadini for the spears.

Marcus and Decurion Princeps Pera had been just outside the fort, exercising their horses when they heard the sound of battle. Decurion Princeps Pera shouted, "Stand to! Turmae Twenty and Twenty-one follow me. Then close the gates. Sound the alarm. Let the Lingones know there is an attack!"

Marcus had drawn a javelin and he waited with Decurion Princeps Pera for the turmae to appear. They had all been exercising their mounts and it took but a few moments. Even as Prefect Glabrio was being hurled into the river the sixty men were galloping along the road. Ahead they could see the battle and, in the river Marcus saw barbarians. He pointed with his lance and Decurion Princeps Pera nodded.

"Twentieth, on me!" Marcus wheeled towards the river. He was lucky that the barbarians armed with the long spear had hurried to take on the turmae further north. He leapt the bank and landed in the river. One of the long spear men heard the splash of Raven in the river and he turned with the long weapon held before him. It was an easy throw for Marcus and the man fell backwards with a javelin sticking through him. Drawing another Marcus urged Raven on. He saw that the Votadini were fleeing. They had achieved their objective: officers were down, troopers were dead and horses lay squealing. Marcus pulled back and hurled his second javelin into the back of a young Votadini warrior who was trying to spear one of the Eighth turma. Up ahead Marcus saw the Prefect, without a shield, trying to defend himself from three Votadini. The Prefect had his sword and a dagger but he was wounded. The First Turma were still watching the road and the other three were chasing over the scrubland after the barbarians. Marcus pulled back his arm and hurled his third javelin. One of the three warriors fell. Drawing his sword Marcus leaned out of the saddle. Even as he swung the Sword of

Cartimandua into the back of one Votadini, the last barbarian caught the Prefect a blow to the head. He fell. Raven knocked the last warrior into the water. Marcus leapt from her back and as the barbarian rose took his head in one blow.

He heard Decurion Princeps Pera shout, "Sound recall!"

Marcus pulled the half-drowned Prefect from the icy water of the river and shouted, "Capsarius!"

Numerius Helva Licina leapt from his horse and was at Marcus' side as the Decurion hauled the Prefect to his feet. Numerius pulled the helmet from the Prefect's head. "It is a good job he had a thick liner on. It has just stunned him, sir, but that is a bad wound to the leg. If you give me a hand to get him to the bank."

That was easier said than done. There were bodies both human and equine littering the bank. The ambush had worked but the Votadini had paid with dead warriors. Once at the bank the capsarius said, "Thanks, sir. You can leave him with me."

Marcus ran and vaulted over the horns on to the back of Raven. Vexillarius Ralle held the reins. The plain speaking vexillarius said, "That was a cock-up sir."

Marcus nodded, "We were within sight of the fort! I think the Legate has learned a great deal this morning. If he has survived."

Chapter 12

The Legate, First Spear and the Prefect all survived. Decurion Galeo and twenty-seven troopers did not. It was the largest single loss the ala had ever suffered. Confidence was at an all-time low. With three senior officers in the sick bay Decurion Princeps Pera took charge. He ordered the gates of both forts to be locked and barred. They would recover the bodies the next day. No one knew if this was an unlucky accident or the beginning of some new offensive.

The Legate was the first to recover. He waved away the ministrations of the capsarius. His head was badly bruised but he was angry rather than in pain. His first thoughts were for the ones who had been wounded. "How are they?"

Decurion Princeps Pera gave him the butcher's bill. "I estimate thirty dead Votadini sir. The Prefect will live but he has a serious wound to the leg. He won't be riding for a while. First Spear is a bit dazed but the wound to his arm is not serious."

The Legate nodded, "Then you take command of the fort. Decurion Aurelius, I want your turma and one other. We will complete the inspection of the road. I will not be beaten by barbarians!"

Decurion Princeps Pera was about to voice his misgivings when he realised that this would be the safest time to go. The barbarians would be heading back to the forest refuge. "Take Decurion Stolo with you. He wasn't on patrol yesterday."

"Sir." When they reached their horses he said, "Felix, you and Wolf scout ahead of us. Let me know when you smell trouble."

"Sir!" He ran and vaulted on to the back of Flame. He and Wolf sped out of the gates.

"Numerius, get the Legate a clipeus and fetch him a new helmet." The Legate was about to object when Marcus said, "Sir, there is bravery and then there is recklessness. Your helmet is damaged and we may be attacked again."

"You are right, Decurion."

As they mounted Marcus said, "A plain horse and cloak would also have been a sensible option, sir. The barbarians targeted you. The first four men they hit were all officers. That is no coincidence."

As they rode past the site of the ambush every shield was held tightly and every single man expected the clatter of a stone or arrow. The exception was Marcus. Felix had not alerted them. There were no barbarians. Once they were past the ambush site the Legate was able to study the land. He could see why Agricola had picked Bremenium. After they had ridden for eight miles they saw to the east of the road the remains of two large marching camps. "This is a good site but too close to Bremenium. Pity."

They were about to turn back when they spied a piece of high ground which slightly overlooked the road. The road had twisted and turned for a few miles but after the high ground it was straight. Marcus saw Felix sitting by the side of the road eating something. He gestured behind him, "It looks like an old camp up there, sir. It is mostly overgrown but you can see where the ditches were."

The Legate dismounted. He, Marcus and Decurion Stolo walked across to the old marching camp. "This has possibilities. Perhaps not yet but in a year or so. It is what, fourteen, fifteen miles to Bremenium? There is clear line of sight north. Despite the ambush, this has been a worthwhile journey, Decurion, and your scout is to be commended."

The journey back was complete safely and Marcus breathed a sigh of relief when the gates slammed shut behind them.

The Prefect was recovered enough to speak with the Legate. "I am sorry that you lost men, Prefect. As I said to your Decurion Princeps, earlier, I now understand some of the problems you have to deal with. I must confess I did not expect to be attacked while still within hailing distance of the fort."

"I apologise, Legate, I have let you down. Perhaps it is the site." He glared at Marcus.

"The site is perfect. The barbarians were just too clever for us, this time. I have spoken with First Spear. The Lingones can take on the patrol of the land where the river is close to the road. We can do little about the river. There is nothing wrong with this site and your officers and troopers showed exemplary behaviour and courage. I am impressed. We have seen where we can build another fort but, for now, we stop the barbarians using the road. Winter is coming and we have Habitancvm almost ready. Tomorrow I will visit Alavna and view the site. I intend to visit again but by ship." He turned to Marcus. "Rest tomorrow Decurion, the day after I intend for you to escort me back to Coriosopitum."

"Yes sir."

The Legate nodded to the Prefect. "I requested replacements before I left. Hopefully they should be there by the time we return."

The Decurion Princeps and Marcus were left with the Prefect after the Legate had gone.

The Decurion Princeps broached the delicate subject of command. "Sir I am more than capable of running the ala until you are fit. Decurion Dives has had enough of recuperation and is keen to start work. It is important that you get well."

He nodded, somewhat absent-mindedly, "Caesar was the best horse I ever had you know? He had the heart of a lion and could run all day without tiring. I will never see the like again."

"You never know sir. There may be remounts at Coriosopitum too."

Marcus said, "With your permission I would like to send Felix back south to the Dunum. We will not need him until then and he has my family to protect. They need him too."

The Prefect smiled, "He is your scout. I understand the Legate is impressed with him."

"There was only one other like Felix and he is now dead. Like your horse, sir, he is irreplaceable."

That night Marcus sent for Felix. "When we return south to the wall I would have you with us. I need you to carry on to the farm and be with my family."

He nodded, "I won't say sir, that I am unhappy about that for I am not but do you not need me here? Wolf can still sniff out enemies."

Marcus lowered his voice, "I fear that there is danger in the valley. Domina Atrebus is a fine lady and has good people around her but you I trust above all other. Drugi chose you to follow him. He protected me and you will continue to do the same for my family."

"But sir, you do not have Marcus' Horse to protect you."

"These are warriors. The sword will have to protect me. I have neglected my family long enough. I lost my brother and his family. I lost Drugi. I lost my mother. Enough is enough."

"Yes sir. It would be an honour and I have missed the Dunum. This is raw land up here. The Dunum is like tempered steel. This is fresh mined iron."

Marcus was taking no chances escorting the Legate south. If the barbarians were watching they might try to finish what they had started. He went to see First Spear. "Any chance of an escort of a century for the first five miles of the journey with the Legate? After that there are fewer places for them to ambush."

"Of course. Until we were attacked the other day, I thought that you horsemen had all the advantages and now I can see that you have not. Sitting atop a horse you are a bigger target. The horse is a target too. Will a century be enough?"

"It should be. I have Felix with us. He can sniff out the Votadini and my men are well trained. I am just being careful."

When the Legate left it was in a tight formation. Both sides of the road were potential ambush sites. The Lingone centurion was a veteran and he made sure his men all carried their shields on their outside. Marcus emulated him. It felt strange to hold the clipeus in the right hand but it would protect against a sudden attack. Marcus said little. He was studying Wolf and Felix who were four hundred paces ahead of the leading Lingone.

He was almost startled when the Legate asked, "Why do you watch the dog so much?"

"Wolf has been trained to smell barbarians. He will raise his hackles and drop to all fours when he smells them. He senses them. Do you see that his ears are up and he stops to smell the ground to the west? There were barbarians there but they have moved."

"A dog can tell you this?"

"Wolf can." He turned in the saddle. They would be leaving the Lingones in two miles. "Trooper Naso come here and take my place next to the Legate. You can take the barbarian arrow meant for him."

"A pleasure, Decurion. I get a night in the vicus after this! It will be worth it!"

Digging his heels into Raven the Decurion rode ahead to the Centurion. "There are Votadini on both sides of the road but they are mainly to the west."

"I know they are here but how do you know the numbers?"

"Felix's dog. I know I am telling an old hand something he knows but be on the alert on the way back. I would hate for Centurion Sejanus to lose any more men on account of us."

"Don't worry Decurion. I intend to get back with every man in my century but thanks for the warning." They parted just a few miles short of Habitancvm. Marcus suddenly felt naked without the eighty auxiliary soldiers. The good news was that they could travel faster.

Arthfael watched the Roman horsemen part from the Lingones. He had been seeking an opportunity for his one hundred men to garner the glory of killing the red-crested Roman on the white horse. The Roman horseman with the magic sword who led them was cunning. The dog had almost spotted their presence and he had had to pull his men back from the road to avoid it alerting the horsemen. Now the cover became too sparse for an attack. He decided to attack the Lingones. They had no dog. They had no magic sword and they would not be expecting an attack. He turned to his lieutenant, young Aodh. He held up his hand five times and pointed to the east. Aodh was a bright lad and nodded. He tapped twenty-four of the warband and they loped off after him. Arthfael waved the others to close up with the Romans. The undergrowth was twenty paces from the side of the road but with their blackened greased bodies they were almost invisible. Now that the trees were changing colour it was easier to hide in plain sight.

He waited until the road took a sharp turn to the west and passed very close to the river. Aodh and his men would be in the river and well hidden. Arthfael had a bow. It was a good bow and his arrows had been dipped into his own faeces. Even a wound would kill. The Romans were just twenty paces away. They had shields facing the undergrowth but not all of their bodies were covered by their shields. He stopped and pulled back on the bow. Around him those with slings and bows did the same. He released. He sent it on a flat trajectory towards the nearest auxiliary. The arrow tore through his leg. A second arrow hit the man behind. The slingers struck helmets.

The Centurion shouted, "Back to back!" It was a wise decision for Aodh led his twenty-four men to attack the eastern side of the road. The Centurion saw that five men had been hit. Two had been laid out by stones but his men were still in a good position to defend themselves. He turned to the signifer, "Sound recall!"

"But we are all here!"

143

"Sound it, you dozy bugger, there are horsemen close by on patrol."
The signifer did as he was ordered.

Arthfael hit another Roman and he shouted. "Spears and swords,
attack!"

His men were armed with the pole weapons which would outreach
the spears of the Lingones. His slingers and archers were keeping the
heads of the Romans down. Two Romans fell in the first attack and then
there was the sound of a buccina from the north. Decurion Princeps Pera
led a turma into their flank. The troopers were out for vengeance and
their javelins and spears slew many before they even knew that they had
been caught.

Arthfael was the first to die. The javelin struck him in the side. When
he saw the horsemen Aodh remembered his orders, "Flee! Back to the
forest!" It was the right order and it saved many Votadini. Aodh was not
amongst them.

Further south the Legate had stopped to admire the progress of the
fort. He was unaware of the battle to the north of them. Already the
gatehouse was in place and the first two courses of stones had been laid.
There would be one more course of stones and then they would begin to
add the timber. The Principia building was already built as were one of
the barrack blocks. Prefect Tulla pointed to the auxiliaries toiling over
the bread oven. He smiled at Marcus. "When you return we may have
fresh bread for you!" To a soldier fresh bread was almost a luxury.

The last miles were uneventful. The Legate said, "Thank you for the
escort. I pray you come to see me in the morning before you leave. I will
read all the reports tonight. When I have gleaned all the intelligence from
them I will have a message for the prefects of the forts." He smiled. "I
know that the journey home will be faster than the journey south. I
recognise my limitations."

Felix and Wolf took their leave. Felix was not one for a night in
civilisation. The forests and the wild were his mansio. "I will watch over
your family, Decurion. Should I return when the new grass grows?"

"No. I will send word to Morbium if we need you." He watched the
young warrior slip south. He felt better already. With Felix and Wolf to
watch his family he could sleep easier at night.

Marcus took the opportunity of visiting the vicus. This was the
nearest vicus to the ala. Prices might be high but goods could be bought
here that were impossible to acquire further north. He found a wine seller

and bought four skins of decent wine. Marcus was careful with his money and the farm brought in a healthy income. He was not poor. One skin would be for his turma and the other three for the mess. He then found an alehouse where he enjoyed some of the dark beer they brewed here. His turma chose another one. It was not that they did not wish to drink with the Decurion but they respected his privacy. With his winter cloak around him he did not look Roman and he was ignored by the men who frequented the inn. There were Brigante and there were Votadini. There was even a Selgovae.

What attracted Marcus attention was the Selgovae, two Votadini and two Brigante who were sat around a table. Their furtive actions bespoke conspiracy. They were huddled together and kept glancing over their shoulders. It was almost like a joke, 'Two *Votadini, two Brigante and a Selgovae walk into a bar...*' Except that did not happen under normal circumstances. Marcus was in a corner some four paces from them. He did not hear everything. As other conversations became louder they drowned out parts. It was fragments which drifted to his ears. It was like putting a shell to your ear. The sound came and went. He stared at his ale as he tried to pick up every word.

"Chief Haerviu has spoken with the...."

"Gold for the Sword of Cartimandua...."

"When the new grass comes..."

"Cross the Tinea and make their way north. They will join Chief Randel..."

"Rising of the North..."

Just then some officers from the VIth entered and the five men drank up and left. The officers recognised Marcus and came over to speak with him. Marcus did not have the opportunity to follow the five. What he had learned had chilled him to the bone. He did not sleep well. The fragments he had heard had told him that Brigantes were going to head north and cross the Tinea. There would be an attack in the spring. He had learned of the chief who would be leading the attack but the most important phrase had been '*Gold for the Sword of Cartimandua*'. That concerned him directly.

The meeting with the Legate now became of paramount importance. The Legate saw the anxiety on his face. "Is there some news you have heard?"

Marcus nodded, "Last night in the vicus I saw Selgovae, Brigante and Votadini. I could not hear all of their words but I heard the name

Chief Haerviu, an attack in the spring, warriors crossing the Tinea and word that there was a price on the sword I bear."

The Legate picked up a wax tablet. "I was about to give you this, Decurion. My spies have also reported unrest amongst the barbarians and this alliance featured in the news they brought. They also brought word that the Novontae were involved too. Was there no Novontae warrior there too?"

"No, but that is not a surprise. Their land is well to the west."

The Legate nodded, "And this Chief Haerviu was also mentioned." He looked at Marcus. "He claims to be the heir of King Venutius. It seems the tribe believe him but…"

"But he needs the Sword of Cartimandua to legitimize his claim."

"Perhaps you should have gone south with the rest of Marcus' Horse."

"Perhaps, Legate, but it is too late for that now. Men will be seeking the sword."

"You could stay here in Coriosopitum."

The Decurion shook his head, "This is too large a place. The vicus is enormous. As you know many travellers and traders cross through it. Any number of knives in the night could slip in. I would not risk others here in the fortress."

"Will your fort be any safer?"

Marcus smiled, "You have been there Legate. There is no vicus. The nearest Votadini settlement is Otarbrunna. The fort is already under threat. Any barbarian who comes close will be scrutinised. If they choose to attack it will not be just because of the sword. I will, however, tell the Prefect and First Spear of the threat. That is only fair."

"You are a brave man. Forewarned is forearmed. I have asked for the recall of Marcus' Horse. Vigilance and security along the wall will be increased. Our sentries will have to look south as well as north. This may act as a spur to Prefect Tullus and First Spear Sejanus. I will have messages for you to take back with you."

"And the replacements and remounts, sir?"

"They are not yet here. They should be here by Mensis October. I promise that they will be there as soon as they arrive. I feel responsible for your losses." He rose, "One more thing, I intend to send a message to Chief Randel. Unless he surrenders himself by the festival they call Samhain then I will have the hostages executed."

"That seems a little drastic sir."

"He has blatantly ignored the fact that they are hostages. Their deaths will be on him. Do not worry, Decurion. No blame will be attached to you."

"Sir, I am curious. How will you get a message to Randel?"

"You are quite right about the fortress being a meeting place. Enough Votadini pass through for the message to reach the chief. I intend to have the news broadcast in the vicus forum. I am giving him plenty of time."

With the messages safely in his saddle pouches Marcus mounted and rode Raven to the stables the turma had used. They were in high spirits. They had enjoyed a night in the vicus. It was not just the ale they had bought; food and women were also readily available. They seized such opportunities with both hands. Enough troopers had died to show them what a perilous existence they enjoyed.

A mile north of Onnum, Marcus reined in. "Gather round."

The Vexillarius saw the serious look on the Decurion's face, "What is amiss, sir? Have we offended you?"

"No, Vexillarius but I learned something last night in the vicus which may put your lives in danger and it is right that you know of that danger." He took out the sword. "As you know this is the Sword of Cartimandua. Last night I learned that a Chief Haerviu has put a price on the sword. There will be men who seek to take it from me. That puts not only you but the rest of the ala in danger."

Trooper Luculla suddenly said, "Chief Haerviu! The whore with whom I lay last night spoke of him. She said a Brigante chief with that name passed through and paid her well. I think she told me to increase the coins I gave her. It did not work."

The Vexillarius said, "Thank you for telling us sir but it does not change anything. We are here to control these barbarians. You are a good officer and we are proud to follow you. We will do all in our power to protect the sword."

Trooper Fimbria said, "I think, sir, that the barbarians want to kill all of us. I am not worried about the sword drawing more men to us."

As they headed north Marcus wondered if the sword was a blessing or a curse. So long as he rode with it at his side then it would draw men like moths to a flame. Other men would die because of him. It had been different when he had ridden with Marcus' Horse; the sword was part of the ala.

Prefect Tullus was stoic about the message from the Legate. "We are north of the wall. This is not Rome. My men and I expect to be attacked.

We will be ready when they come. How about your ala? They have suffered serious losses."

"We are lucky. We have the Lingones close at hand and I have fought alongside those men. They are hard men. We will endure. At least the Legate knows when the attack will come. The problem is discovering where the main strike will be."

Prefect Glabrio was less understanding. Later Decurion Princeps Pera would tell Marcus that it was a result of the wound but he was in low spirits when he read the missive. "We barely survived one attack by a handful of barbarians. How will we manage against four tribes?"

"To be honest Prefect it will, in all likelihood be just two tribes. The Selgovae and the Novontae will attack the western side of the wall. We will have more reinforcements by then and the Legate is prepared for the attack. The VIth will be ready. I understand he has ordered the recall of Marcus' Horse. I am more hopeful than I was." Marcus hid his fears about the sword. This was not the time to give that information to the Prefect. He would tell the Decurion Princeps. He owed him that much.

He waited until they were in the mess having their evening meal. With Felix gone then freshly hunted game would be rarer. After he had told him Marius said, "Thank you for telling me but you are the one in danger. It means that the rest of us know the main attack will be aimed at you and your men. You have told them?" He nodded. "Then you have done all that you can. Soon winter will come and we will be snowbound. That will be hard but it will be harder for the Votadini."

The message reached Randel about the threat to his wife. It took but two days. Sadly for him it also reached his wife, Olwen. She was a strong woman. She did not think that her husband would acquiesce to the Roman demands and she was not afraid of death but when she heard that the death would be by strangulation she took matters into her own hands. Although guarded the Votadini slaves who worked in the fortress were able to speak with her. Olwen was a priestess and knew potions. She acquired some deadly nightshade and gave a draught of the poisonous potion to her family. They died, silently in their sleep. The proud priestess then cursed the Romans, especially the traitor who bore the magic sword and she took her own life. When Randel heard the news, his men feared for his sanity. His eyes rolled into his head and he stormed off into the deepest and darkest recesses of the forest. He returned a day later. When his men looked at him with questions in their eyes he said, simply, "I have made a sacrifice and spoken to the god, Cocidius. The god will help us avenge my family." He took the wolf token he wore around his neck. It was covered in blood. "This is the blood of the wolf I killed in the forest. I ate of his heart. I am now the wolf."

The Legate was as good as his word and all the losses they had suffered were made up by Mensis October. They came with wagons laden with grain and winter supplies. They had no sooner arrived than they awoke to a white world. The snow had fallen. Within days it was so deep that they had to dig a path to the fort of the Lingones. The road was, effectively, closed. They would have to exist on the supplies that they had. They had a whole winter to wait and worry about the attack which would come when the new grass grew. Decurion Princeps Pera had the interior of the fort cleared of snow so that they had a rudimentary gyrus and each turma took turns to exercise. The men lived off their memories of their last visit to a vicus and they gambled. Some, who had the skill, carved bones. The life of an auxiliary on the last frontier was an austere one. The forts were even more isolated than they had been. They were surrounded by enemies both human and natural. All they had was the comradeship of their shield brothers.

Chapter 13

Far to the north, as Samhain approached, the chiefs made their way to Traprain Law. King Clutha had summoned every tribal chief. War Chief Randel was expected to present his plans for the war. As he travelled north he was silent. The Romans had shown him that they could keep their word. They had promised that his family would die if he continued to war. He could do no less. He had promised his people, including his dead wife, that he would rid the land of the Romans and so he would. He had with him the twenty warriors who now formed his honour guard. All had lost families to the Romans. Some had died violently but most had succumbed to hunger or disease. They all blamed the Romans. They found the journey as hard as the Romans who tried to patrol it. There were many drifts of snow. It did, however, afford them the luxury of knowing that they were safe from enemies.

Brennus had become, after the deaths of many of Randel's other lieutenants, his most trusted confidante. Randel said, as they dropped down from the ridge towards the ancient tree line greenway which led to Traprain Law, "Rome is not our only enemy. King Clutha is old and harmless but Creagh, now styled Prince, is a different matter. His father, Agnathus, has told me of his tricks and his deceit. We need to watch him. We only eat food which he eats and we drink from the same ale skin."

"Let us kill him!" Brennus was young and a little reckless.

"That would divide the tribe and we cannot afford that. For the present we pretend that we are his friends but once the Romans are gone then he will pay the price for his treachery. His title will avail him nothing."

Creagh, or as he preferred to be known now, Prince Creagh, was happy with his change in fortunes. King Clutha was becoming more forgetful by the day and relied totally on Creagh. All of the King's bodyguards now owed allegiance to Creagh. The three who had opposed

Creagh had mysteriously disappeared. The rest of the King's household took notice and made sure that they did nothing to upset the Prince. The four men who had been faithful to Creagh now reaped their rewards. All had titles and all had coin. Kerryn, the most faithful of Creagh's men, was now Steward and controlled the treasury. Lugubelenus controlled the King's bodyguards and Judoc the King's warriors. Madoc had but one purpose. He was Creagh's bodyguard and never left his side. At night he slept across the door to his chamber. Creagh was cunning, sly and deceitful. He assumed the worst in others. He would take no chances. Only his inner circle knew his plan. It had been cunningly crafted in the time he had spent at court. He had not been dismayed at Randel's success. In fact it suited him. He had one small detail to attend to and the gathering of the chiefs would allow him to do just that!

As the chiefs arrived they were greeted warmly by Creagh. He had arranged for gifts for all of them. It had cost him nothing for it had come from the King's treasury. King Clutha took the warm greetings of the chiefs as an acclamation of his benevolent rule. He did not know it was joy at the gifts they had received. Creagh was attempting to win over the support of the chiefs. It was not vital to his plan but it would certainly make it easier if they were on his side, albeit briefly.

As he had hoped Agnathus and Randel were amongst the last to arrive. It was to be expected. They had the longest of journeys and would wish to spend the minimum amount of time at court. There were no gifts for his father nor the War Chief. He did, however, greet them with a warm, if hollow smile, "Welcome. I hope that we can put aside our previous disagreements. What we do this Samhain is for the tribe."

Randel did not smile back. He had too much honour for that, "Everything that I do is for the tribe. Can you answer as truthfully?"

"As the next King of the Votadini it is in my interest for the tribe to be successful. Remember Randel, you are my War Chief."

"But that does not mean that I have to do as you command."

Creagh scowled and then remembered that Randel's views did not matter. His plan would negate any influence Randel had. He turned to his father, "No words for me father?"

Agnathus said, simply, "I have no son. He died in the attack on the Roman fort. His body was taken by a shapeshifter and soon the gods will answer my prayers and end the life of the creature who has stolen his body." It was an acrimonious greeting but Agnathus had not left his son in any doubt about his feelings.

The meeting began at noon the next day. After the priests had made a sacrifice Randel and Agnathus were invited to speak to the chiefs. Agnathus did the speaking. Randel had been busy fighting and it was Agnathus who knew the details of the promises made.

"Fellow chiefs, King Clutha, I come here bearing great tidings. We have an alliance of the four great tribes. The Brigante, Selgovae and Novontae will join with us at Eostre to simultaneously rise and drive the Romans from our lands." This was greeted with great applause. Creagh was the only one who was muted in his praise. "As a mark of their commitment the Brigante have sent a thousand warriors who, even now, are with Chief Randel's men. There are almost three thousand warriors close to the invader's road and their forts. We have a fortress in the forest and the gods provide us with animals to hunt and protection from the Romans." This was greeted by the chiefs standing and banging their daggers on the table. When the acclamation died down Agnathus continued "Further, Chief Haerviu has promised that he will pay a chest of gold for the sword which is borne by the Brigante who serves the Romans."

When the applause had died he sat and Randel stood. "Agnathus has told you the easy part. He has not told you what we expect of you!" Randel was not in the least conciliatory. He spoke aggressively almost belligerently. He challenged them to argue with him or to defend themselves. The fire in his eyes prevented any such challenge. "I need every clan to provide armed warriors. There must be slingers and archers amongst them. There must be men with shields and, most importantly, I want one man in four armed with a long pole weapon or long lance. We have learned that they are most effective at hurting Roman horse warriors. There are now four Roman forts in our land. We will attack all four simultaneously."

Creagh said, smugly, "And we leave the wall alone?"

Randel stared at Creagh. The man was obviously a fool. "Were you not listening, Creagh? The Brigante will attack the wall."

"I was listening and it is Prince Creagh!"

"I assumed, as I was not addressed as War Chief that we were not using titles. Surely, they do not matter. What matters is that you will be there with King Clutha's warriors attacking the Romans with us."

"I fear that I must stay with the King's guards to protect him. With so many warriors fighting the King of our tribe needs protection."

For the first time there was no approval from the chiefs. Creagh had given them gifts but they had assumed that he would be fighting with them. The fact that he was not worried them.

However, the tribe were united in their desire to fight the Romans. Creagh had arranged a feast. The priests were happy that Samhain was being respected and the food and the drink flowed. If Creagh thought that Randel and his men would become drunk he was wrong. Other chiefs ate and drank so much that they fell face down in their food. Randel, Agnathus and Randel's inner circle kept apart. Madoc stood at the only door to the hall. If any left Madoc would follow them. He trusted no one. Witan and Góra had joined them. They told of the gifts which had been given by Creagh. Agnathus was worried. "I know my son. He is up to something!"

Brennus said, "Worry not, Agnathus, to get at our War Chief they will have to come through us. Madoc watches them. When they leave, he will follow. See, all of Creagh's men are still with him."

Randel noticed that Creagh was being frugal in his drinking. He appeared almost unblinking. King Clutha, in contrast was in his cups and passed out half way through the night. Agnathus and Randel watched as Creagh and his men carefully carried the King to his quarters. Madoc disappeared from the door. When Creagh and the others reappeared so did Madoc. He nodded. All was well.

Brennus said, "I am certain that they will not try something here with everyone present."

"Perhaps you are right but until our chief is safely away from here I will not sleep easy."

For Randel this was a dull night. He was a warrior and, for him, it was time wasted. He could be slitting Roman throats. He watched Creagh and was uncomfortably aware that the would-be prince never took his eyes from him. Randel rose. He needed to make water. When he reached Madoc he said, "Watch Creagh and his men, if any follow then come to me. I go to make water. Have any left lately?"

Madoc shook his head, "I have them all in my sight. If any follow then the Votadini will need a new Prince."

Randel left the hall. He walked a few paces and then dropped his breeks. He smelled something different. Even as he did so the cudgel smashed against the side of his head. Madoc waited for the return of his chief. He wondered if he needed more than to make water. After what seemed like an age he waved over Brennus. "The Chief has not returned. I will go and seek him. Watch Creagh. No one has left."

Madoc had seen his chief head to the right. He walked down the side of the hall and almost tripped over the body. It was Randel. He knelt next to him. He was still breathing. He half lifted him.

"What happened?" Randel was confused. The side of his head was bloody.

"I know not Chief. No one left and yet you must have been struck."

Randel's hand went to his belt. His father's sword and the Roman sword he had taken were gone. The wolf amulet had been ripped from his neck. "Help me to my feet. This is Creagh's doing."

"Neither he nor his men left the hall."

"Then he had men waiting but why did they not kill me? Take me back inside. Perhaps they think that they killed me. Watch them!"

Creagh's face was one of triumph as Randel returned. Agnathus saw the bloodied head, "What happened?"

"Someone attacked me when I went to make water. They took my weapons and my wolf amulet yet they let me live. Why?"

"Because my son still needs you to win the battle so that he can attain the throne and rule the tribe."

"I have had enough of this. We will return to the warrior hall. We leave when day breaks. If I see my father's sword again then I will know who is my enemy." What worried Randel more than anything was the loss of the wolf. He had made a sacrifice. He had killed a wolf. It had not been easy and the wolf had almost killed him. When he had eaten the heart, he thought that Cocidius would help him. He had been wrong.

Creagh was happy when he discovered that Randel had left. Bricius was a warrior who had come from the north and offered his services to Creagh. He was a killer. Creagh had kept his presence hidden from all. Even his closest lieutenants knew nothing of him and the men he brought. Bricius brought the wolf amulet, the two swords and the dagger to Creagh even as Randel and his men headed south. "I could have killed him, lord!"

"His death would not serve my ends, Bricius. You have done well and now my plan can be put into action. Return to your hideout. I will send word when I need your services again."

All the way south Randel brooded about the attack. No matter how much he analysed it he could find no reason for it. That Creagh was behind it was obvious but how could he gain from two swords, a dagger and wolf amulet? The sooner he was back in his forest the better. Amongst his own men he felt safe. The harsh winter meant that no insects would bite and they were safe from the Romans. He would feel safer there than amongst a conclave of chiefs.

Agnathus had not left with Randel. He, too, was curious. He knew his son was at the heart of the attack but, like Randel, he could not understand the nature of it. He stayed at court. It enabled him to talk to those like Witan and Góra, as well as others and to build an opposition to Creagh. His son was not as secure as he thought. Even if the King died then Randel would still have more supporters than Creagh. Agnathus knew that he was no warrior but he could help Randel to defeat the man who had been his son.

Winter in the land of the Votadini was when the old died. The very young died too. The druids and the priests said that this was the god's way of making the tribe strong. It was also the time of the short days and the long nights. The long nights were feared by all the tribes. Only Creagh seemed happy about them. The winter solstice had been celebrated. Time passed but the snow still retained its icy grip on the land.

King Clutha was in a happy frame of mind. Since he had appointed Creagh his heir his life had been better. His new chamberlains led him to his bed. He could no longer satisfy the young women they brought to him but he enjoyed their giggles. As he was laid in his bed he wondered if his new War Chief would drive the Romans from his tribe's land. He had seemed passionate enough. The slight prick in his side felt almost innocuous and then the pain coursed through his body. He put his hand down and it came away bloody. Even as he died he wondered who had done this.

Creagh and his men were in the sacred grove with the priests when the King was killed. They spent the night in a sacrificial ritual for victory against the Romans. When Creagh and the priests went to wake the king, to their horror they found him slain. In his side was Randel's sword and in his hand the wolf amulet Randel wore. It was clear proof that Randel had killed the King! Footsteps in the snow led south. The priests turned and acclaimed Creagh as King.

Only those who lived close to Traprain Law attended the funeral. As they were the chiefs who owed the most loyalty to the new King that allowed King Creagh the opportunity to put the last part of his plan into operation.

Holding the wolf amulet and the sword high before the chiefs he said, "We know who has done this. It is Randel, our War Chief! He has violated the sanctity of Traprain Law. Violence is forbidden here. For that alone Randel should die but he has killed our rightful King and for that, too, his life is forfeit." He dropped his head as though overcome by grief. "However, I am King now and I need to think of the tribe. Randel's execution, though justified, would serve the Romans for there are many of our people misguided enough to follow this man and I would not have civil war. Judgement on Randel will be postponed until we have driven the Romans from this land and then he can answer for his crimes."

The priests and the chiefs were impressed by the mature words of the young King. He had overcome his grief and done that which was right. He had thought of the tribe first.

Deep in his forest fortress Randel was unaware of the death of the King for half a moon. He and his warriors were preparing for the war which would soon be upon them. He had had a new wolf amulet made and the druid who lived in the forest with them had cast a spell upon it. Randel had yet to make the blood sacrifice which the gods demanded. This time it would not be a wolf. He would find some other beast. The choice of animal was crucial.

It was Agnathus who brought the news. Living on the coast where the snow was lighter he had received the news just days after the murder. It had taken him seven days to cross the snow-covered land. "King Clutha has been murdered. You have been named a murderer."

For the first time, Randel was taken aback, "But I have not left the forest since we returned from the council of war!"

"They found your Roman sword and your wolf amulet close by. Creagh and his men were with the priests. I know that he commanded the death but he has managed to place himself where he could not be implicated."

Madoc shook his head, "He has killers we know not of. I should have followed War Chief Randel when he went to make water. This is my doing."

Agnathus sighed, "My son that was is clever and he is cunning. If it had not been then it would have been another time." Looking at Randel he said, "You have been sentenced to death but the punishment is postponed until we defeat the Romans."

Randel laughed, "Your son is clever. I win the kingdom for him and then I die. He knows that I must lead the tribe against the Romans for I gave my word to the chiefs."

Agnathus looked suddenly old, "I am sorry Randel. I have spawned a viper."

Randel squatted by the fire and fingered his amulet. He was thinking. Creagh was cunning but Randel was clever and thoughtful. He suddenly stood. "If I stay here in this forest then I look guilty. We will go to Traprain Law and I will confront the King." He held aloft his wolf amulet. "This needs a blood sacrifice. What better sacrifice than Creagh! I will challenge him to mortal combat. He is known as a champion. He will believe he can beat me. We will let Cocidius decide!"

Agnathus cautioned, "My son is sly and devious. He won most of his combats in an underhand way. He uses poisoned blades and other such devices."

"Agnathus do not think me reckless. I know that he will try to outwit me. I do not believe that he will kill me. When I dreamed that Morrigan made me a dragon and gave me fire I knew that I would lead a vast army against the Romans. Neither she nor Cocidius will let me die to a creature like Creagh!"

Leaving Agnathus in the forest to continue the training, Randel took his oathsworn north.

In the fort at Bremenium First Spear Sejanus was aware that the snow, which was heavier than he could ever remember was having a demoralising effect on his men. Optio Laevinius was a keen hunter. His centurion suggested to First Spear that the Optio take ten men and hunt some game. It would make the food a little more varied and it would enliven the barrack room talk. There had been no signs of barbarians. The daily patrols found no footprints save those made by caligae. The forest to the north of the ala's fort teemed with game and so Optio Laevinius and his ten men set off to hunt. They did not take their shields but they took swords, hunting spears and javelins. As they passed the ala fort they waved cheerfully to the troopers on watch.

"Don't get lost ladies. We are cosy in here and wouldn't want to have to search for you."

"When we bring back the wild pigs and deer we will make sure that the wind is in the right direction so that you can enjoy the smell! It will take away the smell of horse shit!"

The banter was good-natured. The ten men tramped through the snow. It had not snowed for some time. The land had frozen, partly thawed and then frozen again. This was a day with a partial thaw and their caligae broke through the icy crust. It was a three-mile hike to the trees. Once they reached the forest the snow was not as thick. The partial thaw made the ground slippery. Laevinius knew how to hunt. As soon as they entered the forest he knelt to examine the snow. The partial thaw and the thinner covering of snow showed him the distinctive marks of deer tracks. It was a doe and her young. They would need more than that but deer are sociable animals and like to herd. He decided to follow the tracks. The slight breeze was from the north and so the smell of the animals would tell them when they were close.

Randel and his men crossed the Roman road five Roman miles north of the horse fort. They had worked out that less than five miles was the limit of each patrol. It was a route they often took. His men carried icy snow to drop in their tracks as they crossed. It disguised them. On the other side they walked along the icy stream until they reached the forest. Once in the forest they did not bother hiding. The Romans were predictable. Their patrols went south for five miles and north for five miles. They did not deviate from the road. It proved to Randel that his men would win for they were unpredictable. Kerryn, who was leading, held up his hand as they crossed the trail left by the auxiliaries. Randel knelt. The marks of the hobnails were clear. He had choices. They could retrace their steps and find another way north. That would add time. They could follow and see what the Romans were doing or they could return to the forest. Randel chose to follow. He drew the sword he had in his belt and his men did the same. He waved them left and right. The forest was their home. They knew how to move silently. None were wearing mail nor did they have helmets. They were the hunters. The Romans used garum to flavour their dull diet. The fish sauce was pungent and it was that smell which alerted the Votadini to the Roman presence.

Ahead of them Laevinius and his men had found the small herd of deer. They were eating the lichen on the trees. The Romans were so focussed on the deer that they did not notice the Votadini closing with them. Optio Laevinius had his men in a half-circle with spears poised. They were approaching stealthily. They needed to be within twenty paces to be certain of a hit.

The first that they knew of the attack was when one of the auxiliaries plunged face forward. The two men next to him thought he had just tripped and then they saw the blood seeping from the sword wound to his back. Even as they fell Optio Laevinius was shouting, "Ambush!" and turning, he came face to face with Randel

Randel rammed his sword under the groin protector and into the Optio's guts. He tore his blade savagely to the side to eviscerate him. The deer had fled at the noise and, soon, the ten Romans lay dead. Randel knew that the Romans had been sent to him by Cocidius. "Take their heads and impale them on spears. The Romans can enjoy that sight when they find their men. Strip the bodies. We will now have mail and weapons. Cocidius has sent me another Roman sword and this one will kill Creagh."

When the Optio did not return by dark First Spear Sejanus feared the worst. He went to speak with the Prefect. "We have ten men missing. They went hunting yesterday."

The Prefect could now walk about but the ache brought on by the cold made him grumpy. "Why you sent men hunting is beyond me! What would you have of me?"

"A turma of horsemen could search quicker than a century of my men. This may be something more sinister than just men becoming lost."

Decurion Princeps Pera said, "It would not take much to send a second patrol out sir. We could send Decurion Aurelius. He seems to be a good tracker."

"Very well but tell the Decurion that he is not to risk the turma. If the Legate's intelligence is right then we can expect an attack by Mensis Aprilis."

The Decurion Princeps found Marcus and said, "Take four spare horses with you. If any have survived the night in the cold the horses might be useful and if they have not..."

"Sir."

Marcus left the fort with Decurion Stolo. It was his turn for the road patrol north. The winter had actually helped the young Decurion. He had learned to manage his men and to get to know them. As he rode next to Marcus he asked, "Do you think they are still alive?"

"I hope that they are but I fear that they are not. According to First Spear Laevinius was a good hunter. The cold would not catch them out. I do not think that they would be so foolish as to try to spend a night in the forest and as none have yet returned, I fear the worst."

"But the Votadini have been quiet over winter."

"It is just that we have not given them much opportunity to cause mischief." He pointed north. "Perhaps we should have extended our northern patrols." He shrugged. "When you look back you always have perfect vision. We shall see."

They parted where the virgin snow began. As they rode north Marcus saw that it was not exactly virgin. There were prints. They were the prints and marks of animals and birds. Then he reined in. The snow was disturbed ahead.

The Vexillarius said, "What is amiss, sir?"

"Someone has been across here and disguised their passing." He looked northeast and saw a stream. "We will ride up the stream. Look for signs at the side."

It was the capsarius who spotted the tracks which left the stream. "Sir tracks heading to that wood."

Marcus drew a javelin, "Keep a good watch." The tracks led to the wood and Marcus saw more prints further east. They were not in single file and they were hobnailed. He pointed, "The auxiliaries came there and the barbarians found their tracks. I fear our mission is doomed to failure." It was obvious that the auxiliaries had arrived first for their hobnails were obscured by the Votadini prints.

As if to confirm it they had not been in the trees for long when the flock of crows and magpies took flight in a squabbling cacophony of flapping wings and squawks. The auxiliaries had been stripped of their armour. Their weapons and helmets had gone. Their sightless eyes stared at them from the spears.

The Vexillarius said, "Bastards!"

"Put the bodies on the horses."

"What about the heads sir?"

Marcus took off his cloak. He would endure the cold. He would not leave the skulls as Votadini trophies. "I will deal with them." The cold had frozen them and made them easier to handle. He wrapped them in his cloak and then tied it around one of the saddle horns. While his troopers dealt with the bodies Marcus followed the tracks. They led north. The barbarians had not returned to their forest. Where were they going? He knew it was impossible to gauge numbers. They were running in each other's tracks but he noticed that they were making a deeper imprint.

They were wearing the mail. He made his way back to his troop and they had the bodies loaded.

"Have they cleared off then sir?"

"Yes, they headed north."

He shook his head, "Looking at the footprints I think the auxiliaries were just unlucky. The Votadini look to have been heading north in any case and they stumbled upon the hunters."

The Vexillarius spat, "I will stick to porridge flavoured with a little garum and salted meat. It isn't the best taste in the world but it is safe."

First Spear was angry when they rode into the fort. Marcus was apologetic, "I am sorry First Spear as near as I can make out the ten men were surprised by Votadini heading north. As we found no other bodies your lads must have been surprised."

"I am tempted to take the cohort into the forest and destroy their camp!" He looked at Marcus. "Could you find it?"

"Probably but would it be what the Legate wanted, First Spear? You lost a handful of men and that is sad but if we went into the forest you could lose a century. Is that wise when there will be an offensive against us in the next couple of months?"

"No, Marcus, it would not be sensible but sometimes you need to say to hell with sense"

"You became First Spear because you use your head, don't change now. The men who did this will be far to the north."

"You talk sense. When these Votadini attack there will be no quarter!"

Marcus said, sadly, "When they attack quarter will be last thing on their minds."

Chapter 14

It took Randel some time to reach Traprain Law. The snow was thawing and that made travel even harder than normal. During that time, he worked out a strategy. He had spoken with Agnathus before he had left. He was uncertain of the protocol of a challenge against a King. Neither Randel nor Agnathus thought of Creagh as King but Agnathus knew he had been anointed by the priests and therefore he was legitimately the King. Randel needed Creagh to accuse Randel of murder. When he did so the ancient laws of the Votadini allowed a challenge. As it was not a challenge for the throne Creagh could not refuse. Randel would have to make it quite clear that he had no desire to be the King.

They timed their arrival to be as close to dusk as possible. Randel wanted surprise on his side. He did not think that Creagh would expect this course of action. Creagh's iron hand could be clearly seen. The walls were manned and the gates were closed.

Randel banged on the gates, "Open the gates. We are here to greet the king."

It was a crucial moment. If the sentries refused entry then all was lost for Randel. The sentries, however, had not been given any orders regarding Votadini. They opened the gates and admitted them.

Kerryn came from the King's hall and saw who it was. He turned and hurried back inside. Creagh was cavorting with two young Votadini maidens. He was enjoying the power he had attained.

"Your majesty, it is Randel! He is here!"

For the first time in a long time Creagh was surprised. He had not expected this. "Have Judoc ready the men then fetch the priests. We will need to do this legally. I must be seen to be the one in the right." He glanced down at the two maidens. "Put some clothes on and make yourselves scarce. I will send for you when I need you."

162

He donned a fur and left the sleeping chamber. He went to the warrior hall. He saw that Randel had with him less than twenty men. Lugubelenus had his bodyguards watching them. It was obvious that one wrong word would result in a blood bath. The new King did not mind others dying but in such an encounter he might be hurt. Creagh smiled as he awaited the priests, "I am surprised to see you, War Chief Randel. It is not the time of year for travel and I would have thought you were deep in preparations for the attack."

Randel noticed a golden torc around Creagh's neck. He had heard it had been given by King Clutha. It was a visible symbol of Creagh's rise to power. "I came because I heard disquieting news. I heard that King Clutha had been murdered."

The priests arrived and formed a wall behind Creagh. The King felt on firmer ground. "I thought you would have known that. After all you were the murderer."

"You accuse me of murder?"

Creagh could not understand Randel. He seemed so calm. He had expected him to fly into a rage and attempt some harm to him. If he had done so then the King would have sheltered behind the priests and Judoc and his men would have butchered Randel. The War Chief was not playing the game Creagh expected. He went on to the offensive, "Of course I accuse you! We found your swords and your wolf amulet. It was you."

"Then I demand the right to trial by combat. I am innocent and the only way to prove it is to confront my accuser. The one who has accused me is you."

Creagh had been outwitted, "I am King. I will have a champion fight for me!"

Randel looked at the priests. "Tell me, holy ones, what is your judgement? I do not fight the King. I would not fight the leader of the Votadini. I fight the man who accused me, Creagh. Unless, of course, he can produce witnesses who saw me murder the King."

Ninnian was the most senior of the priests. "He is right King Creagh but you will win for the gods will favour the one who speaks the truth. You will not be harmed."

Randel allowed a thin smile to crease his face and he saw Creagh pale. Creagh knew the truth. It was a small thing but there would be doubts in his mind. He nodded, "Very well."

Ninnian said, "It cannot be inside Traprain Law. It will be on the hill of the King."

The hill of the King was a small mound where a square of flat stones stood. It was the place where kings were anointed. Ninnian thought he was doing Creagh a favour for the gods would surely protect the rightful king in that most holy of places. Randel and Creagh knew otherwise.

Randel said, "My men and I will stay outside of the court. It is only right." The priests nodded. "Could I make a request, Holy One?"

Ninnian nodded. Randel went to him and spoke quietly. The priest smiled and nodded. "Of course, but it will not aid you. The gods will decide."

Randel smiled, "That is what I am counting on."

There was a settlement outside of Traprain Law. A warrior hall and alehouse were there as well as the homes and workshops of those who made a trade from visitors coming to the holy shrine. As War Chief, Randel was afforded great honour. He and his men were given their own section of the warrior hall. They ate in the alehouse and they kept together. Until the combat Randel was in great danger. Madoc and the others feared an attack in the night. To that end four men slept around Randel when he retired. Bricius and his two killers sent by King Creagh were thwarted. With poisoned blades they had crept into the hall but there were two men awake at all times and Randel slept with two torches burning. Bricius reported his failure to Creagh.

Kerryn could see that his lord was worried. "Your majesty. We will just poison the blades. It has worked before."

Creagh nodded, "My enemies before were not as dangerous as Randel. I will wear King Clutha's armour and his helmet." The king had metal armour made of plates sewn onto the leather jerkin. The looked like fish scales. The King's helmet was also well made but on the top was a bear. It was a weakness.

Aedh said, "Are you certain, lord? It is heavy and you have not fought in it before."

"It will afford me protection. My mind is made up. Make sure the blade is well coated." Creagh had not fought for a long time. The easy life at Traprain Law had made him soft and flabby. His body was not the muscled torso it had been.

When dawn broke Madoc and the other warriors were relieved that Randel had not been attacked. They helped him to dress. He donned a leather jerkin and then the Roman mail shirt. He did not wear the helmet.

He had two Roman swords and Brennus had made two scabbards which he could wear over his back. He regretted not bringing a shield and knew he would have to use a dagger as an improvised shield.

The warriors of Randel and Creagh formed a circle. Ninnian and the priests waited in the middle. Randle and Creagh approached. Creagh was wearing armour for the first time in such a combat and a helmet but he felt confident. The poison on the blade would ensure victory.

Ninnian waved both warriors forward. "Show me your blades." Creagh's forehead showed a frown. "Touch your blades." They did so. Then to Creagh's horror the priest took out a water skin and poured water down both blades. "This water is from the spring of Morrigan. Let the goddess help decide the fate of these two warriors." Randel had asked the old priest to use the water from Morrigan's spring to ensure that all of the gods were appeased and that they would decide the contest.

Randel gave Creagh a cruel smile. Even if all of the poison on the blade was not washed away, enough of it would be to render its effect harmless. Randel was grateful for Agnathus' advice. He had known his son and his tricks. As the priests made an offering to the gods on the hill of the King all eyes were on the two men who faced each other. Only Creagh's inner circle knew the secret of the poisoned blade. The others were banging their shields in anticipation as they headed to the place of the anointing of the King. All felt that the gods would aid Creagh. He was King and Randel was a murderer. Few of his men had seen Bricius. He and his two killers were shadowy.

The priests finished their sacfirice. The chicken lay mangled and butchered in the middle. The place would be bloody before they started. Ninnian and his priests stepped away. Randel was under no illusions. Creagh may have cheated his way to the throne but Agnathus had told him that his son was a strong warrior and a skilful one. He was almost half a head taller than Randel and broader in the chest. Facing each other Randel saw that Creagh had a long sword. His height allowed him to use the longest of blades. He also had a shield. With just a sword and dagger Randel would need as much of his experience as he could muster.

Creagh was worried. He hefted his shield a little tighter to his body and whirled his sword. He had counted on the poison doing his dark deed for him. He had intended a swing at Randel's breeks. His blade would have scored a line in the material and broken the skin. Randel would have been a dead man walking. Creagh knew that there would be some poison remaining but not enough to kill. He would have to use his skill

165

and strength to win. He saw that Randel had no shield. That made his opening strategy clear. He pulled his arm back and swung it at Randel's left side. It was a long sweep and a powerful one. The length of Randel's sword would keep the War Chief at bay.

Randel was more comfortable than Creagh. Unlike Agnathus' son Randel had trained, exercised and fought every day for the last two years. The last fight Creagh had been involved in was the battle of Bremenium when he had not even drawn his sword. He had fled. Randel had anticipated the sweep. He did the only thing he could. Holding his dagger before him he stepped inside the blow. Creagh's sword hit the dagger not at the end where it had the power but at the stubby sword guard where the dagger stopped it easily. More than that the sharp blade slid over the inadequate hilt and scored a line along Creagh's hand. Blood dripped.

Randel's men shouted. Brennus roared, "First blood!"

Creagh used his strength to push his shield at Randel. Randel was happy to step away. As he did so he flicked his sword at Creagh's breeks. It was the same blow Creagh had planned. Randel's sword came away bloody. It was an annoying wound. It would neither incapacitate nor kill but the blood seeping into Creagh's boot would be a reminder that Randel had scored two hits and he had not landed one. Angered Creagh stepped forward and brought his sword from on high. To prevent Randel stepping in Creagh held his shield before him. Randel had no intention of trying to block the blow. He spun away from it and the sword landed in the hardened ground which Randel had just vacated.

Creagh whirled around to face Randel. The War Chief had seen the sweat on Creagh's face. He was out of condition. He was unfit. Tiring after two blows was not a good sign. Randel knew that nerves would be playing their part. He decided, in that moment, to make the contest as long as he could. The long battle of Bremenium and the battle by the river had made Randel tireless. His blade would dull before he tired. Creagh tried a different tactic. Instead of a sweep he tried a lunge. There was a tip on the sword and Creagh hoped that some remnant of the poison might remain there. The sword came at Randel's throat. It was bare. His lack of helmet saved him. He swayed to the side and the sword slid over the mail armour on his shoulder. He heard the blade rasp through the mail and score a line on the leather beneath. As it did his quick reactions enabled him to stab with his dagger. The armour worn by Creagh was held together by pieces of thong. The plates overlapped and the thongs were covered. As the dagger stabbed upwards it sliced through three of the leather thongs and five pieces of metal fell to the ground.

As Randel stepped away the vision of the dragon came into his head. A dragon had scale armour. It protected the winged monster. The hole in Creagh's armour was a weakness. Creagh was becoming desperate. Randel was like a flea. He would not stand still and allow himself to be killed! He forced himself to slow down and use cunning. He saw the remnants of the dead chicken. The ground there was slippery. He began to edge around. Randel had shown that he would only respond to attacks. He would not initiate them. When the War Chief stood with the slippery ground behind him then Creagh launched his attack. He punched with his shield as he swept his sword in a long arc. Randel took a hurried step backwards and lost his footing in the chicken's guts. He began to fall and Kerryn and the rest of Creagh's men roared. The King would win.

The fall drove the air from Randel but he had enough wit to roll. As he rolled he swung his sword. Creagh's blade came down. It struck Randel in the back. It ground through the mail and sliced into the leather. The leather jerkin held. Randel's sword struck Creagh below the knee. It ripped through the breeks and across the shin. The blow was painful but it also cut to the bone. Creagh roared in agony. Both legs now had a wound. He lifted his sword as Randel took another roll and then leapt to his feet. His left shoulder had been hurt. Creagh was suffering. The blood from the new wound was clearly visible and the King was struggling. It was then that Randel went on the offensive. He used his speed. He darted in, feinted with his sword and as Creagh blocked the blow, Randel lunged with his dagger to the hole where the scales had fallen. His dagger found flesh and scraped along Creagh's ribs. As Randel pulled it out he twisted it. The roar from Creagh was almost primaeval. The man who would be king now had four wounds. The last two were the most serious and the blood was clearly visible.

Creagh knew he had to finish the contest quickly. The longer it went on the more chance he had of losing. The trouble was he was finding it hard to move his legs. Blood was sloshing in one of his boots. He saw that Randel was closing to strike with his sword and so Creagh punched at the War Chief's unprotected head. Instead of blocking it with his sword Randel brought his left hand across and took the strike with his dagger and left arm. Creagh still had strength and Randel's arm felt numb. He stabbed down with his sword. It pinned Creagh's left foot to the ground. The pain was excruciating. Bones were broken. Creagh

167

punched harder and Randel fell backwards. He rolled over. Randel's sword was torn from the mangled foot. Had Creagh been mobile then Randel would have been dead. He lay sprawled on the ground but Creagh could barely stand let alone run.

Randel stood. Creagh was sweating, panting and bleeding. He waited. Now Randel could not risk the contest lasting longer. Creagh had almost got lucky. Randel walked up to Creagh purposefully. He kept his eyes on Creagh's face. What Randel had was speed and mobility. He ran. Creagh swung his sword at neck height. Spinning beneath the flailing blade Randel brought his own sword across the back of Creagh. The scale mail held but the blow jarred Creagh's spine. As he tried to turn Randel lunged with the tip of the Roman sword. Creagh's neck was unprotected save for the King's torc. Randel's sword went beneath it and into the throat of Creagh. Randel pushed. The blade hit something vital and a fountain of blood spurted out. The life went from Creagh's eyes and he fell. There was a heartbeat of stunned silence and then Brennus and Randel's men all cheered. Looking down on the body Randel reflected that none of Creagh's blows had broken skin. The poison would not have worked. Creagh had lost because he no longer relied on his warrior skills. He had tried to use deceit. The gods had decided.

Randel knelt and took the golden torc from around Creagh's neck. He turned and, lifting the torc aloft as a symbol of his power, said to Ninnian, "I have been proved innocent. The gods have spoken." Even as he was speaking Kerryn and Creagh's inner circle turned and ran. Brennus and Randel's oathsworn followed them.

Ninnian nodded. Randel could leave Kerryn and the others to Brennus. "Would you be King?"

"I did not fight this false King for his crown. I have no desire to be King. I am War Chief. When the Romans are driven from this land then the chiefs can choose a king. That will not be me." He turned to the men who had guarded King Clutha. They had not fled with Kerryn for they knew nothing of the murder. "You will now join Chief Agnathus. I command you, as War Chief of the Votadini, to make your way to Ammabile."

Their leader, Carrick, nodded, "Aye War Chief. This was meant to be. You are a true warrior. We saw that today."

Ninnian protested, "But what of Traprain Law? Who will guard it?"

Randel smiled, "These were the King's guards and he is dead. The ones who will guard this holy place will be you and the gods. The gods have shown today that they know the truth and that they are capable of protecting their own."

The feeling began to return to Randel's left arm and he sheathed his dagger. His shoulder ached. He knelt down and took the torc from Creagh's body. "I take this torc so that all will know that I killed Creagh in fair combat!"

Ninnian nodded and asked, "You will not stay?"

"No, I have a war to begin. When my men return we make our way south." He slid his sword into the soil. "Already the ground becomes warmer. Soon it will be the time of the new grass and the north will rise to devour the Romans. When that is done we will return here and give thanks to Morrigan and Cocidius for their help."

Brennus and Madoc returned some time later. "Kerryn escaped. There were three men waiting with horses. They headed north. The rest are dead."

"Did you recognise the three men waiting?"

Madoc shook his head, "No, War Chief. I think they were the ones who attacked you. We will know them again. If we see them then they will die."

Randel nodded. "We will leave in the morning. There are horses in the King's stable. We will use those. I would travel back as quickly as we can. Creagh's plots have served no one save the Romans."

As the snow melted and the roads became clearer so the ala began to take longer patrols. Their horses had survived well the harsh winter. They had eaten grain. What they needed was exercise. The Prefect, now on his new horse, had two turmae at a time on patrol. The attack on the auxiliaries still rankled with both forts and the patrols were aggressive ones. The patrols went to the eaves of the forest. The Lingones took axes and, on each patrol would cut down more trees at the edge. In the grand scheme of things, it did not diminish the size of the forest by much but the trees were hauled back to the forts and used to strengthen them and there were fewer places for the barbarians to hide in ambush. It also showed the Votadini that the Romans had not forgotten where they lay.

Alavna was finished. Ships could now sail up the river and the Legate arrived unannounced one day in Mensis Martius. He had had a few reports during the winter but he was keen to see the progress of this northern outpost. He listened as the Prefect and First Spear told him all that had happened during the winter months.

"We did not manage to stem the flood of Brigante warriors heading north. We caught or killed a hundred but we lost men in mile castles. They have learned our weaknesses. I have half of the VIth ready to respond when the attack begins. From our spies and the prisoners we have questioned we know that the attack will begin across the whole of the northern frontier. The barbarians are bold and have a network of spies. They ambushed the wagons with the pay for the legion."

First Spear said, "So they have gold to spend! That is not a good thing."

Prefect Glabrio said, "You have a strategy, Legate?"

"Aye. We weather the storm of the initial attack."

"We do not leave our forts to fight them?" The Prefect was a horseman. He wanted to take the fight to the enemy.

"Marcus' Horse is still fighting the Ordovices. They will not be here until Mensis September at the earliest. That means we have just your horsemen and the one hundred and twenty Gauls to defend the road. We cannot risk them in open battle. When the Votadini have wasted themselves attacking our forts then we attack them. Prefect, you have to trust the VIth Legion."

"But surely they will be defending the Wall and Coriosopitum!"

"They will." The Legate nodded towards First Spear Sejanus. "We learned much when the Votadini attacked last time. Habitancvm and Alavna now have three ditches. They have more bolt throwers. Bremenium was isolated last time. Now there is Ala Petriana here to support the Lingones. Keep your horses safe Prefect. What you and your horsemen need to do is give warning of their attack. The feast of Eostre lasts a whole month. We do not know exactly when the attack will start. Your horsemen will be able to observe their men as they approach the road."

"And what about Alavna?"

"You need not worry, First Spear. I have three ships of the Classic Britannica constantly patrolling the coast. They will both support the garrison as well as warning of an attack."

The Prefect seemed satisfied. "And how do we know when we should attack?"

"I will be marching at the head of the legion. I will bring the news. It will be as the last time we relieved a siege. The difference is I will have four times the number of men with me. When the Brigante are destroyed then I will bring the full weight of our forces against the Votadini. This time we will follow them into their forest stronghold and we will root out and destroy every one of them. Rome will show the barbarians the price of insurrection. It will be a high price they pay."

The Prefect had had the winter to think things through. "Suppose we could initiate the Votadini attack."

"I do not understand."

"There is a hillfort at Otarbrunna. There are few people there but if we were to destroy it and drive the villagers hence it might anger their chief."

First Spear said, "And it would be vengeance for the men they slew in the forest."

Quintus looked at the map before him. The insurrection had begun close to Otarbrunna. The Votadini had not taken the partial destruction of it as a warning. They needed something more destructive and dramatic. The Legate nodded, "It cannot hurt and, if you destroy the defences completely then it can never be used again. Make it so." He left for Alavna and the ships.

Prefect Glabrio and First Spear Sejanus wished to be there for the destruction. First Spear took two centuries of auxiliaries and the Prefect, four turmae. It would not be a swift job. The auxiliaries would have to flatten the ramparts. One of the centurions had the bright idea of putting the soil from the ramparts in the stream. It would, effectively, flood the valley. Decurion Princeps Pera was worried about an attack from the forest while they were destroying the defences. The Prefect agreed to four turmae, under the command of the Decurion Princeps, to be positioned on the road so that they could forestall any attack by the Votadini.

The raid was meticulously planned. The thaw had melted almost all of the snow and so the soil would be easier to work. None the less they took plenty of tools for the job. The auxiliaries and their escort left before dawn. Decurion Princeps Pera, Marcus, Decurion Stolo and Decurion Scaura all left at dawn. That was the normal time for patrols to set out. They knew that the Votadini would be watching the fort. The Prefect and First Spear had both slipped out of their east gates in the dark. It was doubtful that they would have been seen. When the Decurion Princeps led his one hundred and ten men south on the road they knew that men would be running to take the message into the forest that the horse warriors were doing something different.

Decurion Stolo did not need warning this time. He had learned of the dangers of the forest. Decurion Princeps sent Decurion Scaura five miles ahead of the main body. He would ride almost to Habitancvm and then turn to rejoin the other turmae. They stopped on a line which led from the forest to Otarbrunna. There was a crude bridge which crossed the river. An open and ancient greenway led to the hillfort. In times past, when the hill fort had first been built the greenway had been a path used by the Votadini to take shelter in the citadel. No one thought the Votadini would be foolish enough to use the path with the Romans there but the alternatives were to cross further north where they could be seen from the forests or further south and that was where Decurion Scaura and his men rode.

The three turmae dismounted and watered their horses. Four men remained as mounted pickets and they sat on high ground. The troopers ate their rations and chatted. It was good to be out of the fort.

"So, we may not have you for much longer, Marcus."

"You will have me until this offensive is over for my ala will not be coming home until after the summer. I will miss this ala. The Twentieth Turma is a good one." Decurion Stolo no longer reacted adversely at such comments. He had grown and he and his men were now a team.

"And your sword has not attracted the attention you feared."

"Not necessarily true, sir. I did not expect them to take it in winter but come the battle it will be a lure for them. My turma know. They understand the risks."

Just then Decurion Scaura returned. "Decurion Stolo, your patrol."

When Scaura dismounted he said, "We met a patrol of Gauls. We told them what we were about. One of their scouts said that he had seen barbarians watching the fort."

"Aye, it is getting close to the time when they will attack. The waiting will get to some men."

"And we fight from behind the walls?"

"Yes, Decurion Scaura. I for one am happy for it means our horses will be safe. We have twelve bolt throwers now and more bolts than I have ever seen. The Votadini will rue their rebellion."

The patrol proved to be uneventful. The hillfort was destroyed in one day and it became a boggy and inhospitable land. The area could be cleared and drained but not without the permission of the Romans. Roman authority had been established. They had changed the land; such was their power.

The refugees joined Randel and Agnathus in the forest. They were in the final stages of planning. Brennus said, "We should have attacked the Romans while they were destroying the fort."

Agnathus shook his head, "And that is just what they wanted, Brennus. The War Chief was right to be restrained. Had we attacked then the horsemen who watched the road would have pounced and we would have lost irreplaceable warriors and for what? A hillfort we can no longer defend. When the Romans are gone we will rebuild it bigger, better and stronger than ever."

Randel was distracted. This was his plan and he had done all that he could to ensure its success. The four thousand men he had at his disposal would attack the three forts by the road. Agnathus would lead fifteen hundred men to attack Alavna. He was confident that his part would succeed but he was less confident about the other attacks. The Brigante would attack Coriosopitum and Onnum. The Selgovae had promised to attack Cilurnum and Magnis. What happened west of there was not a priority for Randel. He hoped it would keep the legion busy while they dealt with the auxiliaries. He and his chiefs were waiting for dark of moon for their attack. Much had been learned from their first attack. Randel knew that they could not trick the Romans and an all-out assault might succeed but would bleed the tribe dry. He and Agnathus had devised an attack which would minimize the casualties. Already the men were in the forest building what were, in essence, giant ladders to cross the ditches. The shields had given them the idea and Randel had just developed it.

Far to the South Chief Haerviu was meeting with his chiefs. They met at Stanwyck. It had been the capital of Queen Cartimandua's realm and given that the sword was at the heart of the attack it seemed appropriate. It had become an armed camp. His chiefs were happier about the attack than they had been when the witches had determined their strategy. They all knew that they had tried to attack too many forts at the same time. Chief Haerviu had chosen just two, Coriosopitum and Morbium. They would have to take Morbium in order to get to Coriosopitum. Morbium only had a small garrison. Coriosopitum was a different matter. True it had the legion based there but they had the river to aid them. It would allow men to get closer before the deadly bolt throwers decimated them. They would attack every side at once.

However, Chief Haerviu was no fool. He knew that the Romans expected an attack and that they knew it would be at Eostre. He had used the gold from the paymaster to bribe the Selgovae to attack Cilurnum first. He had hoped that the Votadini would do so but the bribe of the young warriors had not proved to be the incentive Haerviu had hoped. Chief Randel was fighting his own war and not the one the Brigante wanted. The Selgovae were a poor tribe. The gold from the paymaster had been greedily grasped. The Selgovae would attack Cilurnum and threaten Onnum. The legion would have to respond and when they did then the Brigante would strike.

The Selgovae chief who had promised to attack was an old man. Scarth had eight sons. He wanted them to be rich men. He took the gold knowing that many of his men would die when they attacked. He hoped to keep the deaths to a minimum but if the result was that his sons had a better life than he then the gods would approve. He was no coward. He would lead the attack. The coughing at night and the blood he found in his mouth and beard each morning told him that he was not long for this world. He would go out in a blaze of glory. He had eight hundred men ready to attack the fort. His sons had another four hundred in reserve. They would not be needed. When the Romans came from their fort to sweep them away they would melt in the forest which covered the heartland of the north. The forests were their home and they would pick off the Romans as they pursued them. Scarth knew they could not defeat the Romans but the chest of gold would secure the future for his sons and the clan.

As Eostre approached so the patrols from the two exposed forts increased. The horses had regained their fitness and the troopers were well practised in their patrols. It fell to Marcus to spot the first hint of the attack. He was returning from the north. He had taken his troop further north than normal. It had been just a prickle at the back of his neck which had made him deviate from the standing orders. He never ignored such feelings. Drugi had said it was just another sense which was as useful as sight, sound, smell, hearing or touch. After two miles riding down the road, all that they found was a dead bird. It was a raven. When he looked in the sky Marcus saw a hawk. He wondered. Could that be a spirit? After searching the ditches and undergrowth to the side of the road he turned the patrol round and headed south.

Trooper Naso grumbled, "We will be late for evening meal now, sir! All for a dead bird."

His friend, the vexillarius, snapped, "It was worth investigating. Besides, there is always plenty of food. Stop complaining."

Marcus smiled. Complaints were a healthy thing. When men did not complain it was a sign of danger. "I am afraid, Trooper Naso, that our return will be even later. We need to take it easy with the horses."

"Don't worry sir. We have a day off tomorrow. Naso can be first in the queue."

Aelric and his warband had been given the routine followed by the ala. They had waited in the forest to the north of Bremenium. Randel's messenger had told them to bring the warband just before dark. Then they could cross without fear of being spotted by the Romans. Aodh, his scout, pointed to the horse dung on the road. "That is still warm, chief. The horse warriors have passed already. We could cross now. The sun is lowering in the western skies."

Aelric agreed with his scout but he had been told to wait until dark. However, he was anxious to reach the forest fortress and he took a fateful decision. "Very well. Single file."

The fifty warriors stood and headed towards the road. They began to trot across the ditch and the cobbled Roman Road. Already the sun was dipping towards the west.

It was the moaning Naso who spotted them, "Sir, barbarians four hundred paces down the road."

Marcus took out a javelin, "Follow me."

As soon as they began to gallop the hooves of the horses sounded like thunder on the paved road. The barbarians heard them. Only ten men had crossed. The twenty on the road turned and looked in horror at the thirty horsemen galloping towards them. Aelric was amongst those who had crossed. He hesitated. That cost some of his men their lives. He shouted, "All of you, run across the road. Get as far in the forest as you can!" The fear of the dreaded horsemen made the chief forget how to be a warrior. The delay was fatal. The rest of the warband hurtled across the road. Four were caught out by the ditches. In their panic, they stumbled across them and fell on the road. The troopers covered the four hundred paces faster than the Votadini could cross the road. Marcus and the first six troopers all hurled their javelins. Four barbarians were hit. Capsarius Licina led two men to slay the four who had fallen foul of the ditch. Marcus drew another javelin and did not even have to throw it. He rammed it in the back of a barbarian who was racing towards the forest. Pulling his arm back he then threw it ten paces into the back of a luckless Votadini who had almost made the trees.

The auxiliaries had been clearing the trees which lay close to the road and Marcus took a risk. "After them!" Taking another javelin, he threw it at a Votadini who managed to dive over a fallen log. The javelin pinned his leg to the tree. The three warriors who had been with him turned to face the horsemen while the unfortunate youth attempted to pull the javelin from his leg. In one motion Marcus picked up his shield and drew his sword. He did not break stride but swung his sword sideways to slice through the skull of one of the three men. He took a blow from a sword on his shield as Raven tried to bite the third. Trooper Piso's javelin hit the warrior who had struck Marcus' shield and Marcus leaned out of his saddle to plunge the Sword of Cartimandua deep into the chest of the third.

Looking around he saw that the Votadini were too deep in the woods to risk following. "Sound recall!"

He dismounted and went to the pinned youth. In his struggle to free himself he had torn a larger hole and his lifeblood was pumping away.

"What is your clan and who is your chief?" The youth tried to spit but the effort was too much and he expired. Marcus reached down and pulled the amulet from the neck of the Votadini. It was a bear. He tossed it to the Vexillarius. "Clan of the bear. See how many died. I estimate there were fifty or so who crossed the road."

It was pitch black by the time they entered the fort. The Prefect, Camp Prefect and Decurion Princeps were all waiting anxiously.

"We were worried. What happened?"

"I went further north than normal. I thought something was wrong. As we came back south we surprised a warband making their way to the forest. They were the clan of the bear. We managed to kill twenty-eight of them. Twenty-two or more escaped. We had no casualties."

"Then our regular routine is making us vulnerable. Decurion Dives, beginning tomorrow I want the times of the patrols and the length of them varying. We will begin to be unpredictable."

Over the next few days their changed times yielded results. None were as dramatic as Marcus' but messengers were intercepted and small warbands hunted down. Decurion Princeps Pera thought it was a drop in the ocean but it had to have a demoralising effect on the barbarians.

176

Chapter 15

It was Scarth who began the attacks. He had agreed that it would be
Eostre when they attacked. He knew nothing about the dark of moon and
he was an honourable warrior. He sent four men on ponies to ride to
Stanwyck and tell Chief Haerviu. That had been three days since. He had
coughed up more blood lately and that had influenced him. He gathered
his warband around him. He would not risk a frontal assault on the fort.
That would invite slaughter. He intended to take as many men back north
as he could. The fort guarded the section of the Tinea where the wall
went across it. There was a bridge and it was a vital crossing. Scarth had
some young warriors who were good swimmers. He spoke to them first.
"Go to the river north of the bridge. Use the debris from the trees and
float down. Your task is to scale the bridge and attack the guards there."
He smiled at the young warriors. "Do not waste your lives. You are there
to draw the Romans to that side of the fort. Once we hear the Roman
horns then we will attack.

The fifty or so youths were excited to be given the honour of
initiating the attack. "We will show the Brigante that the Selgovae know
how to fight!"

They left for they would have a long journey to reach the river and
then enter the water. The old chief addressed the rest, "The Romans have
a ditch and they have their ramparts. We will attack before dawn so that
we can get close to the walls. It is their bolt throwers which are the
danger. There are gates at the small towers. I intend for us to attack
those. We know that each of the gate forts has eight men. The towers
between have six. I would have us capture four of the gate forts and
destroy their gates. Once we have captured the gates then you, Burgos,
will head towards the west and capture as much of the wall as you can. I
will take the rest east. We can then use the Roman's own wall to attack
the fort."

His men were more confident of success than the old warrior was. He had no doubt that they could capture the four gate forts but Cilurnum was a different matter. "One hundred men will attack each gate fort. The rest of the warband will be in reserve. When the gates are down then they can head south and raid." The warband had some hill ponies. Once the gates were open then the land to the south was ripe for raiding.

His men moved through the trees until the white wall could be seen ahead. The fort lay to the east. Between the gate forts were small towers. In total, the Selgovae would have no more than a hundred men to fight. In theory, it would be easy but they had a ditch to cross. His scouts had reported that there were no stakes there. The sides were steep. He had slingers and archers ready to keep down the heads of the Romans when his men attacked. The glow in each turret showed that there were men inside and they were keeping warm. He raised his sword and they moved forward. Scarth had a shirt made of metal plates sewn onto the leather. His helmet was old but comfortable and he had a large round shield. He raised his sword and waved his line of men forward. They crept over the open ground.

The sentry was clearly visible. They had watched his routine. He left the turret of the gate fort and walked to the next turret. There he waved at the sentry who watched from the turret. That done he walked back. Scarth and his men timed their movements so that they only moved when the sentry had his back to them. Then they froze like shadows on the ground. In this way they approached the ditch. It was when they reached the ditch that they heard the buccinas to the east. His boys had attacked. The Romans must have had some sort of system for the sentries looked to the fort when they heard the buccina. It meant something to them. In those few moments the men in the mile castles signed their own death warrants for the Selgovae swarmed across the ditch and reached the wall. Using shields, they boosted warriors up and over the walls. Scarth was the first. Already dawn was breaking in the east. Aelric brought his sword around. It struck the auxiliary's shield but the man knew his business. He jerked his spear forward and it tore through Scarth's left arm. The old chief ignored the blood and brought his sword down across the soldier's neck. He fell to the passageway below. More of his men had joined him. The Romans fought bravely. There would be no surrender and ten of the Selgovae died before they took the turret.

The Romans who had been asleep now ran up the ladder to fight their attackers. They knew the interior of the mile castle and eight more

Selgovae died before all opposition ceased. They had taken their first gate fort. Scarth was on the wall. He shouted down, "Open the gates and bring the reserves." Opening the door to the wall he led his oathsworn to the small turret which lay ahead of them. "Grab as many Roman shields as you can. They have bolt throwers and they will try to use them against us!"

The handful of men in the small turret had seen the fate of the milecastle and they had fled to the fort. The two turrets were empty. There was no opposition but the Romans in the fort had been warned. The Selgovae could expect opposition.

The young warriors who had swum the river had exceeded all of Scarth's expectations. The old chief had expected to distract the garrison and allow his men to get close to the fort before discovery. Instead, the lithe young warriors had managed to kill the sentries at the bridge and capture it. They even managed to turn the bolt thrower around and use it on the gate into the fort.

Prefect Decimus Porcius Sura had been awaiting an attack. He slept with his mail close by his pallet. Hearing the alarm, he had dressed, grabbed his sword and run to the river. The buccina had told him where the attack had begun. When he reached the centurion at the gate he saw three men slain by a bolt and the bolt thrower wrecked. Centurion Helva said, "It was lucky hit Prefect. They have the bridge and they are using the bolt thrower. Luckily, they are slow at loading. Down sir!" A bolt flew towards them. The first ones had been killed because the Romans were not expecting to have their own weapons used against them. Now they were watching.

"Centurion Helva, take two centuries and clear the bridge."

"Sir."

He turned and shouted, "Centurion Vetus fetch another bolt thrower. Bring one from the north-east tower."

First Spear hurried up the ladder, "I was making sure the sentries in the other turrets were all closed up sir."

The Prefect nodded, "This must be Brigante. They are coming from the south." Another bolt flew from the bridge. This time it was aimed across the fort. The barbarians were learning. Once again luck was with the half-naked warriors. It tore through three Vangiones on the turret just forty paces from them. "How in Hades did they capture the bridge? Were the sentries asleep?"

179

First Spear peered across the river. "Sir, we still hold the far end of the bridge. These came down the river. They aren't Brigante. They are Votadini or Selgovae."

Just then there was a cry of alarm from the north-west turret. A voice shouted, "Sir, the barbarians have crossed the wall. They have captured the milecastle."

It was the most disastrous of news. The Prefect turned to Centurion Vetus as he and his men hauled the bolt thrower into the turret. "Centurion Vetus, take charge here. When the bridge is cleared have Centurion Helva bring his two centuries and reinforce the west wall."

"Sir!"

"Come on First Spear you and I will earn our pay this day."

By the time they reached the turret they could see the barbarians racing down the wall to the north-west turret. The garrison of the small turret were there. First Spear knew every man in the fort. He jabbed a finger at the Optio who had been in the turret. "Optio Flaccus, report."

"They must have sneaked close to the mile castle, First Spear. The first that we knew was when we heard fighting. They took Cotta's turret. I knew we had to warn you sir and so we barred the doors and came here." The Optio was worried. To abandon a turret on a wall was a grey area.

First Spear nodded, "You did the right thing Optio." He turned to the men who had been guarding the turret. "Get that bolt thrower. Aim it at the door on Optio Flaccus' turret."

The Prefect peered west. The new day was not far away and the light was becoming greyer. He could make out barbarians on horses flooding out of the gates. They appeared to be a large warband. The wall had been breached. "Take charge here, First Spear." The Prefect hurried down the ladder. He waved over a Decurion from the horse section. "Decurion Pavo, send two troopers to Coriosopitum. Warn the Legate that the wall has been breached. Barbarians are heading south."

"Sir."

By the time he had returned to the turret the Selgovae had broken through the gate. Whoever was leading them was not a wild unthinking barbarian. The men who advanced had taken the time to grab auxilia shields and were advancing in what looked remarkably like a Roman tortoise. Behind them came the rest of the warband with the own shields held aloft.

First Spear said, "Right Optio, let's show them that there is more to being a Roman soldier than just carrying a shield."

"Sir!" The optio adjusted his aim and then shouted, "Release!"

The bolt flew straight and true. It ploughed through the shield as though it was not there. Scarth's wound had slowed him down but he still led his warband. The bolt tore through his mail and his body. He would not die of the coughing sickness. The bolt carried on through the next two men and finally stopped when it struck the spine of the fourth warrior. Their chief was down but his oathsworn had their blood up. They closed ranks and moved faster. The ageing chief had slowed them up and now they were able to run. It affected the bolt thrower. The next bolt did not hit the Roman shields but struck those following. Once again it hit five men.

First Spear shouted, "Javelins!"

As the javelins struck there was a rattle like hailstones on a roof. They were less effective than the bolt although they made the shields unwieldy. The warband struck the gate below the turret. First Spear said, "I'll go below sir and give them a Vangione welcome!" He turned and shouted, "Centurion Helva! I need your men now!"

The Prefect admired the courage of the Selgovae. They were coming up against disciplined men who wore mail and were well armed. He saw that most of the barbarians were half-naked. Any strike would cause a wound. The bolt thrower cracked again and another file of barbarians fell. The javelins were having more effect against the ones with the small Selgovae shields and their numbers were being thinned. The Prefect was amazed when one warrior, struck by a javelin merely pulled it from his arm and hurled it back. It missed the Prefect by a handspan.

In the turret below the Prefect, First Spear was organising the men to welcome the barbarians. The turret was wide enough for eight men: a contubernium. "Helva with me. I want three lines of men. Listen for my command! Second and third ranks, use spears. The rest give them your swords!"

They would fight like legionaries. They did not have the scuta of the legions nor the short stabbing sword, the gladius, but First Spear had served with the IXth and knew how to fight. The door gave way with a crash and the barbarians poured in. The narrow door meant that they had to come in one at a time and that guaranteed their death. The first one was skewered by Centurion Helva as the exultant Selgovae physically hurled himself at the waiting Vangiones. With their chief dead and their most experienced warriors slaughtered the barbarians had no one to organise them. They entered the turret and they died. By the time dawn broke the attack on the fort was over.

Prefect Decimus Porcius Sura descended the ladder to First Spear. "Take Centurion Helva's men and clear the wall. I will take the horsemen out and we will try to plug the gap."

"Sir."

The Prefect stepped into the parade ground and shouted, "Decurion Princeps Celsa, mount your men." This was where a mixed cohort was like gold. He had over a hundred horsemen. He would ignore the ones already south of the fort and the wall. His task was to regain control of the frontier. He led his men west. They did not gallop. With javelins held at the ready they rode down any Selgovae they came across. The Prefect glanced over to the wall. He saw that First Spear had recaptured the first milecastle. He waved his javelin. "Decurion Dorsuo, take your turma and take the next milecastle."

As the turma peeled off the Prefect hoped that First Spear and the Decurion would arrive at the same time. He saw that the next two mile castles had also fallen. Their gaping gates shouted it loud and clear. He knew that the Prefect at Broccolitia was a sound commander. His Tungrians would hold on but they had no horses. Prefect Sura had to plug the gap.

As they passed the next milecastle he sent another turma to take it. He now had just two turmae. If they had taken more than one more milecastle then he would struggle to retake them. Then he saw, in the dawning light that only one more mile castle had its gates open. A battle was taking place at the next one. Early sunbeams glinted off swords and spears.

"Decurion Princeps, let us retake this mile castle!" They wheeled to the north and headed towards the gate. The Selgovae had already left and the milecastle was empty.

The Decurion Princeps shouted, "Horse holders! Chosen man, get those gates closed."

Prefect Sura shouted, "Second turma, with me." He hurried up the ladder. The dead garrison lay butchered and naked. Their weapons and mail had been taken. The prefect knew that the assault on the next mile castle was his priority. He led the thirty men of the Second Turma towards the battle at the next mile castle. Each turret they passed told the same story. The auxiliaries had fought as long and as hard as they could but Roman courage had not been enough against overwhelming numbers. By the time they reached the mile castle the Tungrians had prevailed. The Selgovae had simply run out of men.

The Prefect greeted the bloody centurion he met, "Well done, Centurion. The gap is closed. I will take my horsemen and hunt down those who are south of us. Have the turrets and mile castles garrisoned. This is just the beginning."

Hours later when Prefect Sura finally rode into Cilurnum with his weary horsemen it was with the satisfying knowledge that they had hunted down and killed every warrior who had crossed the wall. The Selgovae had paid a heavy price but so had the Romans. More than a hundred and twenty Romans lay dead and the wall was now more thinly manned than it had been.

In Coriosopitum the Legate heard the news of the attack. He had expected it and, in some ways, it was a relief that it had come. He now had to worry about the attack from the Brigante. When would they strike? He sent messengers north to warn Habitancvm and Bremenium of the insurrection and then walked the walls with First Spear.

"Now we play the game, Quintus. Do I commit the VIth north to Cilurnum or wait here?"

"I know you have made that decision already sir. We wait. It is as clear as the nose on your face. The Prefect at Cilurnum will tell us if they need help and we have heard nothing from Onnum."

"You are right Quintus, I am just seeking reassurance that our plans are the right ones."

"It is those poor buggers to the north I fear for, sir. We have help all around us here. Those four forts are little islands in a sea of barbarians."

When Chief Haerviu received Scarth's message he put his plan into operation. Like the other tribal leaders, he had learned to respect the Romans. Frontal assaults did not work. He had a large warband waiting to the south between Cataractonium and Morbium. He wanted the road cut. The rest of his warband were gathered at Morbium. The fort there was not a large one but it was vital. Chief Haerviu planned on destroying the bridge and cutting off the wall and the north-eastern corner of the province. Like Scarth he did not plan on waiting for dark of moon. He assumed that Chief Randel and the Votadini would be rising already. Eostre had been the time they had all agreed.

The Legate had sent for the Cohors Primae Aquitanorum some time ago. They had been delayed in Lindum where there had been some unrest. The Prefect was keen to reach the wall. He knew how urgent his mission was. Perhaps it was the fact that they were not only south of the wall but also south of the Dunum but whatever the reason the cohort was not as alert as it might have been. They knew that Morbium was just five miles away and, in their minds, they were already enjoying a hot cooked meal and a night where they did not have to build a marching fort.

The Brigante had good intelligence. They could move faster than the Romans and they had tracked the cohort as it had first marched to Cataractonium and then left. Consequently, the warband was in place even before the cohort had left the Roman fort. The Brigante had chosen their ambush site well. There was a rocky crag which overlooked the road. The IXth Legion had built the road as straight as they could and had used the high ground whenever possible. The crag was not in the way of the road and so they had left it there. It was covered in scrubby gorse, heather and bracken in equal measure. On the other side of the road were stands of scrubby bushes. Elisedd led the warband. He was a seasoned warrior. He had enjoyed victories and suffered defeats. He had learned from both. He had his slingers and archers amongst the rocks of the crag. They would initiate the attack. When the Romans turned to face it then he would launch his main attack with sword and spear.

The first to die was Prefect Lepida. His fine mail and plume made him a target for the young slingers. Four stones struck him and he died instantly. Had First Spear not turned to see where the attack had begun then he too might have lived. As it was he was hit in the face by a stone. The experienced centurion had a mercifully quick death. The next most senior, Centurion Buteo, saw men dying. He took charge. They had been marching in a column of fours. "Second and Fourth Centuries turn right; Third and Fifth Centuries turn left. Lock shields!"

The shield the Cohors Primae Aquitanorum used was not as effective as the scutum but as soon as the shields turned to face the arrows and stones then the casualties stopped.

Centurion Buteo shouted. "Cohors Primae Aquitanorum, hold! Keep tight!"

Elisedd saw that the Romans had not fallen into his trap. He had a choice; he could back off or he could continue with the attack. Chief Haerviu was already in place waiting for darkness to attack the fort. If the Roman auxiliaries reached the fort intact then it would ruin the tribe's chances. "Charge!"

The barbarians burst from cover. They were eager to emulate the success of the slingers and archers. They ran recklessly.

"Third and Fifth Centuries, javelins!"

One hundred and forty javelins flew through the air. The Brigante had little mail. A few had shields and one or two had helmets. Eighty javelins found flesh. "Third and Fifth Centuries, javelins!" Once again the javelins were effective but the Brigante closed with the Romans and hurled themselves at the shields. Many were impaled.

Second Century, turn and support the Third and the Fifth."

As the Brigante tried to fight and claw their way into the auxiliaries ranks the Second Century began to hurl their javelins over the heads of their comrades into the attacking barbarians. The slingers and arches had almost used their ammunition up and they could not resist joining their more experienced comrades. They ran down from the crag towards the Fourth Century. Their centurion had been waiting for just such an opportunity. "Ready javelins!" He waited until the eighty or so boys and youths were just thirty paces away and then he shouted, "Release!" More than half the barbarians fell. The centurion saw the opportunity to end the attack. "At them!" The stunned slingers and archers stood no chance. A dozen managed to flee but the rest were butchered. "About face!"

Centurion Buteo saw that the Third Century was tiring. "Fourth and Second, javelins. Fifth Century replace the Third. Third Century retire, now!"

Only the Roman army could perform this manoeuvre. It required great training and trust in the men behind you. One hundred and forty javelins sailed through the air as the Fifth Century stepped into the places vacated by the Third.

Elisedd saw that his ambush had failed. Along the road more than two hundred of his warriors lay dead or wounded. He shook his head in disbelief. The control the Romans had over their men was remarkable. He took the cow horn from around his neck and blew two blasts. Most of the Brigante heard it and obeyed. A dozen had blood in their heads and they fought on until they were butchered. Elisedd pulled his men north to block the road.

When it was clear that the barbarians had fled Centurion Buteo said, "Capsarii, see to the wounded. Optios report the numbers of dead and wounded. Fetch any undamaged javelins. We may need them."

Centurion Buteo would need all of his experience to extricate the cohort from this disaster. The sun was setting. There was no chance of making a camp while the barbarians stood blocking the road. He shouted, "Centurions, to me!"

The four of them moved away from the men. What Centurion Buteo had to say was not for the ears of all. "First of all, well done. Not many cohorts could have survived an ambush like that but we are not out of it yet. We have a couple of choices. I will be honest I don't fancy any of them. We could try to make a camp here but I doubt that the Brigante will let us. We could head back to Cataractonium. That is a long walk and I have a feeling that we were stopped for a purpose." He saw one of the capsarius give one of the auxiliaries a warrior's death. They had been hurt. "The last choice is to eat and wait until dark. Then push on to Morbium."

"In the dark?"

"What difference will the dark make? We march, double time with shields protecting our sides and our heads. We have five miles to go. If we double time we can be there in just over an hour."

"What about the Prefect and the other dead?"

"We leave them. They would understand. So, what do you think?" The other three nodded their agreement. "Good then have the men eat. Take the valuables from our dead and all of our weapons. I don't want to leave anything the barbarians can use."

His optio came up to him, "Twenty-five dead, sir including First Spear and the Prefect. Forty wounded. We will need litters for four of them."

"Right. We leave when it is dark. Have the lads fed and watered. We are going to fight our way to the fort."

Chief Haerviu received the message that Elisedd had managed to stop the Roman reinforcements. It made the attack on the fort even more vital. As soon as it was dark he waved his arm and the order was repeated by his chiefs. All around the fort men moved forward. It was a single line. They knew the effect of a bolt sent through a mass of men. Men would die but they would die singly. The river was not particularly deep at Morbium. Before the Romans had come men had forded it. There was a small island in the middle where travellers made offerings to the gods. The first ones across each had an offering. The sound of the water disguised the sound of men splashing through the water. On the three landward sides men were creeping in the dark towards the walls. Those who moved through the vicus had the advantage of cover and shelter. Even so they were spotted. The Prefect had been warned of an attack and he had double sentries.

"Stand to!"

The fort was filled with the sound of running feet as the rest of the garrison ran to the towers and the walls. Prefect Bassa had three javelins already to hand. The barbarians were too far away for them to be of use yet but he heard the snap of the bolt throwers. The fort had twelve of them. The two at the bridge gate had the most effect. Although the bolts only hit two men the two men pulled their comrades with them as they fell to their deaths. The next warriors to the bridge did not even make it half way. If the Brigante were to succeed it would not be over the bridge. When they reached the ditches, they came within range of the javelins. Without armour the Brigante died but sheer weight of numbers meant that they reached the walls. They began to climb up. Now that they were close their slingers and archers began to take their toll of the defenders. Prefect Bassa saw eight of his men, within twenty paces tumble backwards as stones hit them full on in the face. As he hurled his last javelin he drew his sword. This would be a test of the discipline of his men. He blocked the blow from the barbarian's sword as he rammed his sword into the man. He pushed him over the wall and his body knocked two more climbing men in to the ditch. The stakes had injured and wounded scores but still they came.

The greatest danger came from those who had forded the river. There was no ditch and the bolt throwers had killed less there. First Spear shouted, "First and Second Centuries, to the south wall! On the double." He knew that the odds were in the barbarian's favour but he hoped to take as many with him as he could.

Centurion Buteo waved his men forward. The Cohort was able to run in time without the need for words. The sound of their hobnailed caligae on the stone road was like a death knell for Elisedd and his men. The last thing they had expected was for the Romans to attack. They came up the road with javelins used as spears. It was like a giant metal hedgehog. They simply ploughed through the Brigante. Those who were not speared were trampled to death. When Elisedd himself was killed the heart went from the Brigante. They melted away.

"Don't stop. Pick up any of our wounded!"

They had been lucky. None had died and only a few had suffered wounds. No one wanted to stop. As they neared the fort they heard the sounds of battle. Morbium was under attack. Centurion Buteo decided to ride their luck. He shouted. "We go straight over the bridge. I will make a decision when we get to the other side."

The Brigante who were waiting to cross the bridge wondered what the noise was behind them. As they turned the Romans hacked, slashed and stabbed their way through them. In the fort the bolt thrower crews saw the column of men coming. "Optio is that a Brigante trick? Are they dressed in our lads' mail?"

The optio laughed, "Brigantes could never run like that. Prefect! Reinforcements!"

The Prefect almost ran to the gate. He saw the cohort running across the bridge. He shouted to them, "Centurion, have half your men take out the Brigante by the river. The rest are needed in the fort!"

Centurion Buteo raised his sword and shouted, "Second and Fourth Centuries, clear the river bank. The rest take the wounded inside the fort."

He joined the Second as they attacked the flank of the Brigante. With First Spear on the wall hurling javelins down and two centuries hacking through them the Brigante broke off the river attack and returned south of the river. The extra men who suddenly filled the walls swung the battle and Chief Haerviu called off the attack. They could have carried on fighting but his men were becoming demoralized. He would regroup. This was just the first part of the war. When the Votadini captured the four forts in the north then the balance would swing in the favour of the Brigante. The Romans would have to send the VIth legion north and Coriosopitum would fall. He would return to Stanwyck and they would lick their wounds.

Chapter 16

The Legate received the news about the Morbium attack just as the last of the Selgovae were rounded up by the Gauls. He sat with First Spear. "And still the Votadini do nothing. Perhaps our intelligence was wrong."

"No sir, I fought these bastards. This Randel is clever. I reckon your strategy is a good one. We sit tight. We have stabilized the wall and Morbium is safe, for the moment. So far we have heard nothing from the west. It may be that we need to defend an attack from there."

"You may be right. However, just to be on the safe side I will send a turma of Vangiones to Habitancvm."

In the west the barbarians had had even less success than in the east. Even though most of the wall was turf from Luguvalium west the barbarians had not even taken a mile castle. They had attacked during the day and been slaughtered. The Novontae and the Selgovae had withdrawn north of the rivers to lick their wounds. They would attack again. The news of Scarth's success had given them hope. Scarth's sons were seen as heroes. They had breached the wall. That was no mean feat. When they pulled back to lick their wounds it was to learn from their attacks. The insurrection was not over. All along the wall the garrisons of the turrets and forts had lost men. Those in the west were even less likely to be reinforced. The nearest help was at Deva and there they were busy dealing with the Ordovices.

Randel and his men knew little of the battles to the south. Agnathus and Randel had made their plans. The recent change in routine by the Romans had upset them somewhat. They had lost more men than they had expected. Even so they had more than enough to launch their attacks. As dark of moon approached Randel divided his command into three. He retained half of the warband. The other half was divided between Brennus and Agnathus. With two forts and the ala to attack Randel had the harder task. Agnathus had the hard task of taking his men well north before turning east to approach Alavna. Brennus was the one with the apparently easier task. He would be attacking Habitancvm. His problem lay in the forts of Onnum and Coriosopitum. If the warriors in the south had not done their job then the legion would be marching north.

"For the two days before the attack we attack their patrols. Ambush them. Cause as many losses as you can. That will both weaken them and distract them. We have been quiet for too long. They will expect us to attack now that the new grass is here. They know of our rising. Let us make them think that our pinprick raids are the main attack. Do not waste men!" Randel turned to Brennus. "When we have destroyed the two Roman forts then we will march south. Agnathus, you will hold Alavna. We know the Romans send their ships there. Do not let them reoccupy it."

Brennus had risen from one of Randel's oathsworn to lead a quarter of the tribe. He was excited. It manifested itself in an inability to keep the silence of Agnathus and Randel. "Perhaps the Selgovae and Brigante have succeeded. Eostre began two days since. They may be heading north even as we sit here. Perhaps we should start our attack early."

"Brennus you have courage but you do not have wisdom. Randel has thought this out well. We wish this attack to succeed. That means we must use the gods to help us. They will darken the moon and we can attack unseen. Do not be foolish enough to attack early. Keep to the plan."

Brennus was a little hurt by Agnathus' words. It sounded as though he was being chided like a child. "I know the plan, Agnathus. We use stealth to approach their ditches. We cross them with the bridges we carry. We used shields to climb the walls and we do not shout, cry or cheer. We use silence."

Randel smiled, "And you shall succeed. It is right that you are concerned. I would not have it otherwise. When this is over the Roman Road will be covered by grass and the Romans themselves will be but a memory."

The Decurion who led the depleted turma from Cilurnum found the road north remarkably free from barbarians. Prefect Tulla had heard nothing of events to the south. "The attack there is over?"

The Decurion had been charged with one message and he had
delivered it. "I know not. The Selgovae lost many men but they breached
the wall. To the south Morbium is still surrounded by the Brigante." He
pointed south. "I can tell you that the road between here and Onnum is
clear of barbarians."

"Then return and tell the Legate that we have not been attacked yet.
We watch each day and our patrols are alert. I will tell Bremenium and
Alavna."

Two turmae of the Gauls headed north. Prefect Tulla was a veteran.
The fact that there had yet to be an attack meant nothing. The two turmae
which headed north watched each leaf and blade of grass for sign of
Votadini. It was with some relief that they met the road patrol from the
north. Decurion Scaura escorted them back to the forts.

In the forest the Votadini warriors who watched the road were
disturbed at the sight of over a hundred horsemen heading north. They
were used to the patrols but they had fewer men in them. One of them
began the journey back to the heart of the forest to speak with Randel.

First Spear and Prefect Glabrio heard the report together. Decurion
Princeps Pera was present too. First Spear nodded after he heard the
reports. "Then we can expect no help until the wall and the road to
Eboracum is under control again. Prefect, would you send a turma to
Alavna with the news. The garrison there is isolated."

A year ago the Prefect might have been annoyed at such a request
from an officer of lower rank. Now he knew that the forts were
interdependent. "Of course. I will increase the road patrols."

The Decurion who had brought the news nodded. "Prefect Tulla is
patrolling south to Onnum and north along the road."

"Then we are doing all that we can."

It fell to Marcus and his turma to make the ride to Alavna. They were
not chosen especially, it coincided with their turn. They would have to
spend the night in the fort for it was over thirty miles. The road had yet to
be properly paved. When the Lingones had travelled east to rebuild it
they had made the road more serviceable as they had gone but they
needed a summer free from fighting to complete the task. The road
passed the now desolate and ruined hill fort of Otarbrunna. Marcus knew
that there were Votadini watching them. They would be a tempting
target. He and his men were vigilant.

Centurion Vibius Durmius Celsa was coming to the end of his enlistment. This last posting as commander of the fort at Alavna was an honour and the high point of his career. He had no intention of losing the fort which had cost his cohort so much tragedy and dishonour. He listened to Marcus' words. "And you, horseman, what is your opinion?"

"This Randel is a cunning foe. He is planning an attack but he does not waste his men. I doubt that it will be a frontal attack. He could weaken the fort by attacking the patrols. With the wall under threat then we are in an even more perilous position."

Centurion Celsa nodded, "That makes sense. We are lucky. Every couple of days ships from the Classis Britannia pass by, if we are attacked then we can summon help quickly."

The turma left the next morning. They accompanied the half century which patrolled the road for five miles. Leaving the Lingones to head back to their fort Marcus led his turma up the valley with the bubbling river. He had no doubt that the locals had a name for it but he and the troopers just called it the bubbling stream. It emerged from the side of the ridge and, once they had crossed it, they were heading down towards Otarbrunna and the road. As soon as they began to descend storm clouds appeared from the east. They meant an early dusk and icy sleet filled rain. If the rain was from the west it would just be wet but the east rains always seemed colder. Marcus and his men were still using their winter cloaks and Marcus pulled it tighter about himself.

It was easy to feel cocooned with a cloak wrapped around you but Marcus still kept his senses tuned to the land around him. The forest was closer to the road than Marcus would have liked. The road had been built merely to allow men to build the fort. As Alavna could be supplied by sea it was unlikely they would ever need the normal sized road. Marcus felt uncomfortable. His hand went to his sword. Suddenly Raven stopped with her ears pricked. There was danger. Marcus drew his sword and raised it. As he did so he pulled his clipeus up. It was not before time.

The Votadini had been waiting for the horsemen. When they had passed Otarbrunna the previous day they had sent a warband to ambush them. It had been a long wait but they knew that the Romans had to return. Marcus' drawing of the sword had initiated the attack. The young barbarians who made up the band were too pent up after a day and night waiting for a chance to strike at the Romans. Stones and arrows flew. The rain helped Marcus and his men. The bow strings were not as taut as they should have been and the sling shots were soaked with water. Even so Trooper Merga was struck and killed by a stone.

Marcus' turma were well trained and highly experienced. When Marcus shouted, "Charge to the right!" None hesitated. They hurtled towards the trees. Marcus had to use his sword. Others hurled their javelins. The slack bow strings meant the javelins had the same range as the Votadini weapons. The young barbarians who had begun the attack were stranded close to the road. Marcus swung his sword back and when he hit the Votadini he split him from his stomach to his neck. He leaned forward to bring it down a second time on a mesmerised young warrior who seemed transfixed by Raven. His life was ended when Marcus brought his sword down to split the man's skull. Trooper Nerva had used his three javelins and he, too, leaned from the saddle to kill a Votadini who thought his own sword and shield would protect him. He was wrong. Once they were in the trees then any advantage that the Votadini had had was gone. The trees here were not as closely packed as in their forest home and they did not have the advantage of arrows and stones to keep the Romans at bay. The horsemen were moving so quickly and there were so many trees that the troopers were able to stab and spear the Votadini at will.

Dusk was falling rapidly but Marcus wanted to make sure that the threat of this warband was over. He glanced over his shoulder. Vexillarius Ralle was still there. He sheathed his sword and took out a javelin. He had no intention of throwing it but he would use it like a lance. A barbarian had been hiding behind a tree and he stepped out, swinging his sword two handed at Marcus. Marcus pulled Raven to the left while leaning to the right and he rammed the javelin so hard into the man that he pinned him to the tree.

The Vexillarius shouted, "That looks to be most of them, sir."

"You are right. Sound the recall." He turned his horse and stopped by the Votadini he had pinned to the tree. He tore the amulet from around his neck. He examined it when they reached the road. It was the clan of deer. He knew that there were twenty clans. They had found evidence of at least ten clans so far. This was the start of the uprising here in the land of the Votadini.

They placed Trooper Merga on his horse while the capsarius dealt with the wounds the men had suffered. As they rode down the road, towards the setting sun, Vexillarius Ralle said, "They hurt some of the horses, sir. I am not certain we will be able to take a full turma out tomorrow."

"If this is the start of the offensive then that may be a moot point! If they attack then the horses will be in the stables and we will be on the walls."

When they reached the fort, they discovered that every patrol from both forts had been attacked. Men had died. The barbarians had managed to take their dead with them and the Prefect did not know how many had been killed. He and First Spear spoke. "Do we keep the patrols inside the forts tomorrow, Prefect? The enemy may be massing for an attack."

"And then again they may not or they be attacking Alavna and Habitancvm. From what Decurion Aurelius told me the fort at Alavna has protection from the sea but Habitancvm is isolated. We will patrol south only tomorrow. I suggest double strength."

"I agree."

Decurion Princeps Pera came to speak with Marcus as the Decurion groomed Raven, "Marcus, tomorrow I am leading the patrol along the Alavna Road and the Prefect will be on the south road. We would like you to have two turmae ready to respond to any attacks close to the fort."

"I only have twenty fit troopers and horses, sir."

"I know. Decurion Stolo has a full troop. Fifty men should be enough."

Marcus nodded, "We were ambushed on this side of the ridge, sir."

"I know. That will be the extent of our patrol. It is the Lingones you will need to protect. We can get out of trouble quickly. They move slowly and the Votadini are fast."

Marcus went to the barracks and sought out Vexillarius Ralle. He had become, in effect, Marcus' Chosen Man. "Pick the fittest twenty troopers and horses, Manius, we are on call tomorrow. We and the Fifteenth are the reserves."

He nodded, "They will all want to go, sir. They think you are lucky!"

"Lucky? We got ambushed today!"

"And you got us out of it. These Votadini all have coins, bracelets and the like. The lads are doing well out of it. Some of the other turma wish you were their officer."

"I appreciate the vote of confidence but this time next year I shan't be here. I will be back with my ala."

"Aye sir, and more's the pity."

There was an air of anxiety the next morning as eight turmae prepared to ride out. Few had full complements. Marcus went to the gatehouse to watch them leave. He saw the Lingone patrol parade before the fort as they began their patrols. One century would head north and the other south. As usual they took axes with them so that they could clear more trees. In theory, every patrol made them a little safer. Marcus wondered at the wisdom of sending a century north when there would be no horsemen there.

It was the third turma which was on duty and Marcus said to Decurion Macula, "Anything unusual, Aulus, let me know. The Votadini are up to something."

"Will do."

The turmae who were in reserve were in the parade ground. All of them were examining their horses and saddles. A loose girth could be fatal! Decurion Stolo approached Marcus. "Do you think we will be needed today?"

"Let us say I hope not but I expect that we will be needed. Every patrol was ambushed yesterday. The same will happen today. When we ride we will need to be quick and decisive."

He nodded, "I think I have learned, Marcus. Thanks for being so patient with me. I must have been annoying when we first met."

Marcus laughed, "You were young. We all have to learn. The trouble here is that the lessons are paid for in blood and death."

The barbarians had watched the auxiliaries and seen their routine. They knew that when they stopped and twenty took off their helmets that they were about to hew down trees. They had also counted the two hundred and fifty horsemen who had ridden to patrol. The leader of the warband, Seisyll, deemed the risk worth taking. They had shadowed the patrol and kept deep in the woods. The sound of the hobnails marked the movement of the auxiliaries. When the marching stopped and the orders were shouted Seisyll raised his arm. He and his men had no intention of fighting a battle, their aim was to inflict as many casualties as they could. The twenty men without helmets and holding axes were an easy target. As the twenty men advanced to the woods another forty spread out to watch the trees. The slingers and archers targeted the twenty axemen and more than half fell. A second volley hit another four and six of those supporting them.

"Sound the buccina! Shields!"

The centurion took the correct action. Firstly, he had to present a solid wall of shields. Then he would assess the enemy and finally, he would attack.

In the fort Marcus heard the buccina. Decurion Macula shouted, "Stand to! Patrol to the north is being attacked." In truth the Decurion could not see the fighting but he could hear the sound of battle. He could hear the cries of the wounded and the dying.

Marcus vaulted onto the back of his horse. He turned to Decurion Stolo. "Ride to the aid of the century on the road. I will take my turma and cut them off!"

The sentries opened the gates and they galloped out. Without seeing the ambush Marcus knew that the Lingones would be able to defend themselves. The arrival of Decurion Stolo's turma would make the enemy run. Their camp lay to the south-west and Marcus wanted to catch as many of them as he could. When they reached the road, he saw that the century had a shield wall and the barbarians, having seen the Fifteenth Turma hurtling up the road were melting into the forest. They galloped across the road and leapt into the river. It was shallow enough for horses to ford. Raven took it so well that she made the other bank in just two strides. The Votadini on foot could be seen, further north. They were slower at crossing the river. It came up to their chests. Their bowstrings would be soaked. Once they reached the thin trees before the forest proper began Marcus headed north. He only had twenty men with him but they knew their business.

"Spread out and get as many as you can. Do not pursue them into the forest."

As he looked north Marcus saw that Decurion Stolo had grown. His turma was also leaping into the river and they were herding the Votadini towards Marcus.

Seisyll realised he had made a mistake. The line of horsemen heading towards his men would hit them. He could have ordered them to make a shield wall but only half had shields. He shouted, "Every man for himself. Run!"

It was the last thing he said. Vexillarius Ralle's javelin struck him in the chest. The death of their leader made the young warriors panic. They ran hither and thither. The fifty horsemen hurled their javelins and then used their swords. When Marcus could see no more foes he shouted, "Sound the recall!"

While his men made certain that all of the Votadini had been slain, Marcus joined Decurion Stolo and the Lingone centurion. "Well done, Servius. You handled your men well."

"Thank you, Marcus."

The centurion nodded his thanks too, "And I am grateful to you both. They could not hurt us more but you wrought vengeance upon them. I have lost good men today."

"We will wait here while you take your dead back to the fort."

When the other patrols came in all had lost men. Others had been wounded. Their casualties were not serious but the attacks were worrying. That night they had even more sentries on the walls.

Deep in the forest Randel was pleased with their attacks. They had weakened the Romans. The warriors they had lost had been expendable. They were young and inexperienced. The heart of the warband, the veterans, armed and mailed like Romans, remained intact. Two hundred and fifty of them had mail shirts. Another five hundred were seasoned, hardened warriors. They were the ones who had destroyed Habitancvm. They were the ones who had ambushed the auxiliaries. They were the best.

"Tomorrow night we attack. I want every warrior deep in the forest tonight in case they decide to come in after us. By late afternoon, when the patrols have returned to their forts every warrior will be in position ready to attack. Today and yesterday we did well. The fort to the south lost forty men and the ones close by lost another forty. We can replace our losses. Thanks to the attacks in the south the Romans cannot reinforce."

The Legate and his garrisons had endured night time attacks as well as attacks on the road. Those Brigante who supported Rome and the soldiers who had retired there had been attacked. Farms had been burned and families butchered. The Legate was not happy.

"It is time that we took the offensive. The good news is that the Tungrians have finally left Morbium and they will be here tomorrow. I want the forts at Brocolitia, Onnum and Cilurnum to send a cohort each to Vinovia. I intend to sweep south to Stanwyck. My spies tell me that is where Chief Haerviu hatches his plots. We will cut off the head of the snake and we will destroy his hill fort."

First Spear nodded, "And the Legion?"

197

"I will take the Second and Third cohorts south to Vinovia. When the Tungrian Cohort arrives, you take the First north. Have the Gauls, Lingones and Ala Petriana join you and sweep into the forest. This insidious insurrection is bleeding us dry. Trade has stopped and people are losing faith in the Pax Romana!" He handed a wax tablet to the First Spear. "Here are my orders."

As the day dawned the garrisons on the wall were on the move. They were heading south. Along the road the Gauls, Lingones and Ala Petriana marched up and down the Via Trajan. They watched and waited for an attack which never materialised.

Vexillarius Ralle commented as they parted from their gallic counterparts, "I tell you this sir. This road is well named!"

"Via Trajan? He was just the Emperor who named it."

"No sir, not the official name; the name every soldier in the north used, Via Hades, the road to hell!"

Chapter 17

Bremenium

As the patrols returned, unscathed, there was a strange atmosphere in both forts. Although they were pleased that they had not lost men the fact that the Votadini had not attacked had them all perplexed. For once the Prefect seemed unsure of his plans for the next day. Unusually for him he called a meeting of his officers. For the autocratic officer this was a rare departure from the rules and regulations he lived by.

"Have we beaten them? Were the attacks of the past few days the insurrection?"

Decurion Scaura said, "We hurt them, sir. They have lost men in every attack. Perhaps we have torn the heart out of them."

Marcus shook his head, "I spoke with the Lingones who have been going into the woods to cut down trees, sir. They tell me that they have seen the tracks of many hundreds of men heading into the forest. They were easier to see when there was snow on the ground but they saw them. The fact that they were not hiding their numbers shows their confidence. They are in the forest."

Decurion Princeps Pera said, "Decurion Aurelius is right, sir. When was the last time we killed one of them wearing a mail shirt? Carrying one of our shields? They have all been boys. We might have lost fewer numbers than they did but the numbers we lost were more valuable than the slingers and archers."

The Prefect sighed, "You may be right, Decurion Princeps but why no attack today?"

"If I was to hazard a guess I would say because they intend a bigger attack in the next couple of days."

"Then we stick to the routine we have had. Double watch tonight and double patrols tomorrow. I know it is taking its toll on the horses but that can't be helped."

Coriosopitum

First Spear had briefed Centurion Buteo. "We will be leaving first thing in the morning. Your men can guard the fort. I know your lads will be tired but with the legion heading north and south you should have an easy time of it."

"Don't worry about us First Spear. I was convinced that we would be in the Otherworld when the Prefect and our First Spear died. All of the lads did. For us this is as though we have been reborn. A night standing a watch on the walls is nothing. The ones we left behind would trade what they have for it in a heartbeat."

Morbium

The Legate gathered his officers together. He had three cohorts of auxiliaries and two cohorts of the VIth. He had just one turma of cavalry and they would have to do the work of an ala. He was ready to march south. They had just three miles to go. The Vangione turma was already in position across the road two miles south. Their task was to be a screen and prevent the Brigante from discovering that a huge force of Romans was ready to pounce.

"We are going to catch the Brigante unawares. There will be no buccina. We will use hand signals. We need to have complete surprise. Our one turma of Vangiones will have to catch and kill any sentries they find. We surround the hill fort and end this insurrection here and now. Then we can march north and deal with the more serious problem there."

Stanwyck

Chief Haerviu was pleased with the offensive thus far. A messenger had arrived from Randel and Agnathus telling him that the attack on the four Roman forts would be at the dark of the moon. That suited Chief Haerviu. He had two thousand warriors in the hillfort and they were ready to strike at Morbium, Vinovia and Longovicium. They had weakened Morbium and the last news they had had from the vicus, two days ago was that the cohort they had attacked had moved north to Coriosopitum. The Votadini attack would mean that no Romans would be able to relieve any of the forts he and his men planned to attack! When the Sword of Cartimandua was in his hands he would be King of the Brigante! The Romans thought they had defeated them but Chief

Haerviu had yet to unleash the full force of the men gathered at the hill fort.

The forest close by Bremenium and Habitancvm

Brennus and his men crouched by the edge of the forest. All of them had blackened their faces, arms, legs and in some cases, chests. He was keen to get across the road and begin to work their way closer to the Roman walls but he knew they had to wait until halfway through the night. The sentries would be tiring. He had a hundred warriors who had mail shirts, helmets and shields. He had another two hundred who had a shield and helmet. The ones who were less experienced would carry the bridging ladders. In the half darkness of dusk, he identified the position of the bolt throwers and their crews. He crept down the edge of the forest and pointed them out to the slingers and archers who would follow. Their job was simple. They would kill the crews of the bolt throwers.

Randel was close by the Lingone fort. Teutorigos was leading the attack in the ala fort. The War Chief was more strategically minded than both Brennus and Teutorigos. He had gone over the attack with his lieutenants time and time again while they had been in their forest fortress. He did not need to tell his men whom they should target. They could identify the threat for themselves. He closed his eyes and thought back to his wife and family. He had kept their faces from his mind until now. He needed the added hatred that their untimely death had created. His wife had taken her life and that of his family but the Romans had caused it. He had kept his anger hidden. Now, with battle about to begin he dragged it to the surface. When the forts were razed to the ground and every Roman slain then Olwen and his family would be avenged. The Roman armour he wore, the sword and shield he carried and the helmet upon his head were reminders of the enemy and what they had done to him. When the forts were gone then he would discard the Roman trappings. With the land of the Votadini free he would need them no longer.

He opened his eyes and looked at the sky. It was black. The gods were on their side. He crouched and began to move towards the road. The many hundreds of men rose as one with him. They were in awe of their War Chief. He had killed Creagh and everyone knew he had been the greatest Votadini champion. The fact that he had also defeated Creagh's treachery and avenged King Clutha merely added to his aura. None would dare to let him down.

The warriors with the broad ladders had reached the ditches and laid them down. One of the two men who had carried them crawled across to hold them safe on the far side. The first ones to follow them were the ones carrying the ladders for the second ditches. Randel nodded to the warrior who commanded the slingers and archers. They would crouch by the ditches and they would listen for the sound of alarm. When it was heard then they would clear the men manning the bolt throwers.

Randel crawled like a child first learning to move across the wooden bridge. It was undignified but necessary. He kept crawling and began to move across the second ditch. He could hear the Lingones talking on the fighting platform above him. He did not understand the words but the tone suggested that they were not alarmed. His mailed men all made it across and then the alarm was given. It was Teutorigos and his men who had made a noise and the sentries in the ala fort had heard. Above him, at the Lingones' fort, he heard orders being shouted and then there was the crack of stones and the sound of arrows. Cries from above him told him that the bolt thrower crews had died.

He stepped onto the shield held by his two tallest men and they lifted him up to the wall. A Lingone raised his javelin to end the life of the War Chief and an arrow knocked him into the fort. Randel sprang over the top of the wooden palisade and brought his sword across the head of the optio who raced to repel the attackers. The whole of the wall was filled with Randel's mailed men. The Lingones hesitated for in the dark they could not tell friend from foe.

First Spear was only half asleep. When he heard the alarm, it was like a recurring bad dream. He grabbed his shield and his sword. As he stepped out of his quarters he saw the rest of the garrison. They were running to the walls. He shouted, "Lingones! Shield wall!" He knew that they needed a solid, disciplined wall of men. The barbarians might be wearing Roman mail but they had no discipline. "Second Century, guard the gate! Third Century, support the west wall! Fourth Century, support the south wall." He had six centuries left. They were in four lines and filled the parade ground. Raising his sword, he shouted, "Forward!"

On the fighting platform, Randel was confused. Why were the Romans not racing to the walls? They were dressing their lines and marching forward. This was not the way he had envisaged the attack going. They had attained their first objective. The west wall was in their hands. That part had gone well but the bolt throwers from the horse fort had stopped his men from attacking the north wall. The plan had not gone smoothly but two of the walls were his. Now he needed the gate.

The Decurion Princeps had been on duty when the attack began. It was he who smelled the barbarians. Marcus had told him of the smell of the Votadini and now he had learned to recognise it. He had gone to the edge of the wall and seen a movement. None of his men were outside and he had hurled his javelin at the man who appeared to be crawling across a ladder. When the man screamed he knew there was an attack.
"Stand to!"
Teutorigos had not managed to get men across the ladder. The bolt throwers and the javelins of the four turmae on duty hit the mailed warriors who were approaching the ladders. Some panicked and ran. The ladders were meant to be crawled upon and they would not bear the weight of a large number of mailed men running across them. Two ladders broke, throwing the warriors to the sharpened stakes below. Teutorigos was luckier than most of his men. He made the wall. As he looked up Decurion Princeps Pera hurled a javelin. It hit him in the face. He fell backwards and was impaled on a stake. The ala fort was larger than the Lingones fort and Teutorigos' men faced more troopers. Had the Decurion Princeps not spotted the warrior things might have been different. The Votadini attack relied on them getting inside the range of the bolt throwers before the alarm was given. Teutorigos had failed. His men now had fewer bridges across the ditch and there were more than two hundred men facing them. The bolt throwers kept up a steady rate of bolts and the mass of men trying to get to the remaining bridges died.

The attack did not materialize on the east side of the fort and the bolt throwers there were able to send their bolts at the warriors attacking the west side of the Lingone fort. Although the range was extreme the bolts struck lines of men who were crossing the wooden bridges towards the Lingones' fort. It had the effect of weakening Randel's attack.

Alavna
Agnathus had been forced to attack the one side of the fort which was not protected by the river which bent and twisted around the fort. In many ways, that problem helped him for he was not distracted by trying to attack two walls at the same time. The chief was able to concentrate all of his men on one wall. He knew he had the smallest of the forts and garrisons to attack. He outnumbered those within. He and his men

managed to get the bridges across the ditches and they reached the walls before a sentry saw them. When the alarm was given the Votadini were already being boosted up the wall. The buccina in the fort sounded. The garrison had been ready for this and, even as the Votadini tried to swarm over the walls they were racing to the fighting platform.

The bolt throwers hurled their bolts at the men trying to cross the ditches. When one of the bolts hit a large warrior and he fell heavily one of the weakened bridges broke. Centurion Vibius Durmius Celsa's old and wise head came to the rescue of the beleaguered garrison.

"Centurion Helva, take two centuries and reinforce the west wall. Turn the bolt throwers there to hit the men on the walls."

"Sir! Centuries Eight and Nine, with me!"

"First Century, let us earn our pay. Tenth Century, back us up!" The grizzled old soldier led his men to the south wall and they headed up the ladder. The sentries had been from the Seventh and Thirteenth Century. They were being forced back by sheer weight of numbers. They could not make a shield wall. Centurion Vibius Durmius Celsa turned to his men. "Three men abreast!" As they formed up the Centurion shouted, "Signifer sound advance!" He smiled as he saw that Centurion Helva had done the same. The two bodies of men were closing like a pair of nutcrackers on the Votadini. The men who were fighting the barbarians on the wall would have to hold them up until the two metal giants met.

Agnathus hacked his sword through an auxiliary's arm. He felt blows strike his mail but they appeared to do him no harm. He felt invincible. They had lost many men but he had done what he had been asked. He had taken a wall of the fort. He had enough men left to exploit the breach. Once the gate was taken they would flood in and do as Randel had done at Habitancvm; he would slaughter every Roman and his son's dishonour would be expunged. As the Seventh and the Thirteenth Centuries died, their sacrifice was not in vain for the two columns began to hack their way through the barbarians.

Centurion Vibius Durmius Celsa and the two men next to him were using their spears more effectively than the barbarians. They held their shields before them and stabbed down and over the top of the shields. Even the Votadini who wore Roman mail had no defence against that. The three Romans protected each other and the Votadini fought as individual warriors.

Agnathus felt another blow to his back but he brought his sword over to strike the auxiliary. The Optio blocked it with his shield. Agnathus began to feel weak. He could not understand it. He was wearing Roman mail. He was supposed to be invincible. Chiefs Witan and Góra had just reached the wall and were looking to exploit Agnathus' victory. Witan saw that the chief's men had been slaughtered and Agnathus was wounded. They saw Agnathus' arm weakly raised to strike the Roman officer. Instead, a sword appeared through his body and the chief fell.

"Let us avenge Agnathus!" With fresh warriors Witan was certain that they could succeed. The hard part had been accessing the wall. They had done that. Suddenly a bolt appeared through Góra. It continued through and hit Witan's lieutenant. It had not come from the fort. He looked to the river and saw three Roman ships. Their bolt throwers were sending their deadly bolts at the men attacking wall.

Centurion Vibius Durmius Celsa shouted, "Signifer sound hold. Seventh and Thirteenth, withdraw!" He knew what the ships would do. They would clear the wall. He and the rest of his century dropped to one knee. The bolt throwers on the ships were lower than the walls of the fort. The trajectory would be a rising one. The Votadini began to fall. One warrior, filled with the desire for glory, suddenly ran at the officer with the red horsehair crest. Centurion Celsa calmly rammed his spear into the throat of the screaming warrior. When the barbarians lost the wild warrior who tried to charge the First Century they jumped back over the wall. The three ships changed their aim. They targeted the men waiting to ascend the walls and the centurion led his men along the walkway. Picking up javelins they hurled them at the Votadini who were trying to pick their way across the ditches. It was a slaughter. As dawn broke the battle was ended. The Legate's decision to use the Classis Britannica had worked.

Stanwyck

The Legate was in position before dawn. It was a short distance from Morbium to Stanwyck. They were marching down a good Roman Road. It did not take long. The old hill fort had been formidable once. It had been successfully stormed before and the wooden palisade torn down. Now it was a series of ramparts and a newly built gate. The auxiliaries he had brought now surrounded the hill fort. He was with the VIth. They would take the gate. The dozen or so sentries who were on the walls were taken out by the auxiliaries as the Legion marched towards the gate. Their dying cries alerted Chief Haerviu and his warriors. They raced from their warrior halls to the ramparts. By then it was almost too late.

The auxiliaries excelled in overcoming obstacles. The ditches were wet but they were neither deep nor trap filled. They swarmed up the ramparts. The legionaries would have struggled to make the top but the auxiliaries reached the ramparts at the same time as the Brigante. The Brigante were half asleep. The auxiliaries were ready.

At the gate, ten legionaries with axes made short work of the poorly made gate and the Legate led a column of men eight men wide through the gate and into the heart of the hill fort. With just one gate in and out Chief Haerviu had nowhere to go. He was no coward and he called for a shield wall. The ones who were not already on the ramparts made a large circle. They locked their shields and held their weapons ready to fight. The Legate was in the front rank. All the leaders the Legate had admired, Marcus Brutus, Julies Caesar and Agricola had all done the same. They led from the front. He was a hardened warrior and, in his hand, the gladius was a deadly weapon.

The men who marched with the Legate were in perfect time. They stepped together. Their shields were presented and punched as one. Their gladii ripped up underneath the small round shields of the Brigante. The column began to carve its way into the heart of the Brigante. The auxiliaries joined in. They stood on the ramparts and hurled javelins into the body of the Brigante. The VIth hacked its way closer to the skull topped standards where the chiefs gathered.

The signifer was behind the Legate. As more Brigante fell the Legate shouted, "Signal double line!"

Only the Roman army could perform such a manoeuvre in combat. The front two ranks held. The third rank hacked their way left and the fourth rank right. Each line of eight did the same. Gradually the line of eight men became sixteen, thirty-two, sixty-four and finally, one hundred and twenty-eight.

"Forward!"

Chief Haerviu knew what was coming. He might have surrendered if he thought he would be given the opportunity. He knew he would not. His ancestor Venutius had not surrendered. Chief Haerviu would not either. His wife was in the south with his sons and daughters. His eldest son Venutius would have to regain the sword and the crown. The VIth Legion had done for him and his men. The Brigante died. They died because they had nowhere to go and, despite their numbers, they were not good enough to fight men of the VIth legion.

Habitancvm

As dawn broke Prefect Tulla thought they were going to die. The barbarians had managed to capture the gate tower. The bolt throwers on the west wall were either broken or in the hands of the barbarians. It was a matter of time before they were overwhelmed. His horsemen could not use their horses for the barbarians were attacking the wall close to the stables.

Brennus had lost many men attacking the wall but he was proud that they had captured the gate. He and the last of his oathsworn were fighting their way to the gate. It was only a matter of time before they opened it. They had split the defences of the fort. Brennus had been wounded but they were minor wounds. "On, my warriors! One more push and we have the gate!"

First Spear Broccius, marching from the south, heard the sounds of battle. It had a familiar ring. It was like a dream. This was Bremenium all over again. He saw the mass of warriors at the gates and, as the sun broke, he saw, to his horror, that the gates were opening. "Follow me, double time. Signifer, sound charge!" They were in an eight-man wide line and they would hit the mass of barbarians attempting to get into the fort. The buccina was to give hope to those within and to dismay the Votadini.

The warriors at the rear of the warband had heard the buccina but did not associate it with danger and they knew nothing until the legionaries hurtled into them. Eight spears stabbed and skewered. The Romans were efficient. As they twisted the bodies away they were already pulling back their arms to thrust again. Inside the fort Prefect Tulla heard the horn and knew that help was at hand. "Form four ranks on me!" The survivors of the centuries who were close by knew what was expected of them and they hurried to join shield brothers. Some were wounded and all had blood upon them. What they all had was Roman courage. The Prefect saw that the first rank was ready and he shouted, "Forward!"

The opening of the gates proved to be fatal to the Votadini. Every warrior still outside raced to get within the walls. They were met by a wall of auxiliaries and worse was that the Roman VIth legion was chopping and slashing its way through men who could not defend themselves. The two bodies of organised soldiers protected each other as they methodically slaughtered the barbarians jammed between the gate and the Legion.

On the walls, Brennus could not believe the change in fortunes. They had almost cleared one wall. Bolt throwers lay destroyed and he had been about to lead his men into the body of the fort and end the resistance. Now the survivors of the centuries on the fighting platform reorganised themselves. No more reinforcements were joining Brennus on the walls for they were pouring through the gate and being destroyed. The ones in the middle of the warband were unaware of the scale of the disaster. The VIth were methodical and First Spear Broccius was ruthless. Once they neared the first ditch then it became slaughter. The Romans hacked those who stood on the bridge and many Votadini chose to hurl themselves into the stake filled ditch.

Once First Spear neared the gate Prefect Tulla shouted. "Ninth and Tenth Centuries, clear the walls!"

Brennus and his oathsworn found themselves surrounded by Romans. The vengeful auxiliaries, with closed ranks drew closer to them. The eight who survived were wearing Roman mail but they were not Roman trained. Two of his oathsworn hurled themselves at the Romans. It was for a glorious death. Stabbed by four spears the two bodies were hurled to the ground. Brennus touched his torc. Randel himself had given him the copper and silver torc. It was a measure of his standing as a warrior and a chief. He would die honourably. He raised his sword and opened his mouth to curse the Romans. He was not given the chance. The auxiliaries threw their javelins and Brennus and his oathsworn died. This attack had failed.

Bremenium

As dawn broke it became obvious that the attack on the ala fort had failed. Prefect Glabrio had not dared believe they had escaped destruction until dawn showed the ditches filled with the dead and the dying. The survivors had joined those in Bremenium. There Randel had won. The survivors of the Lingone were in a square. They were surrounded by Votadini and Randel had visions of Habitancvm when he and his men had butchered the garrison there. He knew nothing of the failed attack on the ala fort.

Decurion Princeps Pera said, "Prefect, we can still save the Lingones."

The Prefect shook his head, "The fort has fallen. All that I can see are barbarians."

"Sir, I beg you, let me take out eight turmae. You will still have more than enough to defend the walls. We cannot let our brothers die."

The Prefect was torn but he nodded. "Just eight!"

Decurion Princeps Pera waved over the decurions he trusted the most. Marcus was amongst them. "Get your horses. We are going to the aid of our brothers!"

It did not take long to saddle the horses. Marcus and Decurion Princeps Pera were the first out of the gates followed by their turmae. Marcus held a javelin at the ready. The only barbarians outside the fort were the wounded. They were being tended to by their priests and druids. They were ignored by the horsemen. As the two decurions rode through the gate they saw the scale of the problem. There were hundreds of Votadini. The only advantage they held was that the barbarians were facing the Lingones.

First Spear Sejanus saw the horsemen arrive. There was hope. He shouted, "No retreat! We hold the bastards!"

The two decurions did not shout orders, they waved the javelins and the other horsemen fanned out. The noise of the horses alerted the barbarians and, as they turned, the troopers began to hurl their javelins. The troopers had a thousand javelins between them and more than half of the first two hundred they threw found flesh and men died. Some Votadini ran at the horsemen but they were easily killed by javelins used as spears.

As Marcus threw his last missile, he drew his sword. "The Sword of Cartimandua!" He shouted in the language of the Brigante and the Votadini. At the front, Randel heard the cry. It seemed to be ominous for the Lingones began to push against Randel's men. The attack of the horsemen had weakened the barbarians. They did not have the overwhelming numbers any longer and the heart was going from them. Randel knew they were losing. He cursed the horsemen who had, once more, done for his people. He especially cursed the officer with the red horsehair crest and the Sword of Cartimandua.

Keeping his shield tight Marcus urged Raven on. He leaned forward to hack through helmets, shields and bodies. His turma kept as tight to him as they could. They were brave men and loyal to Marcus. Troopers Ruga and Curva died but not before ten barbarians had fallen to the two Gauls.

Some of the wounded Lingones on the fighting platform had managed to get two of the bolt throwers working and bolts began to tear

209

into the body of the Votadini. This time the barbarians were tightly packed and the bolts hit four and five men with each strike.

Randel had fought and run before. There was no dishonour in withdrawing. They could regroup. He would not be able to take the fort this time but he had hurt the Romans. "Fall back!"

Marcus heard the horn and the words. He shouted, "Watch out, they are retreating!"

The ala lay in the path of the barbarians. It was Marcus and his men who were now on the defensive. They had to back their horses away from the gate or risk being torn from their saddles and butchered. It was a sea of barbarians. Even though they were fleeing the Votadini still died. Chased by the angry Lingones they were speared, stabbed and skewered by the Ala Petriana as they passed. As the last ones fled the insurrection was effectively over but the Roman army had paid a terrible price.

Chapter 18

Marcus and the Decurion Princeps were all for pursuing the Votadini back to their forest fortress but Prefect Glabrio forbade it. In some ways he was right. Both forts had suffered damage and needed repairs. The Prefect sent a turma to Alavna and a second one to Habitancvm. This had been the much talked of rebellion. Prefect Glabrio wondered how the other forts had fared. If they had fallen then the ala and the remnants of the Lingones would be isolated. Even after night had fallen men were still working. The bonfire of barbarian bodies was kept fuelled as the Votadini were gathered and hurled on to it. The Prefect and his officers were watching the last body being incinerated when the turma returned from Habitancvm.

Decurion Stolo reported, "Prefect Glabrio, the enemy have been routed. The VIth are here tomorrow with orders from the Legate."

The relief was palpable. Troopers and officers smiled for the first time since the attack had begun. Bremenium had come close to falling. More than half of the garrison had died or were seriously wounded.

"Well done. The Ala Petriana can hold its head up high!"

The Decurion Princeps gave Marcus a wry look. The Prefect had sung a different tune when things had been the bleakest. "And tonight sir? Double sentries again?"

"I think not, Decurion Princeps Pera. The barbarians have been given a bloody nose. Our fort's walls were not damaged, neither were the gates. I fear the Lingones will have work to do."

"And tomorrow sir?"

He smiled, "We will rest and recover. Perhaps Decurion Aurelius and Decurion Stolo could take a patrol out eh?"

When the Prefect had gone Marcus said, "I think he is in for a shock sir. I can't see the Legate leaving the Votadini to remain free. I did not see Randel amongst the dead. I saw him when we attacked but the man is slippery and he escaped. He has nothing to lose now that his wife and family are dead. The rebellion will only be over when War Chief Randel is dead."

"I fear you are right. As you and Servius are on patrol tomorrow you two can have the night off."

Deep in the forest men were gradually returning to their camp. Randel's contingent was the largest. He had his own men and the survivors of Teutorigos' attack. Barely a hundred returned from Habitancvm. The priests and druids who had survived saw to the wounds of the survivors. The ones they could not save were given a swift warrior's death. Randel did not even feel the stitches as his leg was stitched up. He could not even remember receiving the wound. None of his lieutenants had survived. All were dead. Cragus was the only one of his oathsworn left alive. He looked around the fire and saw that only twenty warriors wore mail. When they had gone to war there had been far more. Before the rising, he had lost only the young warriors. Now he had lost the veterans. The young ones had called them 'the tattoos'. All of them had tattoos which marked a victory. Many had had totally blue bodies. He allowed himself a smile as he saw a few of the younger warriors tattooing each other. To them the battle of the forts had been a victory. All had tasted Roman blood.

Vinicius was one chief who had survived. He came and sat by Randel. "It is over then?"

"No Vinicius. Had none returned here then it would have been over. These men have not given up the fight. I have no doubt that there are many others who will not fight. I see no Brigante here. Although many were killed more survived and they will be heading south. I do not blame them. They served a purpose. We rebuild. We have a forest which feeds us and gives us shelter. The Romans would never dare to come in here after us. They will stay to guard their road and we will begin our pinprick attacks again. We may not destroy their forts by direct action but we can strangle them by stopping their supplies. That will be our war."

Vinicius nodded, "Then tomorrow I will go north. We have no king. The council of chiefs will have to appoint one. You should come."

"I could have had the throne when I killed Creagh. I am content to be War Chief. Go, although I would rather have your spears with us."

"When we have chosen a new king, I will return but it will not be this year. My warriors and I need to make new warriors. We have youths and boys to train. I learned much in this war." He gestured with his arm. "I fear that many more chiefs will do as I have done. They will want a voice in the appointment of a new king."

Randel tapped his leg, "Fear not: until my leg heals and our wounded are fit then we will not be able to fight. This is better. The Romans will think that they have won. They will relax their guard and when the snows come again we will begin to hurt them. I just ask you to return when the new grass appears."

"That I promise."

When Prefect Glabrio rose, he was surprised to find that First Spear Broccus and Prefect Tulla had ridden north with the Gallic turmae. "First Spear. I thought you would have been recovering after the battle. Congratulations on relieving Habitancvm. My turma has yet to return from Alavna but I hope that they, too, have weathered the storm."

"The storm is not yet over. I bring orders from the Legate." He handed over a wax tablet.

The Prefect read it and his mouth dropped open, "This says I am to take my ala along with the Gallic horse and the Lingones. We are to destroy the Votadini camp!"

First Spear nodded, "And he wishes you to make a start today."

"But we have wounded! What if the forts are attacked?"

"The wounded can guard the forts. I have a cohort of the VIth heading north to guard your forts and help to rebuild them. Until they arrive then the wounded can guard the forts. I will go and tell the Lingone First Spear. I know you will have to saddle your horses." With that he turned and left.

The Prefect seemed too stunned to give orders and Decurion Princeps Pera said, "Decurion Aurelius and Decurion Stolo your horses are saddled for you were due to patrol. Head to the forest and find the trail to their camp."

Marcus nodded, "Yes Decurion Princeps." He turned to Vexillarius Ralle, "Go to the kitchens and bring me a large oil skin, a mortarium and as much garlic as you can find."

"Are we eating first, sir?"

"No, we are going to make a potion to stop us being eaten alive!"

When the Vexillarius arrived, Marcus pounded the garlic to a paste and then mixed it with the oil. He smeared some on his own face, neck, arms and hands.

The Vexillarius just nodded, "You heard what the Decurion said, get smearing!" It did not take long.

When they crossed the river and reached the forest Marcus realised he should have sent for Felix. The Brigante scout would have made a better job of finding the trail. However, they were helped by the fact that the Votadini had fled and they had not used their normal technique of running in single file. In addition, men had been wounded. They had cut a swathe through the forest. Lower, spindly branches had been broken off. There was blood on some of the trees where wounded men had brushed against them. Once he found the trail he waited. There were just forty men left in the two turmae. Going into the forest risked a meeting with hundreds of barbarians. Having identified where the barbarians had entered the forest he waited.

Decurion Princeps Pera arrived first with the Gallic turmae. "The Prefect is bringing the rest. He is going at the same pace as the Lingone. He wants us ahead as a screen. What have you found?"

He pointed to the prints on the ground, "The trail is fairly clear. They did not disguise their path."

"Then if your turma follows the trail we will spread out on both sides of you. You will have back up from the Prefect and the rest. We will be like hunters and sweep them up. Use that nose of yours." He slapped his face. "These damned midges! Why aren't they bothering you? Is it your Brigante blood?"

"No sir, oil and garlic. They can't stand the stuff!"

It suddenly felt lonely as Marcus and his twelve men headed deep into the forest. Behind them were a thousand men but, in the gloom and the darkness of that primeval forest it felt as though they were alone.

Randel had had his scouts out and they had run into the camp to tell the War Chief that the Romans were coming. He had two choices: run deeper into the forest or ambush them. He chose the latter. He used the best four warriors he had left to each take a fifth of his men and to spread out along the line of the Roman advance. He and the remaining warriors used charcoal from the fire to black themselves up and then he led them towards the Romans. They would hide in plain sight. This was his territory and not the Romans. He was astounded that they had dared to breach his forest fortress but they would learn that this was not the same as fighting on the walls of a fort.

Gripping his shield tightly to him Marcus took out a javelin and waved it in the air so that his troopers could see. They each drew one out. As they followed the trail Marcus found that they were descending. There was a slightly lighter patch of forest to his left. Marcus guessed that was a waterway. All the rest was like walking through dusk or dawn. It was a shadowy half-light. He had no idea how long they rode. With no sun time was hard to measure. Raven's hooves were the only measurement as she picked her way through the forest. The trees were so close together that it was almost impossible to ride in a straight line. He knew that each of his troopers would ride in a pair. One would watch the leader's back. His was watched by the reliable Vexillarius Ralle. Every five hundred or so paces Marcus would stop and sniff the air. He was seeking the scent of the barbarian. The trail beneath Raven's hooves was still clearly visible, even in the half-light. If anything, it was getting clearer and that made Marcus even more cautious. They were getting closer to the camp. He could see, from the cleared ground where more of the fleeing Votadini had congregated. He stopped two hundred paces from his last stop. On one of the trees was a mark. He suddenly remembered he had seen other trees with the same mark. It looked natural but Marcus knew that it was not. The barbarians had marked the trail. He was on his way to the camp.

Raven's ears pricked and Marcus saw a shadow just ahead of him. It looked like a patch of mud. Suddenly the mud moved and Marcus knew that it was a man. Even as he hurled the javelin into the man he shouted, "Ambush!" He did not have time for a second javelin for another barbarian, even closer rose and lunged with a long pole weapon. Raven's head whipped around to snap at the man and the blade scored along her neck. The strike saved Marcus' life for it forced the blade beneath his right-hand horn and into his knee. Marcus felt an excruciating pain as the edge tore into kneecap. Raven was falling and Marcus threw himself from the saddle. The triumphant barbarian tried to stab Marcus as he lay on the ground and Capsarius Licina's javelin hit him.

Realising that the ambush had been sprung early by Tagus, Randel shouted, "Attack!"

His warband leapt to their feet. Many had long pole weapons and their first action was to hack and stab at the horses. The Twentieth Turma were outnumbered but they fought. Even before their horses were butchered their javelins were hurled at the rising black shadows. Most survived the fall and, like Marcus, rose and drew their swords.

Marcus' voice rang out, "To me!"

The noise of the ambush initiated the attacks throughout the forest. Other turmae heard the noise and knew that the enemy were close. They saved many Roman lives for the attacks were premature. However, they delayed any support reaching Marcus.

Marcus' men formed a circle. There were just eleven of them left with Marcus. As Vexillarius Ralle rammed the standard into the ground behind Marcus he said, "A shame this garlic and oil doesn't keep away bigger pests eh sir?"

"We will use our swords for that! Sword of Cartimandua!"

The eleven men all responded, "Sword of Cartimandua!"

When Randel heard the cry, he recognised the officer who held the sword aloft. Here was his opportunity to avenge all of the dead. If he could get his hands on the sword then he could go to the Brigante and demand more men to continue the fight. The gods had sent him this red-crested officer. "Get the sword!"

As he heard the words and saw the barbarians rush towards his tiny circle Marcus mentally cursed the sword. It was drawing death towards him and his loyal men. Even as they came he took in Raven bleeding to death before him. Even his faithful mount had paid the price of the sword.

Randel was not the first to reach Marcus, Aodh son of Vinicius did. He had not returned north with his father. He had stayed with Randel and now, as he saw the beleaguered Romans, ripe for the slaughter, he thanked the Allfather for his decision. He still had the long pole weapon; his sword was by his side. He ran, holding his like a lance. A long weapon is hard to keep straight when running and Marcus flicked the head aside with his clipeus and rammed his sword up into the rib cage of the Votadini. He punched the body back and the young warrior fell dying, into the path of the warrior following. As he stumbled Marcus took one step forward and brought his sword down to split the skull of the warrior.

The turma were not having it all their own way, although a ring of dead barbarians showed that the troopers were using all their skills well. When Trooper Naso stabbed one warrior a second lunged in and stabbed his left shoulder with a pole weapon. His clipeus hung from his useless arm. When Trooper Drusus next to him was felled by an axe Trooper Naso swung his sword and took the man's head. A triumphant Votadini seized his chance and impaled the huge trooper with his spear. Even dying Trooper Naso hacked into the thigh of his killer. He would not celebrate the brief triumph. Each warrior who had such a victory paid for it with his life for the troopers who survived avenged their friends. But the circle shrank.

The barrier of bodies was making life difficult for the barbarians. The bloody carcasses were slippery and slick. The Votadini stumbled and were slain. Marcus saw one Votadini use a body to spring into the air. He brought his sword, taken from a dead Lingone, into the neck of Capsarius Licina. Marcus used the Sword of Cartimandua to swing it back hand into the warrior's spine. As Trooper Fimbria trying to aid the dying Capsarius was felled by an axe the circle tightened. Marcus felt the reassuring presence of Vexillarius Ralle next to him. He also felt the blood from his knee seeping down his leg. The wound was already stiffening and he could not move as easily as he had.

Randel saw that one of the troopers next to Marcus was wounded. Watching his feet, he hefted his Roman shield and darted in to gut Trooper Piso. Piso's shield brother, Trooper Nerva, brought his sword around so hard that it cracked Randel's shield. Randel was a wily warrior and he brought his head forward to butt Trooper Nerva in the face. As he lurched back Randel brought his sword up under the groin protector to eviscerate the Roman.

Marcus recognised the torc around the warrior's neck. This was a chief. If he could kill him then the others might lose heart. He was dimly aware that there were just five troopers left. "Vexillarius watch my back! I am going to fight this chief and end this."

"Don't worry sir! If they get to you then it means that I am dead!"

Marcus knew that this chief would not be an easy man to kill. He held the Sword of Cartimandua up behind his shield. The barbarian would not be able to see it. He could disguise his strike. He took in, as Randel closed with him, that the man was wearing Roman mail and an auxiliary helmet. He also saw the crack in the shield.

Randel grinned. He saw the blood now pouring from the officer's wound was being aggravated by movement. "Brigante you will die at my hand and then the Sword of Cartimandua will be mine. Know that your death will free this land from the hand of Rome!"

"And know this, barbarian, that you will never use this sword. The gods gave it to the Brigante. Others have tried to take it and their bones lie across this land."

Randel laughed as another trooper died. "Your men are dying and you are wounded. The sword is as good as mine already!"

He lunged at Marcus. Marcus could not move for his leg hurt too much. He took the blow on his shield but he angled the Votadini sword away from him. His sword, now revealed, lunged at the Votadini. The sharpened tip penetrated the mail and scored a line across the barbarian's right shoulder. The War Chief was tough but he recoiled from the painful blow.

As another trooper died behind him he heard Vexillarius Ralle said, "Best get a move on, sir. The lads are dying!" Wounded himself Ralle swung his sword and took the head of the barbarian who had thought a talking Roman would be distracted. The barbarian numbers were also diminishing and the wall of bodies was a testament to the courage of the Twentieth Turma. They had been faithful unto death.

Randel was now wounded and he was warier. The ground between them was slick with blood. A slip would be fatal. The War Chief swung his sword at the Roman's shield. As he pulled his arm back he felt pain in his shoulder. The blow was not as effective as it could have been. Sensing the weakness Marcus brought his sword in a wide sweep and it smashed into the War Chief's shield. The weakened shield cracked and split.

Iuecher slew Trooper Bucco and saw that his chief was in trouble. He lunged at Marcus' unprotected side and his sword slid through the mail and into Marcus' side. He paid for his audacity with a sword in his throat from one of the last troopers, Trooper Planca.

Randel threw down the shattered shield and held his sword in two hands. He saw that Marcus had two wounds. He saw his chance and he swung his sword around in a mighty sweep. It was powerful and although Marcus' shield held the blow, his weakened leg gave way and he fell to the floor. Trooper Planca stepped towards the two barbarians who came to help their chief. He killed one before falling to the other. Vexillarius Ralle was the last man standing and he slew the barbarian before he could get to the decurion. The only barbarian facing Marcus was the chief and so the Vexillarius turned to face the last eight barbarians who advanced towards him. "Come on you bastards! I will show you how a Gaul dies!"

Randel brought his sword down hard, two handed. Marcus used his clipeus to protect his body. The sword strike was so hard that it numbed his arm. He pulled the Sword of Cartimandua around and hacked into the leg of the Votadini who fell backwards. Marcus used his sword to push himself up. He was aware of the Vexillarius fighting for his life and, in the distance, or what sounded like the distance, the sound of a buccina. His left arm was numb and the shield was useless he dropped it and used his left hand to help hold his shaking sword. Randel was trying to get to his feet but with his calf sliced through to the bone he could not. Marcus held the sword in two hands and fell forward. The sword went through the barbarian's skull pinning him to the ground. The blood loss was too much and, as the barbarian died, Marcus fell forward across the body.

Decurion Stolo looked in horror at the Vexillarius hanging on to the standard. Around the twentieth Turma lay fifty bodies. The Vexillarius was wounded but he managed a wry grin. "A bit late, sir but I am glad you came. I think the Decurion needs your capsarius." The Vexillarius then fell over.

When the Prefect and First Spear reached the scene, having slaughtered every barbarian they had found they could not believe their eyes. First Spear recognised Randel. "It looks, Prefect, like Decurion Aurelius has finally ended the rebellion." The Prefect nodded as he dismounted.

Decurion Princeps Pera rode up and leapt from his horse. He looked at the capsarius. "How are they?"

"The Decurion will live but he will be lame for the rest of his life. The Vexillarius? I am not certain. I have stitched up as many wounds as I can but he has lost a lot of blood."

The Decurion Princeps said, "Then get them back to the fort as soon as you can. We owe this turma a great deal."

"Well said Decurion Princeps." First Spear put his arm around Pera.

The Prefect saw the torc around the neck of the Votadini. He leaned forward, "That will make a good trophy for the ala."

First Spear's voice was hard. He knew he was being insubordinate but he could not help it. "That goes to Decurion Aurelius, Prefect! He has earned it. His men have earned it. That torc is a measure of the Roman blood spilt here today and the Roman courage that won the day."

Shocked by the words the Prefect nodded and handed it to First Spear.

Epilogue

It took Marcus more than two months to heal enough to allow him to travel. Vexillarius Ralle was ready quicker. The capsarius had done a good job. Decurion Princeps Pera and the rest of the ala used much of the coin they collected from the dead to give to the Vexillarius. He would never fight again. The money would give him a new start. He called in to the sickbay to speak with Marcus before he left. "I am sorry to part this way, sir. I have been honoured to serve with you. You were the best officer I ever knew and I am just sorry that you will be leaving the army. The ala needs officers like you!"

"And what of you Vexillarius? Back to Gaul?"

"No sir. I intend to go to Eboracum and buy a little alehouse. The wounds will ache in winter but I can keep a fire going. The lads did all right by me. I have coin in my pocket and back pay. What will you do?"

"Back to the valley. I suppose I will become a farmer."

"I can't see that suiting you, sir."

"I have seen too many men die because of this sword and lost too many friends. Farming and watching my family grow will be good enough for me."

He watched his friend leave with the wagons and the first of the troopers invalided out. Marcus would travel with the most seriously wounded. He knew how lucky he was when he saw men who had lost arms and legs. They were just grateful to be alive. It was First Spear and the Decurion Princeps who gave Marcus the best send-off. The night before he had been due to leave they got drunk with him and, the next morning, the two of them walked him to the cart. Marcus had two sticks. The doctor had told him that, eventually, he would be able to walk without sticks but that would be some time in the future and he would always have a limp.

First Spear handed a sack to him, "This is the torc from the chief you killed. We thought you should have it. You have nothing from the army for all the years of service."

"I have my life and that is more than most of my turma. I am content. I have my brother's farm and I am not poor. I have saved my pay."

Decurion Princeps Pera gave him the warrior's grasp. "Thank you, Marcus, you have made this a better ala. Decurion Stolo would not be the leader he is without you."

Marcus took First Spear's helping hand into the cart. "Take care you two. This is still the wild frontier up here."

First Spear nodded, "Aye but we have broken the back of the Votadini. It will be the next generation who are able to rise. By then we will have done our twenty-five years and be enjoying retirement."

The Legate greeted Marcus at Coriosopitum. He was given accommodation in the Praetorium and dined with the Legate. He looked concerned. "I am sorry that your career has ended. You had a future."

"I did my duty, sir and I was luckier than most. I came out of it alive."

The Legate nodded, "I have asked for the Gold Crown for you. In addition, I have sent a letter to the Governor asking for an annual stipend. Everyone who fought alongside you could not speak highly enough of your behaviour and deeds."

Marcus smiled, "Even Prefect Glabrio, sir?"

The Legate inclined his head, "The Prefect was less fulsome in his praise but as it was more praise than anyone else received; you should be happy."

"I am sir."

"And now you go to your farm?"

"I do sir."

"When I travel south I may well visit."

He was dropped off at Morbium. Already the auxiliaries were rebuilding the fort and repairing the bridge. When First Spear saw Marcus, he was shocked. "We had it bad here but when we heard of the battles north of the wall, well, I was surprised that any survived. We heard of your exploits. It is an honour to meet a hero." He seemed to see the sticks for the first time. Then his eyes went to the bags and weapons. "You are going home?"

"Eventually. First, I need to go to my wife. She is at the farm of Rufius Atrebate then we will go to my farm. My days as a warrior are over."

"And how will you reach the farm?"

"I was going to leave my war gear here and walk."

"You will do no such thing. Optio, fetch a wagon and take this hero where he wishes to go."

Marcus was both touched and relieved. He had not relished the thought of the walk. Scealis saw the wagon and frowned. When he saw Marcus being helped down he ran to fetch Frann. Marcus' wife had heard nothing save that there had been battles. When she saw her husband, there was relief that he was alive and then shock at his gaunt frame and the two sticks. Neither could speak and they held each other for the longest time. Macro and Ailis clung to their father's legs and Marcus felt tears coursing down his cheeks. When Felix and Wolf ran to greet him too he knew that he was home.

Marcus stayed at the farm for a month. Rufius' wife and Scealis were happy for him to stay there permanently.

"No, for I must begin my new life. I can now ride and only need one stick. This is good. I will ride to the fort and have my war gear sent to the farm. When I have spoken with Arthfael I will send a message back."

Reluctantly they all agreed but Scealis insisted upon sending two of his largest men with the former officer. Both were ex troopers and knew Marcus well. The former Decurion was pleased to have Aelius and Cornelius with him. They had both been wounded many years earlier and forced to leave the army but their wounds were not as bad as Marcus'. The three of them rode to Morbium and First Spear sent the wagon with them, along with a contubernium of auxiliaries. He explained, "After the insurrection, we found many farms where the occupants had been butchered. Other farms were destroyed. If you need help to rebuild then these men can aid you and if your farm has been taken by rebels they will secure it for you."

In the event none of that was necessary. Marcus found Arthfael but there was no family. There were just slaves working in the fields. He looked pleased to see the Decurion. "I am delighted that you survived, lord. You have come to reclaim your farm?"

"I have but I expected your family to be here."

He looked a little embarrassed. "After the insurrection, I made a bid on a farm at Forcett, just north of Stanwick. I had made much money in the year I ran the farm. With the rebellion prices were high and our crops did well. The price of the farm was low for most of the owners and their families had been killed by the Legion. The house is a fine one and my family live there. I visit here once every seven days. You are lucky to have found me."

"I am pleased that someone came out of this well."

"The Allfather smiled on me. All of your animals are here. You may keep the slaves until you have some of your own. Tadgh is my overseer. He can help you buy more."

"Thank you Arthfael."

"No, thank you, sir. You helped me to become a farmer. You helped me realise my dream."

The auxiliaries helped to unload the wagon and store Marcus' war gear. Marcus sent Aelius back to fetch his family the next day and he and Cornelius made the house habitable.

That evening, just before the sun set Marcus said, "Prepare the evening meal, Cornelius and we will have some wine. There is something I must do." He went to his room and fetched his helmet, armour, bow, quiver and dagger. He still wore, about his waist, the Sword of Cartimandua in the decorated scabbard. He had left a shovel by the door. He headed from the farmhouse to the stable. He went to Raven's stall. He would not replace Raven and this stall would remain empty. He began to dig a hole. It was hard work but he needed to make it deep. First, he placed everything in sacks save for the sword and the scabbard. He laid in it his scale armour. His mail armour had been rendered scrap metal by the battle. The scale armour was his dress armour. He put in his bow, quiver and dagger. He laid them in the bottom of the hole. Then he placed his helmet there. Finally, he took the oiled cloth he had brought and wrapped the sword and scabbard in it. That done he put the sword and scabbard in a sack. He laid them on the top and began to shovel the soil back on top. He walked up and down it. He used his good leg to stamp and tamp it down. Then he took straw and strewed it over the top.

When he was satisfied with his handiwork, he laid down his shovel. "Father, Ulpius Felix, Queen Cartimandua, the sword was passed to me and I have maintained the honour you gave it. Now it is becoming a liability. I do not fear death but it is causing the deaths of others. I do not think that any of you would wish that." He sighed, "It is my decision and if I am wrong then when we meet in the Otherworld you may berate me.

Perhaps I am not the man you all hoped I was. I did my best and I fought for Rome. I defended this land. I can do no more." He lifted his arms, "Belatu-Cadros, watch over this horde and protect it from those who would use the sword for evil. Protect it until the land is under threat and one of my blood will return to finish my work. When they are needed they will save this land from its enemies."

That done he returned to the farm. The sun had set. Cornelius was laying the food on the table as Marcus washed his hands. Cornelius looked at Marcus' waist, "Where is the sword, sir?"

"The Sword of Cartimandua has gone from this world. When this land needs it then someone of my blood will find it."

Cornelius nodded, "Aye sir. What is meant to be will be."

Marcus sat at the table and felt, for the first time in a long time, at peace.

The End

Glossary.

Fictitious characters and places are in *italics*.

Name-Description

Acetum- the sour wine issued to every Roman soldier as part of his rations

Ammabile- Amble, Northumberland

Appius Serjanus-Governor's aide

Aulus Platorius Nepos-Governor of Britannia

Belatucadros – a Celtic god of war

Briac-Brigante prince and descendant of Venutius

Capsarius (pl) capsarii-Medical orderly

Carnyx- Celtic war horn

clipeus – oval shield used by auxiliary horsemen

Cilurnum-Chesters (on Hadrian's Wall)

Coriosopitum-Corbridge

Decurion Princeps Marius Scaeva Pera -Ala Petriana

Decurion Servius Hirtius Stolo-Ala Petriana

Decurion Vibius Seneca Dives-Ala Petriana

Decurion Scaura -Ala Petriana

Dunum- River Tees

Felix-Brigante Scout

Frann- Marcus' wife

Frumentarii- Roman Secret Police (frumentarius singular)

Gaius Culpinus-Tungrian Prefect

Habitancvm-Risingham, Northumberland

Imagnifer-a standard-bearer, similar to signifer

Itauna Aest -Solway Firth

Julius Demetrius-Legate

Julius Longinus-Ala Clerk

Macro-Marcus' son

Manius Balba Ralle, the vexillarius -Ala Petriana 15th Turma

mansio-State inn for travellers

mansionarius-The official in charge of a mansio

Marcus Gaius Aurelius-Decurion Marcus' Horse.

Mercaut- Lindisfarne (Holy Island)

Nemesis-Roman Fate

Numerius Helva Licina, capsarius-Ala Petriana 15th Turma

Oppidum- Tribal hill fort
Otarbrunna-Otterburn
Pons Aelius-Newcastle
Quaestor-Roman official or tax collector
Quintus Licinius Brocchus-First Spear VIth Legion
Roaring Waters- High Force Waterfall
Rufius Atrebeus- Decurion and former Explorate and frumentarius
Samhain – Celtic/Druidic festival on October/November
sesquiplicarius-Corporal
signifer- The soldier who carries the standard and also acts as the turma banker
Tinea- River Tyne
Titus Plauca-Camp Prefect Eboracum
tonsor-Roman barber
Trierarch-Captain of a Roman warship
Vedra- River Wear
Vercovicium-Housesteads (Hadrian's Wall)
Via Claudia-Watling Street (A5)
Via Hades-Road to Hell- Dere Street (A1)
Via Trajanus-Dere Street (Al)-Eboracum North
Vicus (pl)vici-Roman settlement close to a fort

Maps

The Wall and the Forts c130 A.D.

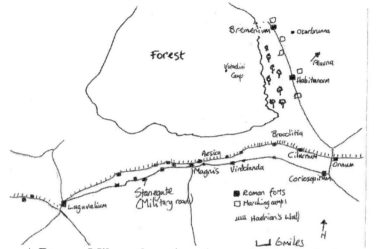

A Roman Milecastle such as the one Aelric attacked.

All maps hand drawn by the author

Historical Background

For those who like authentic maps, I used the original Ordnance Survey maps of the areas made in the nineteenth century. These maps are part of a series and are now available. They are the first Government produced maps of the British Isles. Great Britain, apart from the larger conurbations, was the same as it had been 800 years earlier.

I also discovered a good website http://orbis.stanford.edu/. This allows a reader to plot any two places in the Roman world and if you input the mode of transport you wish to use and the time of year it will calculate how long it would take you to travel the route. I have used it for all of my books up to the eighteenth century as the transportation system was roughly the same. The Romans would have been quicker!

I found a couple of good sites for research:

The first is:-http://dare.ht.lu.se/places/22980.html

Digital Atlas of the Roman Empire © 2015 Johan Åhlfeldt, Department of Archaeology and Ancient History Lund University, Sweden

This is an interactive map giving excellent information.

The other is http://roman-britain.co.uk/places/index.htm. This gives all the information about everywhere in Britain where the Romans built or lived. For the forts and the walls it even gives the units.

I use two sites for Celtic names and Roman names:

https://www.behindthename.com/names/gender/masculine/usage/ancient-celtic

http://www.novaroma.org/nr/Choosing_a_Roman_name

The last one is the best site for names as it shows you how to create a real name.

Roman Calendar
Calendar of Romulus

English	Latin Days	Meaning
March	Mensis Martius 31	Month of Mars
April	Mensis Aprilis 30	Uncertain

May	Mensis Maius 31	Uncertain
June	Mensis Iunius 30	Month of Juno
July	Mensis Quintilis 31	Fifth Month
August	Mensis Sextilis 30	Sixth Month
September	Mensis September 30	Seventh Month
October	Mensis October 31	Eighth Month
November	Mensis November 30	Ninth Month
December	Mensis December 30	Tenth Month

Books used in the research:

- The Armies and Enemies of Imperial Rome- Barker and Heath
- Rome's Enemies-Wilcox and McBride (Osprey)
- Celtic Warrior- Allen and Reynolds (Osprey)
- The Roman Army from Caesar to Trajan-Simkins and Embleton (Osprey)
- Hadrian's Wall- David Breeze (English Heritage)
- Chesters Roman Fort-Nick Hodgson (English Heritage)
- What the Soldiers Wore on Hadrian's Wall- Russell Robinson
- Roman Army Units in the Western Provinces- D'Amato and Ruggeri
- Roman Auxiliary Cavalryman- Fields and Hook
- Rome's Northern Frontier- Fields and Spedaliere
- Roman Legionary Fortresses- Campbell and Delf
- Ordnance Survey map of Roman Britain.

Griff Hosker December 2017

Other books by Griff Hosker

If you enjoyed reading this book, then why not read another one by the author?

Ancient History

The Sword of Cartimandua Series
(Germania and Britannia 50 A.D. – 128 A.D.)
Ulpius Felix- Roman Warrior (prequel)
The Sword of Cartimandua
The Horse Warriors
Invasion Caledonia
Roman Retreat
Revolt of the Red Witch
Druid's Gold
Trajan's Hunters
The Last Frontier
Hero of Rome
Roman Hawk
Roman Treachery
Roman Wall
Roman Courage

The Wolf Warrior series
(Britain in the late 6th Century)
Saxon Dawn
Saxon Revenge
Saxon England
Saxon Blood
Saxon Slayer
Saxon Slaughter
Saxon Bane
Saxon Fall: Rise of the Warlord
Saxon Throne
Saxon Sword

Roman Courage

Medieval History

The Dragon Heart Series
Viking Slave
Viking Warrior
Viking Jarl
Viking Kingdom
Viking Wolf
Viking War
Viking Sword
Viking Wrath
Viking Raid
Viking Legend
Viking Vengeance
Viking Dragon
Viking Treasure
Viking Enemy
Viking Witch
Viking Blood
Viking Weregeld
Viking Storm
Viking Warband
Viking Shadow
Viking Legacy
Viking Clan
Viking Bravery

The Norman Genesis Series
Hrolf the Viking
Horseman
The Battle for a Home
Revenge of the Franks
The Land of the Northmen
Ragnvald Hrolfsson
Brothers in Blood
Lord of Rouen
Drekar in the Seine
Duke of Normandy
The Duke and the King

Roman Courage

New World Series
Blood on the Blade
Across the Seas
The Savage Wilderness
The Bear and the Wolf

The Vengeance Trail

The Reconquista Chronicles
Castilian Knight
El Campeador
The Lord of Valencia

The Aelfraed Series
(Britain and Byzantium 1050 A.D. - 1085 A.D.)
Housecarl
Outlaw
Varangian

The Anarchy Series England
1120-1180
English Knight
Knight of the Empress
Northern Knight
Baron of the North
Earl
King Henry's Champion
The King is Dead
Warlord of the North
Enemy at the Gate
The Fallen Crown
Warlord's War
Kingmaker
Henry II
Crusader
The Welsh Marches
Irish War
Poisonous Plots

Roman Courage

The Princes' Revolt
Earl Marshal

**Border Knight
1182-1300**
Sword for Hire
Return of the Knight
Baron's War
Magna Carta
Welsh Wars
Henry III
The Bloody Border
Baron's Crusade
Sentinel of the North
War in the West

**Sir John Hawkwood Series
France and Italy 1339- 1387**
Crécy: The Age of the Archer
Man At Arms (January 2021)

Lord Edward's Archer
Lord Edward's Archer
King in Waiting
An Archer's Crusade

**Struggle for a Crown
1360- 1485**
Blood on the Crown
To Murder A King
The Throne
King Henry IV
The Road to Agincourt
St Crispin's Day

Tales from the Sword

Modern History

The Napoleonic Horseman Series
Chasseur à Cheval
Napoleon's Guard
British Light Dragoon
Soldier Spy
1808: The Road to Coruña
Talavera
The Lines of Torres Vedras
Bloody Badajoz
The Road to France

The Lucky Jack American Civil War series
Rebel Raiders
Confederate Rangers
The Road to Gettysburg

The British Ace Series
1914
1915 Fokker Scourge
1916 Angels over the Somme
1917 Eagles Fall
1918 We will remember them
From Arctic Snow to Desert Sand
Wings over Persia

Combined Operations series
1940-1945
Commando
Raider
Behind Enemy Lines
Dieppe
Toehold in Europe
Sword Beach
Breakout
The Battle for Antwerp
King Tiger
Beyond the Rhine
Korea
Korean Winter

Other Books
Great Granny's Ghost (Aimed at 9-14-year-old young people)

For more information on all of the books then please visit the author's web site at www.griffhosker.com where there is a link to contact him or visit his Facebook page: GriffHosker at Sword Books

Printed in Great Britain
by Amazon

60557860R00142